*She is the woman he shouldn't have . . .
and the only one he desires.*

"Why are you smiling like that?"

"You have a smear of chocolate on your face."

"I do? Where?"

"Right there." He lifted one hand, lightly touching the tip of his finger to one corner of her mouth. But then his smile vanished, and his palm cupped her cheek.

Startled by the contact, Maria froze. His thumb grazed her lips, and her lips parted in utter surprise.

His intense blue gaze was riveted on her mouth, as his thumb began to brush back and forth across her lips in an unmistakable caress. He seemed to know precisely what he was doing.

This was Phillip, after all.

Phillip, who never did anything improper, who never stepped outside the bounds. Phillip, who didn't even like her, who probably wanted her banished to the farthest corner of the globe.

Phillip was touching her.

And, she realized with a wild throb of excitement, he was going to kiss her.

By Laura Lee Guhrke

SECRET DESIRES OF A GENTLEMAN
THE WICKED WAYS OF A DUKE
AND THEN HE KISSED HER
SHE'S NO PRINCESS
THE MARRIAGE BED
HIS EVERY KISS
GUILTY PLEASURES

Laura Lee Guhrke

SECRET DESIRES
OF A
GENTLEMAN

AVON

An Imprint of HarperCollinsPublishers

AVON BOOKS
An Imprint of HarperCollins*Publishers*
10 East 53rd Street
New York, New York 10022-5299

Copyright © 2008 by Laura Lee Guhrke
Excerpts from *Tempted By the Night* copyright © 2008 by Elizabeth Boyle; *Secret Desires of a Gentleman* copyright © 2008 by Laura Lee Guhrke; *All I Want for Christmas Is a Vampire* copyright © 2008 by Kerrelyn Sparks; *To Sin With a Stranger* copyright © 2008 by Kathryn Caskie
ISBN 978-0-06-145682-4
www.avonromance.com

First Avon Books paperback printing: October 2008

Avon Trademark Reg. U.S. Pat. Off. and in Other Countries, Marca Registrada, Hecho En U.S.A.
HarperCollins® is a registered trademark of HarperCollins Publishers.

Printed in the U.S.A.

10 9 8 7 6 5 4 3 2

To my writing buddies
Elizabeth Boyle, Niki Burnham,
Leah Vale, and Terri Reed,
for teaching me truly effective goal-setting.
Cheers.

Chapter 1

If there be no bread, let them eat cake.
Anonymous

London, 1895

This couldn't be right. Maria Martingale came to a halt at the intersection of Piccadilly and Half Moon Streets, staring doubtfully at the shop on the corner. It was in an ideal location, appeared to be in excellent condition, and the sign over the doorway declared the premises had formerly been a tea shop. It was perfect—so perfect in fact that Maria was sure there had to be some sort of mistake.

She glanced down at the order to view in her hands, then back up at the engraved brass kick plate of the door to verify the address: 88 Piccadilly. No mistake. She was in the right place.

Just come into the market, the agent had told her as he'd given her the order to view. Just what she was looking for. Clean, he'd hastened to add, handing over the keys, and freshly painted, with a thoroughly modern kitchen.

Maria had not received these assurances with much enthusiasm. For three months now, she'd been combing through the streets of London, looking for the right place for her *pâtisserie*, and though she'd had little success in her search, she had learned a great deal about property agents and their descriptions. A modern kitchen often meant nothing more than a closed range and a few gaslights, fresh paint covered a multitude of sins, and "clean" was a relative term. Even in the finest neighborhoods, she'd stepped on so many beetle-infested floors and inhaled the noxious odor of bad drains so often, she'd almost given up the whole venture in despair.

But as she studied the building on this particular corner, Maria felt a spark of hope. The location was first rate. It had frontage on Piccadilly, was within the street's most popular shopping area, and the neighborhood surrounding it was prosperous. Wealthy, influential businessmen lived here with their ambitious, social-climbing wives, wives who would willingly pay to provide their busy cooks with the best in ready-made baked goods. And Maria intended to provide the best. What Fortnum & Mason was to the picnic hamper, Martingale's would be to the tea tray and the dessert plate.

It was all due to Prudence, of course. If her best friend, Prudence Bosworth, hadn't inherited a fortune and married the Duke of St. Cyres, none of this would have been possible. Maria wouldn't have been able to leave her position as *pâtissier* to the great chef André Chauvin and strike out on her own. But Prudence had pots of money and had been happy to back her dearest friend in the venture of her dreams.

Maria folded the order to view and put it in the pocket of her blue-and-white-striped skirt, then she walked a few steps down Half Moon Street. As she viewed the exterior of the shop, her hopes rose another notch. There were enormous plate-glass windows on both streets, and the entrance, set at an angle to the corner, boasted a door with glass panels. This design would provide plenty of opportunity for those walking past to be tempted by the delightful confections she would have on display. She could see from the window wells set in the concrete of the sidewalk that the kitchen was in the basement. Steps on Half Moon Street led down to it through a tradesmen's entrance door.

Eager to see the interior of the shop, Maria hastened back to the corner, opened her hand-bag again, and extracted the key given to her by the property agent. She walked up the whitened front steps, unlocked the door, and went inside.

The front room was large, with enough space for the display cases and tea tables necessary to a *pâtisserie*. The fresh paint extolled by the property agent, however, would have to be redone, for it was that peculiar shade known as yallery-greenery, quite fashionable nowadays but most unsuitable for a bakery.

Maria scrutinized the floor and took several deep breaths. No bad drains, and not a blackbeetle to be seen. Perhaps this time the property agents had got it right.

There was only one way to be sure. She tucked her handbag under her arm and crossed the room, the heels of her high button shoes tapping decisively on the black–and–white-tile floor. Upon opening the door to the back rooms of the shop, she found the arrangements typical of a thousand other London establishments. There was an office and storeroom, and one set of stairs led up to sleeping quarters while another led down to the kitchen and scullery. Maria knew she could hardly expect anything below stairs other than the damp, depressing hole that usually passed for a kitchen in London, but when she reached the bottom of the steps, she stopped in her tracks and stared into the most perfect kitchen she had ever seen.

There were oak cupboards, two full walls of them, with shelves, drawers and bins of every imaginable shape and size. Iron pot racks hung from the heavy oak beams that crossed the ceiling. Above the cupboards, the windows she'd spied from the sidewalk above not only let in some natural light, but they also opened at the top for ventilation—something that would be most welcome in the heat of summer.

Maria moved forward into the room, studying her surroundings in amazement. The concrete walls had been sheathed in a fresh coat of white plaster, and the linoleum floor beneath her feet was a soft, cheery yellow. To her right were four coal-fired ranges, each one fitted with burners, a boiler, and a tap. Above them hung a decorative hood of hammered copper.

The back kitchen was equally modern. The scullery had two sinks, a dual water tap, and a long, tin drain board, and the larder was generous, with shelves to the ceiling. There was even an ice room for cold storage.

Maria returned to the front kitchen, pulled off her gloves, and proceeded to examine the stoves. She opened the oven doors, turned the hot-water taps, and lifted the hot plates, feeling a bit like a child in a toy shop. She used the scullery to rinse the stove blacking off her hands, and bravely sampled the water. Of course it tasted fine. This was Mayfair.

She finally stopped tinkering with the various appliances, but she could not quite bring herself to leave. Her father had been a chef, and she'd been in all manner of kitchens during her twenty-nine years, but never had she seen a kitchen quite like this. It was a dream come true.

Here she would create masterpieces—the tenderest, flakiest pastries, the tiniest, prettiest petit fours, and the most amazing wedding cakes London society had ever seen. Countless people, her father and André among them, had told her that because she was a woman, she could never be regarded as a great chef, but here, in this kitchen, she would prove them wrong.

A shadow moved past the window—a pedestrian walking by—and Maria came out of her reverie with a start. She couldn't stand here dithering all day. She had to go see the property agent and make arrangements for the lease. Now, this instant, before someone else caught sight of this lovely kitchen and snatched it away from her.

Spurred into action, Maria grabbed her gloves and raced up the stairs, stuffing the gloves into her handbag as she fumbled for the latch key. Outside, she locked the front door and shoved the key into her pocket, but even in her haste, she couldn't resist pausing for one last look at the shop. Stepping back from the door, she imagined how it would look when it was hers. The name MARTINGALE'S prominently but tastefully displayed in gold letters over the door. Bright red strawberry tarts, delicate pink and white petit fours, and fat golden scones in the windows.

"It's perfect," she breathed with reverent appreciation, still looking at the shop over her shoulder as she started walking away. "Absolutely perfect."

The collision brought her out of her daydreams with painful force. She was knocked off her feet, her handbag went flying, and she stumbled backward, stepping on the hem of her skirt as she tried to right herself. She would have fallen to the pavement, but a pair of strong hands caught her, and she was hauled up against the hard wall of a man's chest. "Steady on, my girl," a deep voice murmured near her ear, a voice that seemed somehow familiar. "Are you all right?"

She inhaled deeply, trying to catch her breath, and as she did, she caught the luscious scents of bay rum and fresh linen. She nodded, her cheek brushing the unmistakable silk facing of a fine lapel. "I think so," she answered.

Her palms flattened against the soft, rich wool of a gentleman's coat and she pushed back, lifting her chin to look up at him. When her gaze met his, recognition hit her with more force than the collision of their bodies had done.

Phillip Hawthorne. The Marquess of Kayne.

There was no mistaking those eyes, vivid cobalt-blue eyes framed by thick black lashes. Irish eyes, she'd always thought, though if any Irish blood tainted the purity of his oh-so-aristocratic British lineage, he'd never have acknowledged it. Phillip had always been a stickler for things like position and place and who were the right sort of people. So unlike his brother, Lawrence, who hadn't ever cared a whit.

Memories came over her like a flood, washing away twelve years in the space of a heartbeat. Suddenly, she was no longer standing on a sidewalk in Mayfair but in the library at Kayne Hall, and Phillip was standing across the desk from her, holding out a bank draft and looking at her as if she were nothing.

She glanced down, half expecting to see the pale pink paper of a bank draft in his hand— the bribe to make her leave and never come back, the payment in exchange for her promise to keep away from Lawrence for the rest of her life. The marquess had only been nineteen then, but he'd already managed to put a price on love. It was worth one thousand pounds.

His voice, so cold, came echoing back to her. *This sum should be adequate, since my brother assures me there is no possibility of a child.*

Shaken, Maria tried to gather her wits. She'd always expected to encounter Phillip again one day, but she had not expected it to happen so literally, and she felt rather at sixes and sevens.

She'd long ago given up any thought she would see Lawrence again, for she'd heard years ago that he had gone off to America. His older brother, however, was a different matter. Phillip was a marquess, and he mingled with the finest of society. Given all the balls and parties where she'd served hors d'oeuvres to aristocrats while working for André, Maria had resigned herself long ago to the inevitable night when she would look up while offering a plate of canapés and find his cool, haughty gaze on her. Oddly enough, however, it had never happened. Twelve years of beating the odds only to cannon into him on a street corner. Of all the rotten luck.

Her gaze slid back upward. Phillip had always been tall, but standing before her was not the lanky young man she remembered. This man's shoulders were wider, his chest broader, his entire physique exuding such masculine strength and vitality that Maria felt quite aggrieved. If there was any fairness in the world at all, Phillip Hawthorne would have gone to fat and gotten the gout by now. Instead, the Marquess of Kayne was even stronger and more powerful at thirty-one than he'd been at nineteen. How nauseating.

Still, she thought as she returned her gaze to his face, twelve years had left their mark. There were tiny lines at the corners of his eyes and two faint parallel creases across his forehead. The determination and discipline in the line of his jaw was even more pronounced than it had been a dozen years ago, and his mouth, a grave, unsmiling curve that had always been surprisingly beautiful was harsher now. His entire countenance, in fact, was harder than she remembered, as if all those notions of duty and responsibility he'd been stuffed with as a boy weighed heavy on him as a man. Maria found some satisfaction in that.

More satisfying was the fact that she had changed, too. She was no longer the desperate, forsaken seventeen-year-old girl who'd thought being bought off for a thousand pounds was her only choice. These days, she wasn't without means and she wasn't without friends. Never again would she be intimidated by the likes of Phillip Hawthorne.

"What are you doing here?" she demanded, then grimaced at her lack of eloquence. Over the years, she'd invented an entire repertoire of cutting, clever things to say to him should they ever meet again, and that blunt, stupid query was the best she could do? Maria wanted to kick herself.

"An odd question," he murmured in the well-bred accents she remembered so well. "I live here."

"Here?" A knot of dread began forming in the pit of her stomach as his words sank in. "But this is an empty shop."

"Not the shop." He let go of her arms and gestured to the front door of the first town house on Half Moon Street, an elegant red door out of which he must have just come when they'd collided. "I live there."

She stared at the door in disbelief. *You can't live here*, she wanted to shout. *Not you, not Phillip Hawthorne, not in this house right beside the lovely, perfect shop where I'm going to live.*

She looked at him again. "But that's impossible. Your London house is in Park Lane."

He stiffened, dark brows drawing together in a frown. "My home in Park Lane is presently being remodeled, though I don't see what business it is of yours, miss."

She frowned at the impersonal address, but before she could reply, he glanced at the ground and spoke again. "You've spilled your things."

"I didn't spill them," she corrected, bristling a bit. "You did."

To her disappointment, he didn't argue the point. "My apologies," he murmured, and knelt on the pavement. "Allow me to retrieve them for you."

She studied his bent head as he righted her handbag and began picking up her scattered belongings. So like Phillip, she thought, watching as he gathered her tortoiseshell comb, her gloves, her cotton handkerchief, and her money purse and began placing them in her handbag with careful precision. God forbid one should just toss it all inside and get on with things.

After her belongings had been returned to her bag, he closed the brass clasp and reached for his hat, a fine gray felt homburg that had also gone flying during the collision. He donned his hat and stood up, holding her handbag out to her.

She took it from his outstretched hand. "Thank you, Phillip," she murmured. "How—" She broke off, not knowing if she should inquire after his brother, but then she decided it was only right to ask. "How is Lawrence?"

Something flashed in his eyes, but when he spoke, his voice was politely indifferent. "Forgive me," he said with an impersonal smile, "but your use of Christian names indicates a familiarity with me of which I am unaware."

She blinked, bewildered. "Unaware?" she echoed and started to laugh, not from humor, but from disbelief. "Phillip, you've known me since I was seven years old—"

"I don't believe so," he contradicted, his voice still polite and pleasant, his gaze hard and implacable. "We do not know each other. We do not know each other at all. I hope that's clear?"

She made a sound of indignation, but before she could form a scathing reply, he spoke again. "Good day, miss," he said, then bowed and stepped around her to go on his way.

She turned, and her eyes narrowed on his back as he walked away. He knew precisely who she was, he was only pretending not to. Arrogant, toplofty snob. How dare he snub her?

"It was delightful to see you again, *Phillip*," she called after him, her voice sweet as honey. "Give Lawrence my best regards, will you?"

His steps did not falter as he walked away.

He'd pretended not to know her, of course. Good breeding demanded it. But even before she'd looked up and he'd seen her face, he'd caught the scents of vanilla and cinnamon, and he'd known it was her. He had maintained the dignity of a polite stranger, assisting her with picking up her things as if they had never met before, keeping up the farce even as he walked away, his strides easy and casual, his pace natural and unhurried. But inside, Phillip felt strangely off-balance, as if a fist had just slammed into him and knocked him sideways.

Maria Martingale.

He hadn't known she was in London. In truth, he hadn't thought about her enough to consider her whereabouts. If he had ever been inclined toward such pointless contemplations, he'd have envisioned her the wife of some poor, hood-winked sod—not a man of the aristocracy, for if she'd risen that high, he'd have heard about it. No, he'd have imagined her married to some florid, middle-aged merchant and living in a ter-race house in Hackney or Clapham. But there had been no wedding ring on her finger, a surprising thing, really, when he thought about it.

Perhaps she was some man's mistress now. He considered that possibility as he crossed Charles Street and entered Berkeley Square, but by the time he reached his destination, Thomas's Hotel, he'd been forced to reject the idea of Maria as a courtesan. Though her bewitching beauty might serve her well in such an occupation, he couldn't quite see her in the role. No, Maria was a pretty flirt, the sort who dangled her virtue and held out for marriage, and there were plenty of men glad to end such torture by offering a ring. His brother had certainly been willing enough to marry her. The idiot would have done it, too, if Phillip hadn't been able to make him see sense.

Thankfully, the elopement crisis—only one of many involving his brother—had been averted. Phillip hadn't expected to ever see the girl again. Not in Mayfair, and certainly not on a street corner right outside his home.

He came to an abrupt halt outside Thomas's Hotel, earning himself a surprised look from the liveried doorman holding the door for him. What was Maria Martingale doing in Mayfair anyway, mooning about by his front steps?

A vision of her came into his mind—enormous hazel eyes in a heart-shaped face, tendrils of wheat-blonde hair peeking out from beneath the brim of a straw boater hat, soft pink lips parted in surprise.

"Surprise, my eye," he muttered under his breath as he entered the hotel and crossed the lobby toward the tearoom. The little schemer had a purpose.

The news that his brother had returned from America and had taken up residence with him in Half Moon Street had been reported in all the society papers. She'd probably read about it, along with the rumors of Lawrence's impending engagement to American heiress Cynthia Dutton. So now she was loitering by his house, waiting for an opportunity to see his brother. But to what end?

She couldn't be thinking to rekindle her romance with Lawrence, not after twelve years? He paused outside the tearoom, contemplating that question as he brushed a speck of lint from his dark blue suit and gave a tug to his silver-gray waistcoat. Perhaps she'd simply been curious. Or she might have come to ask for money, though that would have been a futile endeavor. He'd already paid her enough to support her for the rest of her life, and she had to know he'd never give her another penny. And Lawrence, though much softer of heart, was absolutely flat—the usual case with Lawrence.

He glanced through the doorway of the tearoom and noted that his brother had arrived before him. Lawrence was never on time for anything, but his punctuality on this occasion was no doubt explained by the fact that seated opposite him were the lovely, auburn-haired Miss Dutton and her mother. Miss Dutton was having quite a steadying influence on his wayward younger brother, and Phillip could only hope the trend continued.

He lifted his hand to the base of his throat. After verifying that his pale blue necktie was still a perfect knot between the starched points of his wing collar, he started to enter the tearoom, casting a perfunctory glance at his lapel as he did so. He stopped in his tracks.

"Damn the woman," he muttered, staring down at what had been a pristine white camellia a short while ago, but was now a tattered, mangled mess thanks to Maria Martingale.

Justifiably annoyed, he turned around, retraced his steps back across the lobby, and exited the building. He paused before a flower seller, and as he searched for an appropriate boutonniere, the powerful fragrance of the flowers penetrated his nostrils.

Unbidden, a memory from the past came into his mind. A perfect August afternoon in the rose garden at Kayne Hall. Maria, seventeen, gathering a nosegay of flowers, Lawrence helping her, himself seated on a bench nearby, going over reports from his land agents. Twelve years ago, but Phillip could still see the pair in his mind's eye, standing by the arbor, a bit too close together for propriety, Lawrence playfully tucking rosebuds in her hair and making her laugh. He should have appreciated then how far things had gone between them, but all he'd been able to think about was how her throaty laughter was distracting him from a study of estate expenditures.

"Are you all right, guv'nor?"

The flower girl's query pulled him out of the past, and Phillip yanked a white carnation out of the girl's basket with an aggravated sigh. He dropped tuppence into her palm, and stalked back toward the hotel.

By the time he reached the tearoom again, he had tossed aside the damaged camellia and replaced it with the carnation, handed over his hat and gloves to the doorman, and cast aside any unwanted memories of Maria Martingale. If her intent was to cause trouble between Lawrence and Miss Dutton, Phillip knew she would not succeed, for he would be there to prevent it.

His brother spied him first. "At last!" he exclaimed and stood up as Phillip approached the table. "Wherever have you been? You're twenty minutes late."

"Twenty minutes?" Astonished, Phillip pulled his watch from the pocket of his waistcoat, certain his brother was exaggerating, but to his surprise, he found that Lawrence was right. He was twenty-two minutes late. "My profound apologies," he said to the ladies as he returned his watch to his waistcoat pocket, then he sat down in the empty chair beside his brother. "I was unavoidably detained."

"The planets are standing still!" Lawrence proclaimed with glee. "My brother," he said in a confidential tone as he leaned toward the two ladies across the table, "is as reliable as the British rails. He is never late, so his lack of punctuality on this occasion must mean something catastrophic has happened. Supplies not arriving at the shipyards on schedule? Longshoremen on strike? Cynthia's papa deciding not to let us build his transatlantic liners after all?"

"Don't be ridiculous." Phillip gave a tug to each of his cuffs and nodded to the waiter who was hovering nearby with a silver teapot. "As I said, I was detained, that's all, and not by anything catastrophic, I assure you."

"But it was a matter of business, if I know you, Phillip."

"Perhaps it wasn't," Miss Dutton put in. "Perhaps your brother met a charming young lady and lingered with her longer than he should have."

He stiffened in his chair, but managed to maintain an expressionless countenance. Maria had always been charming, but thankfully, he'd always been able to resist her. Lawrence, however, was a different matter.

Phillip glanced at his brother, feeling another glimmer of uneasiness. What was Maria up to?

"Impossible," Lawrence declared in dispute of Miss Dutton's suggestion. "My brother sacrificing punctuality to romance? Never!"

Cynthia ignored that and turned to Phillip. "Who was she, my lord? Tell us."

He spread his hands, palms up in a gesture of innocence. "There was no young lady, I assure you, Miss Dutton." That wasn't really a lie, since Maria Martingale was not a lady.

"Told you," Lawrence said with a certainty Phillip found rather irritating. "My brother is not a romantic sort of fellow."

The girl shook her head, laughing, her teasing gaze still on Phillip. "My lord, this will not do," she told him with mock severity. "You are a marquess, with titles and estates to consider. You must marry."

Lawrence laughed. "For that, my dear girl, he would have to stop conducting matters of business long enough to conduct a courtship."

"Pay no attention to my brother, Miss Dutton," Phillip told her. "He's always talking nonsense. Now tell me," he added, cutting off Lawrence's cry of protest and deliberately diverting the conversation, "what have the three of you been doing today?"

"We have been shopping," Miss Dutton told him, but she was immediately contradicted by Lawrence.

"No, the ladies have been shopping. I have been relegated to the role of list bearer and package carrier. Only on rare occasions have they solicited my opinion on matters of taste. It wounds me."

"Wicked boy!" Mrs. Dutton said, the indulgent amusement in her voice belying the reproving look she gave Lawrence. "Everyone knows gentlemen do not care about carpets and draperies."

"Carpets and draperies?" Phillip inquired as he accepted the cup of tea poured for him by the waiter. "I thought the house in Belgrave Square was to be let to you for the season fully furnished."

Mrs. Dutton frowned. "Baroness Stovinsky and I seem to have quite different ideas of what is meant by the term 'fully furnished.' Cynthia and I were there first thing this morning to inspect the place before having our things brought over from the hotel, only to find there isn't a carpet or curtain in the entire house. She took them all with her. And the paintings, too! What is she intending to do with them, in heaven's name? Cart them back to Saint Petersburg?"

"She's sold them, of course," Lawrence said with cheer, helping himself to a scone. "What else?"

"You're joking," Cynthia accused with a laugh. "Selling the carpets out from under her tenants? Whatever for?"

"To pay her debts, I should think."

"How shocking! Do you hear that, Mama? And she's a baroness, too." She turned to Phillip. "If your brother hadn't called on us this morning after we had returned from Belgrave Square, I don't know what we would have done. He took us around to all the best shops so that we might select replacements for the things taken by the baroness. We should have been lost without him, my lord."

Phillip studied her across the table, noting the wide smile she was bestowing on his brother. A lovely girl, he thought, so steady and sensible, and so obviously in love with Lawrence. He seemed enamored with her as well, not that that meant anything. Lawrence was in love quite often.

In this case, however, Phillip had reason to be a bit more optimistic. By all accounts, Lawrence had been in her company almost constantly while in New York. She came from a wealthy, well-established family. That connection might prove profitable if her father would allow Hawthorne Shipping to manufacture his new luxury liners. More important, however, was the fact that Cynthia's love for Lawrence seemed genuine and steadfast. She would make him an excellent wife, if only he'd come up to scratch and actually ask the girl to marry him. But Lawrence, allergic to serious commitments, was dragging his feet.

He hadn't dragged his feet about Maria Martingale.

The moment that thought entered his head, Phillip tried to shove it out again, but he could not escape that uneasy feeling. If Lawrence saw Maria again, his once-passionate feelings for the daughter of the former family chef might be rekindled. No doubt that would suit her down to the ground, but it would ruin Lawrence's life just as surely now as it would have done then.

Phillip glanced from Miss Dutton to his brother and back again, and their radiant faces as they gazed into each other's eyes hardened his resolve.

Since the age of sixteen, when his father had died and he had become the marquess, it had been Phillip's responsibility to protect the members of his family. Yet he had been looking out for Lawrence far longer than that, ever since he could remember, in fact. He loved his brother, and he would not allow Lawrence's future happiness to be spoiled. Until his brother and Cynthia were safely married, Phillip knew he'd best keep his eyes open and his wits about him.

Chapter 2

One can't make an omelette without breaking eggs.
French proverb

"*Y*ou're certain it was he?"

That question caused Maria to give the Duchess of St. Cyres a wry glance as she paced across her friend's elegant drawing room in Grosvenor Square. "Phillip Hawthorne isn't the sort of man one forgets," she answered, turning at the fireplace to retrace her steps. "And it wasn't as if I saw him from a distance. I cannoned right into him."

"Not your most graceful moment," Prudence said, smiling as she picked up the crystal flagon on the table before her and poured Madeira into two glasses. She held one up for her friend.

"What are the odds?" Maria demanded, taking the glass as she passed. "I ask you, what are the odds of such a dreadful coincidence?"

"Coincidences do happen," Prudence pointed out, sounding so reasonable that Maria only felt more put out.

"Well, they shouldn't." She sank into a chair. "Such a lovely shop, too. Big plate-glass windows, and Green Park right across the street. And the kitchen—" She broke off, pressing a palm to her forehead as she made a sound of exasperation. "Why did that horrid man have to take rooms next to the best kitchen in London? Why couldn't he have stayed at his house in Park Lane with the other rich toffs? Sorry, Pru," she apologized at once, for Prudence, with her income in the millions and her home in Grosvenor Square, was now among those rich toffs. "I forget sometimes the circles you move in these days."

Prudence waved aside the apology. "Is the Marquess of Kayne truly horrid? I haven't yet met him."

"You haven't missed anything." Maria touched one finger to her chin and tilted her head to the side as Pru laughed. "Hmm, let's see . . ." she teased, "gadding about the globe to places like Paris and New York with your charming, handsome husband, or being stuck in London, meeting snobs like Lord Kayne." She heaved an exaggerated sigh. "Dear, dear. What's an heiress to do?"

Something in those words caused Prudence

to stop laughing. "Are you all right about all that?" she asked, looking anxious. "The money, I mean?"

Maria lowered her hand and stared at her friend in amazement. "Of course I am! I don't begrudge you a penny!"

"You weren't happy about it at first," her friend reminded her.

"Because I was afraid you'd abandon your old friends and become haughty and condescending like Phillip. And money does—" She stopped, but Prudence knew what she'd been about to say.

"Money does things to people," her friend finished for her. "Yes, I remember when you told me that."

Maria thought of how Phillip had used his money—threatening to withhold it from Lawrence should he marry her, offering it to her as a bribe to disappear. She and Lawrence had both succumbed. For the sake of security, they had allowed themselves to be bought. She thought of Phillip's matter-of-fact expression that day in the library, and how he'd taken her acceptance of the bribe as a matter of course. Oh, how badly she'd wanted to tear that bank draft apart and throw the pieces in his face, but a thousand pounds was not something a poor girl, alone in the world, could ever afford to refuse, just for the sake of her pride.

"Rhys might know the marquess already," Prudence's musing voice forced Maria out of the past. "School, perhaps, or if Lord Kayne has ever been to Italy. Rhys lived there for twelve years."

Maria shook her head. "I doubt they met at school. The duke is three or four years older than your husband. Italy doesn't seem likely either. Phillip's father died when he was sixteen, and he became so obsessed with duty and responsibility that he'd never leave his estates unattended and go off to Italy. Still, I'm sure you both will meet him soon enough. You're a duke and duchess, after all." She stuck her nose in the air with aristocratic hauteur. "His lordship only associates with the finest so-ci-eh-tay." She drew out the syllables of the last word as if she were the most condescending of aristocrats, making Prudence smile.

"Then I shan't ever meet him. Rhys might be a duke, but he's always been considered terribly disreputable, and high sticklers don't want much to do with him, especially since he married *me*. I am a former seamstress."

"Marrying you is the best thing the duke ever did, and he would be the first to admit it." She paused to take a sip of her wine, then went on, "You might be right about Phillip, though. Given your husband's devilish past, Phillip shall no doubt do his best to avoid an introduction to you, thereby escaping your acquaintance altogether.

He certainly had no difficulty giving me the cut today."

"I still can't believe it," Prudence said. "You've known each other nearly all your lives. Yet he didn't acknowledge you in any way?"

"Heavens, no!" Maria looked at her friend, her eyes widening in mock horror. "I'm the daughter of the former family chef. He is the Marquess of Kayne. Acknowledging me would mean I *mattered*, darling! One might as well go about claiming acquaintance with scullery maids and hall boys!"

"At least you're taking it all in the proper spirit."

"I don't want to," she confessed and set aside her glass. She slumped in her chair, plunking an elbow on her knee and resting her cheek in her hand. "I want that shop."

"Cheer up, dearest. You can start looking for another one tomorrow."

"So you think I should look elsewhere?"

"Of course. Don't you?"

She leaned back, considering the question. She'd first thought to take the premises straightaway, but after her encounter with Phillip and the way he'd snubbed her, she had hesitated, thinking it might be best to discuss the situation with Prudence and give herself time to mull things over before committing herself to a lease. But now, after telling her friend all about it, after a few sips of Madeira and some time to consider, she didn't see why she should alter her plans.

"I'm not going to look elsewhere," she answered with a hint of defiance. "I've been searching for months, and now I've found the best kitchen in London. I'm not giving it up just because that wretched man is living next door. Why should I?"

"Well—" Prudence began, as if to answer that question, but Maria cut her off.

"He's no threat to me. It isn't as if he can do anything. And he isn't going to be living there forever. Besides . . ." She paused to consider the ramifications. "I rather like the notion of being right under his nose. It will irritate him so much," she added with a smile.

"Are you sure it's wise to stir things up?"

Maria ignored that. Instead, she reached for her glass. "Here's to being the bane of Phillip Hawthorne's existence," she said, but when Prudence didn't respond to the raillery, she lowered her glass again with a sigh. "Oh, Pru, you're not going to spoil all my fun by saying no, are you? Being my financial partner, you could, you know."

"I should," Prudence answered, looking unhappy. "But I won't. Still, I do feel impelled to caution you. Perhaps it would be best to avoid trouble and search for a different location."

"What, go scurrying away like a frightened

rabbit because Phillip Hawthorne said boo?" She shook her head. "No, he forced me to take that course once before. He'll not do it again."

"What about his brother?"

"Lawrence?" she asked in surprise. "What does he have to do with it?"

"You'll eventually encounter him, too."

"Nonsense." She swirled her glass and downed the last of her Madeira. "Lawrence moved to America ages ago. Eight or nine years, at least. Last I heard, he's living in New York."

"He isn't, not anymore. He arrived in London a week ago."

"How do you know that?"

"I read the society pages. I have to. As a duchess, I must pay some attention to the comings and goings of peers."

"Lawrence isn't a peer. He's merely the brother of one. I can't imagine why the gossips deem his return from America worth talking about." She felt a pang of alarm. "He hasn't come home because he's ill, or something of that kind?"

"No, he's not ill. It seems he's engaged."

"Lawrence? Engaged to be married?"

"That is what the scandal sheets say, although no engagement has been officially announced."

"Who . . . ?" She broke off, surprised by this news, more surprised, she supposed, than she should have been. "Who is the girl?"

"A Miss Cynthia Dutton, of New York. Her father is Howard K. Dutton, the shipping magnate. He owns a fleet of those transatlantic liners. Family's got heaps of money."

"So Lawrence hasn't gone off with the wrong sort of girl this time. He's making a creditable marriage." Maria's lips curved in a sardonic smile. "Phillip must be so relieved."

She thought of how he had looked this afternoon and the changes time had brought to his face, and she wondered what marks the years might have left upon his younger brother. An image of Lawrence came into her mind—eyes the same deep blue as his brother's, but brimming with laughter. His hair, a lighter shade of brown, but never as neatly combed. His face, similar in features, but much more carefree, the sort of face that had once made a young girl's heart ache with both pleasure and pain. Just for a moment, she felt again that powerful pang of first love—all the joy, all the longing, all the agonizing uncertainty.

"Maria?" Prudence's voice brought her out of her reverie, and she looked up to find her friend eyeing her with concern. "Are you all right?"

"Of course. Should I not be?"

"I thought you might find this news a bit shattering. You did love him once."

"Passionately," she agreed, and gave a little laugh. "When Phillip parted us, I thought I'd die of a broken heart." As she spoke, the nostalgic, romantic moment passed, and she was herself once more, a mature, sensible woman of twenty-nine, not a love-struck girl of seventeen. "But that was a long time ago."

"There's something else you should know." Prudence leaned forward in her chair, the concern on her round, cherubic face deepening. "Lawrence is staying with his brother here in London."

Maria began to feel rather like Lewis Carroll's Alice, who'd been expected to believe six impossible things before breakfast. "Lawrence is also living next to my shop? Are you sure?"

Prudence set aside her glass, rose, and walked to an elaborate gold-and-white table of papier-mâché by the fireplace where several newspapers had been neatly stacked. She pulled the *Social Gazette* from the pile and opened it. After a moment of flipping through the pages, she gave a nod. "'While in London,'" she read, "'Mr. Lawrence Hawthorne will be staying with his brother, the Marquess of Kayne, who is presently keeping rooms in Half Moon Street while his home in Park Lane undergoes renovation. The Marquess is said to be adding electricity, telephones, four full bathrooms and steam central heating to his already luxurious residence. Mr. Hawthorne will retain the rooms in Half Moon Street once his brother vacates them.'"

"Lovely," Maria murmured with a groan. "That's just lovely."

Prudence refolded the paper, placed it on the pile, and returned to her chair. "So you see? You cannot lease that shop."

Maria thought of Phillip and how he had snubbed her. She folded her arms, feeling a bit contrary and stubborn. "I don't see why not," she said. "Where Lawrence and Phillip live hasn't anything to do with me."

"Maria . . ." Prudence's voice trailed away as she gave her friend a warning glance. "Didn't you make a promise never to—"

"Yes, yes," she interrupted with a hint of frustration. "I promised I'd never see or speak to Lawrence again. But it's a meaningless promise nowadays, surely!"

"Is it?"

"Of course. All of us are adults, mature and sensible. Phillip needn't have any fear his brother will go running off to Gretna Green with me now. It's been twelve years, in heaven's name. Besides, Lawrence is about to marry someone else." She paused to consider how she felt about that, then she shrugged. "And I truly couldn't give a fig. I'm happy for him."

"That's a very generous attitude."

Ignoring Prudence's somewhat skeptical look, she glanced at the clock. "Lord, is that the time? I have to be going. It'll be dark soon," she added as she stood up, "and you know how Mrs. Morris worries if we aren't in before dark. Tomorrow I'm going back to that property agent and arrange for the lease."

Prudence also rose to her feet. "If you're determined to do this, I'll have an account at Lloyd's opened in your name first thing tomorrow so you can write a bank draft for the deposit."

"Darling Pru," Maria said, laughing at her friend's serious face. "Don't look so worried. As I said, that entire to-do with Lawrence was a long time ago. It means nothing now."

Prudence did not look convinced. "I hope you know what you're doing."

"I know exactly what I'm doing," she answered, refusing to believe otherwise.

Considering how long it had taken Maria to find the perfect location for her shop, once that goal had been reached, it was amazing how quickly everything else fell into place.

Within a week, she had negotiated the terms of the lease, opened accounts with suppliers, and moved out of her flat in Little Russell Street. Only ten days after first viewing the shop, she decided it was time to tackle the horrible yellow-green paint, and she began the process by applying samples of various other colors to a wall of the shop's front room.

Once that task was accomplished, she stepped back to study her efforts. Tilting her head to one side, she felt a loose tendril of hair tickle her cheek, and she shoved it absentmindedly back into the kerchief wrapped around her hair as she considered the choices before her. The beige was pleasant enough, but it might be too pink when all the walls were done. The taupe was too depressing, the brown too dark, the lavender too awful. There was nothing wrong with the tan, she supposed, viewing it without enthusiasm. It was only that it was so . . . well . . . so dull. Just looking at it made her want to yawn.

"I heard a rumor there's a new bakery in the West End."

Maria turned toward the door, which was open to ventilate the smell of paint, and she smiled at the elegantly dressed woman standing in the doorway.

"Emma!" she cried with relief and bent to set the brush atop the tin of paint on the tarp-covered floor. "Thank goodness you've finally arrived in town. I'm in desperate need of help."

"Yes, so it would seem." The Viscountess Marlowe laughed, shaking her head and causing the enormous white plumes atop her wide-brimmed green hat to bounce as she crossed the room. "Oh, if only you could see yourself."

"Why? Do I look as discouraged as I feel?"

"That wasn't quite what I meant." Emma paused in front of her, opened her small, white leather handbag, removed a round pocket mirror from the bag, and held it up.

"Good lord." Maria stared at her reflection in dismay. Paint seemed to be everywhere—there were smears on her face, her kerchief, even on the unprotected lobe of her ear. She glanced down and was glad to see no paint on her white shirtwaist and brown skirt, although the big bibbed chef's apron she wore over them and the old gauntlet gloves on her hands were spattered with a variety of colors.

"I look like an artist's palette," she said, laughing with her friend. "How can a person become so covered in paint after only dabbing a few samples on a wall?"

"It happens," Emma said, returning the pocket glass to her bag. "So, what sort of muddle are you in that you need my help? Prudence told me you were moving along with your bakery at breathtaking speed. No problems at all."

"Paint, Emma. Paint is my difficulty. I simply must cover up this awful color."

"Cover it?" Emma stared at her in mock horror. "But Liberty colors are part of the whole aesthetic movement, darling! Still considered by many to be the height of fashion."

Maria made a face. "Including the property agent. The entire place was renovated for the last tenant, who had intended to open a tea shop. But she abandoned the project before the paint was laid on, so the property agent was asked to have the place painted." She waved a hand at the walls. "He chose this."

"Not a very appetizing color for a bakery."

"Just so." She turned to the wall and sighed. "But I don't like any of the colors I've tried either. Can you help me? You're so good at this sort of thing. I remember your flat in Little Russell Street always looked ever so smart."

"Thank you, and I'd be glad to help. But you must first give me a tour of the place."

Maria was happy to comply. She began with the kitchen, unable to resist showing off all her modern cooking devices. Emma was suitably impressed. Then she led the other woman through the upper floors that comprised the living quarters.

"It's larger than I expected," Emma told her as they went back downstairs. "Four bedrooms, a spacious drawing room, maid's quarters in the attic. And that balcony off your bedroom is lovely, even if it does extend all the way along the back of the building."

" 'Even if'?" she echoed. "A spacious balcony is a problem?"

"No, except that you share it with the house next door."

Maria stopped on the landing. Heavens, she hadn't even thought about that. Being Phillip's next-door neighbor was bad enough, but sharing a balcony with him? That did not bode well. She felt a sudden pang of misgiving.

"So nice, too, that the rooms come fully furnished," Emma continued, then stopped, noticing Maria was not keeping pace with her. She glanced over her shoulder. "What's wrong?"

Maria reminded herself that Phillip was pretending not to know her, and she could only hope that meant he would never lower himself enough to speak with her. "Nothing," she said, pushing the glimmer of doubt aside. "What did you think of the bath?" she asked, changing the subject.

"Wonderful," Emma answered as they continued down the stairs. "Very modern. And so conveniently located beside your bedroom."

"Once I saw it, I knew I couldn't wait until the place had been painted to move in," she explained as they returned to the front of the shop. "Speaking of paint . . ." She paused and pointed at the wall of paint smears. "Have you any ideas?"

"You must have some ideas of your own," Emma countered, turning toward her. "How do you see it in your mind's eye?"

Maria glanced around, thinking it over. "I envision the ambience of a French café with tea tables and chairs in the center of the room, so people can take tea here if they wish. I want something very modern, very posh. I intend Martingale's to be *the* place everyone thinks of when they think of pastries. Which reminds me . . ." She paused for a moment, then went on. "If you would feel all right about it, I was hoping you would recommend my *pâtisserie* in *All Things London*."

All Things London was a shopping guide Emma wrote under the pseudonym of "Mrs. Bartleby." The guides were published quarterly by her husband's publishing company and were wildly popular.

"Are you thinking of the spring edition?" Emma asked, and Maria heard a hint of hesitancy in her friend's voice.

She hastened into speech. "I realize that since we're not open for business yet, and you haven't tasted a thing from the kitchens, it's awfully cheeky of me to ask, but a recommendation from you would mean so much and—"

"Cheeky?" Emma interrupted in surprise. "Not at all! You're my friend, and I already know you make the most delicious pastries in the world. I had three pieces of Prudence's lovely coconut wedding cake, if you recall. I'd be happy to recommend your establishment. It's just that the folio is about to go to press, so I shall have to speak with my husband about adding a passage to the text. It's past the production deadline, you see."

"I wouldn't wish to be a lot of bother."

"No, no. Harry will give me his usual speech, of course," she added, her expression softening as she spoke of her husband. "He'll be terribly exasperated with me, and he'll ask me why authors are always wanting to make changes right up to the end, and why can't we just leave well enough alone, but in the end, he'll do it if I ask him to. When do you plan to open?"

"I should be ready in about a week."

"A week?" Emma laughed. "It may have taken you months to find the right place, but now that you have, you're not letting any grass grow under your feet, are you?"

"It's already March. I want to take as much advantage of the London season as I can. That's why the spring edition of *All Things London* is so important."

The viscountess took another look around the room. "What about a color scheme that conveys warm, delicious pastries—a soft, buttery yellow for the walls, for instance, with creamy white for the moldings and doors, and walnut-stained wood for your display cases and tea tables?"

"That's perfect!" Maria cried. "Oh, Em, you've grasped what I want exactly! As I said, you're so accomplished at this sort of thing. I shall use those colors in my insignia. And on a striped ribbon for the paperboard boxes."

"Boxes? To take away pastries?"

"Yes, and for picnic luncheons, too. Green Park is across the street, so I thought I'd offer picnic luncheons during the summer months."

"Intend to compete with Fortnum and Mason's famous picnic hampers, do you?"

"I don't just want to compete with Fortnum and Mason," Maria told her. "I want to surpass them."

A deep, male voice answered her before Emma could. "An ambitious goal."

Maria grimaced at that familiar voice, feeling a hint of dread. Hoping she was mistaken, she turned, but the sight of the tall man in the doorway told her she had made no mistake. Phillip Hawthorne stood there, looking as grim as a Presbyterian funeral.

He glanced down the length of her, a slow, deliberate perusal that made her suddenly, painfully aware of her paint-smeared face and spattered clothes. His own attire was immaculate, of course. His charcoal-gray suit showed not a single speck of lint, his claret-red waistcoat had nary a wrinkle, and his linen shirt was a pure, snowy white.

She shifted her weight from one foot to the other, her face growing hot as his gaze traveled back up her body. She thought he must be appalled, but to her surprise, when he returned his gaze to her face, he didn't look appalled. In fact, there was a faint but unmistakable curve to one corner of his mouth. Phillip, the man who never smiled, the man who never laughed, was laughing at her.

She watched him press his lips together as if to hide it, and she strove to muster her dignity. "There is nothing wrong with being ambitious."

"Perhaps not, Miss Martingale." He entered the shop, moving with the arrogant assurance people of his class possessed almost from birth, not seeming to care in the least that he hadn't been invited to come in. "Though ambition is not always an appealing trait in a woman."

"And eavesdropping on conversations isn't an appealing trait in anyone," she shot back.

"It was hardly eavesdropping," he pointed out, gesturing to the open door with his hat.

"So any open doorway is an invitation to not only listen in on other people's conversations, but also to add one's own opinions?"

The silence seemed to crackle with tension, and Emma made a delicate little cough.

Phillip, ever polite, immediately turned in her direction and bowed. "Lady Marlowe."

"Lord Kayne." The viscountess curtsied in reply, then glanced at Maria. "I was not aware you were acquainted with my friend, Miss Martingale," she murmured, looking from Maria to Phillip and back again. A tiny frown knit her brows, as if she sensed the tension but did not understand it.

If Phillip was surprised that someone as low-born as Maria was friends with a viscountess, he didn't show it, but before he could reply, she spoke first. "Oh, but this man is not acquainted with me, Emma," she said, her voice bright and cheery. "We don't know each other *at all*. At least, that's what I've been told." She ignored her friend's deepening frown of bewilderment and smiled sweetly at the man opposite her. "Acquaintanceship would imply a familiarity with me of which this gentleman is unaware."

His smile vanished, but if she hoped the reminder of his words from the other day would provoke him into an admission that they were indeed acquainted, she was disappointed. "I am here on a matter of business, madam," he said. "The establishment you intend to open here, to be precise."

Emma gave another ladylike cough. "In that case, I should go," she murmured. "Maria, it's been wonderful to see your shop."

"Don't leave yet," she implored, giving Phillip a resentful glance. "If this gentleman wishes to speak with me, surely he can do so in front of my friends."

"No, no, I do have to be on my way. But I shall see you for Sunday tea in Little Russell Street, I hope?"

"Of course! But, really Emma, must you go?"

"I'm afraid so. I am supposed to be at some charity tea in Bloomsbury this afternoon, and you know how beastly the traffic in London is nowadays." She nodded to Phillip and started for the door. "I'll talk with Harry about the new catalogue when I see him this evening."

"Thank you," she said, walking with her friend to the door. "You've been such a tremendous help."

Emma departed, and Maria could feel Phillip's cool gaze boring into her back as she paused in the open doorway. Taking a deep breath, she turned around. "I cannot imagine what matter of business you and I might have to discuss. But I'm sure you will enlighten me."

"I was passing by this morning, and I saw you through the windows. Upon making inquiries, I found you had leased these premises. Needless to say, I was surprised."

And angry, too, she concluded. "I find your interest in me baffling, sir. We don't know each other, remember? You told me so yourself."

"Under the circumstances at the time," he said with haughty dignity, "I thought that action was for the best."

"You thought it best to be both cruel and rude?"

"I—" He paused, and his haughtiness seemed to falter. A shadow of what might have been regret crossed his face, but it was gone before she could be sure. "Forgive me. It was not my intent to be uncivil, nor to wound your feelings. I merely thought to spare us both what would no doubt have been an awkward conversation."

She felt compelled to point out the obvious. "Yet here you are."

"A conversation between us has now become necessary." His eyes narrowed, and his expression once again became hard and implacable. "I thought I made it clear twelve years ago that you were to have nothing to do with my brother ever again."

"Your brother?" She peered about her in pretended bafflement. "Is Lawrence here? I must be going blind. I don't see him anywhere. Is he hiding?"

"It's clear you've not changed, Miss Martingale. Still as impudent as ever."

"You haven't changed either. Still dry as a stick."

He ignored the jibe. "You were paid one thousand pounds, in exchange for which you gave me your word you would keep away from Lawrence."

She gave him her best innocent stare and told the truth. "I haven't seen your brother since I left Kayne Hall twelve years ago. I heard he went to America."

"He isn't in America any longer. At present, he is living with me." He lifted his arm and jabbed it toward the residence next door. "In the house attached to this one, as if you didn't know it!"

She waited a moment before replying, choosing her words with care. "When I decided to lease these premises, I had no idea you or your brother were living next door."

"So you are saying you have not broken your promise? That your presence here is a mere co-incidence?" Before she could answer, he made a sound of derision. "You expect me to believe such a flimsy lie?"

"I don't care tuppence what you believe, and I have not broken my word." *Not technically anyway*, she added to herself, feeling a tiny attack of conscience.

"You can hardly continue to keep it if you are living right next door." He glared at her. "Tell me, do you have no regard for any of the promises you make, Miss Martingale, or just the ones you make to me?"

"Oh, for heaven's sake!" she cried, exasperated not only by his intractable attitude, but also by her own niggling sense of guilt. "It's been twelve years. We are all adults who can behave civilly. Must we all avoid each other like the plague?"

"You *are* a plague," he muttered. "A plague on men's sanity."

She bristled, her momentary guilt vanished, and she opened her mouth to fire off an equally flattering opinion of him, but he spoke again before she could do so.

"How much?"

She blinked at the abrupt turn in the conversation. "I beg your pardon?"

"I had to pay you once to go away. I am attempting to ascertain the amount required to make you go away again. How much?"

"Of all the—" Outrage choked her throat, and it took a moment before she could go on. "You don't have that much money."

"I can assure you I do. Name your price."

"Not everything is for sale, my lord. I am here, I intend to stay here, and there is nothing you can do about it."

"You think not?"

The question was deceptively soft, but Maria was not fooled. She knew from painful experience how hard-hearted Phillip could be. Prickles of warning danced along her spine, but she stood her ground. "There is nothing you can do," she repeated.

"You made a promise to me twelve years ago, Miss Martingale, and by God, I shall see that you keep it. Paying you off would have been the simplest, most expedient course, but since that notion does not appeal to you, I must call upon my attorneys."

"Attorneys? Whatever for?"

"To arrange for your eviction from these premises, of course." With that, he turned and strode away. He was at the door before she could recover from her surprise enough to reply.

"What are you talking about? You cannot have me evicted."

"Oh, but I can." He paused, hand on the doorknob, and gave her a grim smile. "I happen to own this building."

Chapter 3

*Be he alive or be he dead, I'll grind his bones to
make my bread.*

English nursery rhyme

"What?" She stared at Phillip, and she couldn't
help a laugh. "That's absurd. My lease is with a
company called Millbury Investments."

"A company I own, which makes this building
my property. I expect you to be gone from these
premises by this time tomorrow."

He opened the door and walked out without another word, closing the door behind him.

"Oh!" Frustrated beyond bearing, she turned
away from the door and kicked the wall. It chipped
the plaster and hurt her toe, but did nothing to relieve her feelings.

Of all the ludicrous situations to find oneself
in, she thought, balling her hands into fists. Bad

enough that Phillip lived next door, but to find that once again her fate was in his hands was aggravating beyond belief.

"Hateful man!" she muttered and kicked the wall again. "Loathsome, hateful man!"

She grimaced at the pain in her toe and decided kicking the walls of her shop was no way to rid herself of her frustration. She peeled off her work gloves and marched downstairs to her kitchen, and a few minutes later, she was elbow deep in bread dough.

For over an hour, Maria kneaded, punched, and pummeled the ball of soft, white dough, less concerned with culinary considerations than she was with relieving her feelings of frustration, a task made even more difficult when an errand boy from the property agent's offices came to call. He presented her with a very official-looking document.

"That didn't take long," she muttered as she snatched the folded sheet from the boy's outstretched hand, ignoring his amazed stare at her paint-stained clothes, flour-dusted hands and disheveled appearance. She glanced down at the words, EVICTION NOTICE, printed on the outside of the sheet in red ink. "What did he do when he left here?" she demanded, returning her gaze to the delivery boy. "Ring his attorneys on the telephone?"

The boy didn't answer. He simply continued to

stare, his expression conveying obvious doubts about her sanity. Maria heaved a sigh, slammed the tradesmen's door in his face, and broke the seal on the document. She scanned the typewritten lines from Millbury Investments and was not surprised to learn that she was required to remove herself and her belongings within twenty-four hours, just as Phillip had demanded. But when she reached the reason for her eviction, the frustration she'd been trying so hard to eradicate erupted into fury. "Violation of the character clause?" she cried. "Of all the unfair, unfounded accusations he could make—"

Too incensed to read any further, she crumpled the eviction notice into a ball, tossed it into the rubbish bin beneath her worktable, and resumed her task, venting her feelings on the dough with more force than ever.

"I am a woman of impeccable moral character! How dare he say otherwise?" She lifted the ball of dough from the floured board of her worktable, then threw it down again with enough force to flatten it. "And why does it matter to him where I live anyway?" she added, giving the dough a resounding slap with the palm of her hand, wishing she could do the same to Phillip's face. "I don't care tuppence for Lawrence. Why, I haven't even thought about him for years."

The moment she'd said those words, she had to admit they weren't the absolute truth. Even a dozen years after her departure from Kayne Hall, memories of her first love had sometimes stolen into her mind. A particular shade of blue would remind her of his eyes, or she'd catch the scent of roses and remember that day in the arbor when he'd put rosebuds in her hair and declared her the prettiest girl he'd ever seen.

Phillip had been in the rose garden that day, too. "Glowering as if he had indigestion," she muttered. She lifted the dough and slammed it back down. "Stuffy, stiff-necked snob. How dare he evict me?"

Maria stopped, panting, and she knew she had to find a way to fight him. She refused to meekly slink away. She refused to believe that she had found the perfect shop only to lose it before she'd even had the chance to prove herself.

She could call upon Prudence's attorneys, but she was already borrowing a fortune from her friend, and though Prudence didn't care if she ever paid any of it back, *Maria* cared. Pride had always been one of her besetting sins, she supposed, but she didn't want to live on her friend's charity. She was determined to pay Prudence back every penny she borrowed, so she didn't want to run up her debt by any extravagant expenses, particularly the engaging of attorneys.

In any case, she doubted it would do much good. If she remembered the terms of the lease, there was indeed a character clause within it. Her tenancy could be revoked for nonpayment of rent, for infliction of damage to the premises, or for immorality of character. Though there was little explanation of what immorality of character encompassed, it hardly mattered. That sort of fight would ruin her reputation regardless of the outcome, and no one in Mayfair would buy her pastries.

She could find another shop. Maria looked around her beautiful kitchen, with its modern ovens, gleaming copper hoods, and generous cupboards. She could recreate it all somewhere else, she supposed, build cupboards like these, buy equipment just like this. But again, that would be so costly. And she couldn't recreate prime shop frontage on Piccadilly. That particular commodity was as rare as hen's teeth. Still, what else could she do but leave?

She was suddenly swamped by despair. Phillip was a marquess, a man of vast wealth and influence. She was powerless against him, just as she'd been when she was seventeen.

How cold he'd been that day in the library at Kayne Hall when he'd told her of his brother's decision to keep his income rather than marry her. How unmoved he'd been by her tears of heartbreak and fear as she had first protested, then agreed to his terms. How impersonally he'd held out the check in exchange for her solemn promise to never come near Lawrence again.

With sudden certainty, Maria knew what she had to do. She reached behind her and untied the strings of her apron. She pulled off the heavy cotton garment and tossed it onto the worktable, then she left the kitchen. For twelve years, she had faithfully kept her promise. Now, she was going to break it.

Two hours later, there was no paint on her face, nor was there any lingering scent of the turpentine she'd used to remove it. Maria stepped out of the porcelain bathtub and lifted a towel from the mahogany surround. She dried off and squeezed the water from her hair, then hung the towel on the iron towel rail and walked into the dressing room that adjoined the bath.

After donning fresh underclothes, she slid her arms into the sleeves of a crisp white shirtwaist and did up the buttons. For this occasion, she chose her best day dress, a walking suit of blue serge. She combed out her hair, pinned the long, curly strands into a tight twist at the back of her head, and then put on her prettiest hat—a wide-brimmed, dark blue straw trimmed with a froth of cream-colored ostrich plumes and ribbons. After all, she told herself as she slid her hands into knitted white gloves, when a woman intended to see the man who had once been the love of her life, it wouldn't do to encounter him looking drab and down at heel.

Maria went downstairs, retrieved the eviction letter from the rubbish bin and smoothed it out, then folded it and put it in her pocket. She exited the house, and as she locked her front door, she took a peek up and down the street just to be sure Phillip wasn't hovering about, spying upon her, ready to pounce if she came near his doorstep.

She dropped her latchkey into her handbag and bought a newspaper from the boy on the corner, then crossed the street to Green Park. Choosing a bench where she had a plain view of Piccadilly in both directions as well as the entire length of Half Moon Street, Maria sat down, unfolded the newspaper, and pretended to read, but all the while, she kept her gaze fixed on the corner across the street.

She didn't have to wait long. After perhaps twenty minutes, she spied a brown-haired man in dapper, buff-colored flannels and a straw boater coming up Half Moon Street, swinging a walking stick. She squinted, studying him for a moment, then she gave a satisfied nod and stood up. She'd know that jaunty, carefree stride anywhere.

She cast aside the newspaper and hastened back across Piccadilly, careful to do so at an angle away from the corner so that she would not be seen by her quarry too soon. By the time she passed the doorway of her shop and turned onto Half Moon

Street, she had her handbag open and was fumbling within its depths, seeming to any unknowing observer like a woman too preoccupied with the contents of her bag to pay attention to where she was going.

The collision was perfectly timed. Her bag and his walking stick clattered to the pavement, his hat and her bonnet went flying, and even to her own ears, her cry of pain sounded quite genuine.

"I say," Lawrence cried, grasping her arms as if to prevent her from falling, "I'm terribly sorry. Are you all right?"

"I–I'm not certain," she answered. Looking up into his face, she found he had not changed much at all, for his countenance was very much the boyishly handsome one she remembered. But time had changed her, for looking at him now, she felt none of the agonizing sweetness she'd felt for him at seventeen.

She gave a gasp of pretended astonishment. "Why, Lawrence Hawthorne, as I live and breathe!"

Thankfully, Lawrence wasn't like his brother. Not only did he recognize her at once, he freely acknowledged the fact. "Maria Martingale?" he said, laughing as he stared back at her in amazement. "Maria, is it really you?"

She nodded, laughing with him. "Heavens, this is a surprise, isn't it?" she said, hoping she sounded convincing. "How have you been?"

"Well enough. Well enough," he answered and bent down to retrieve their hats. "And yourself?"

"Perfectly well, thank you."

"I'm glad to hear it." He straightened, and as he looked at her again, there was open admiration in his expression, something Maria found quite gratifying in light of his brother's disdain. "By Jove, you haven't changed a bit," he said and winked at her as he put her bonnet on her head. "Still the prettiest girl I've ever seen."

Maria wondered what Miss Dutton might think of that opinion, but she didn't voice her speculation aloud. "And you're still the biggest flirt," she said instead, straightening her hat to the proper angle as he bent to gather the rest of their belongings from the pavement. "My goodness. How long has it been? Ten years?"

"Twelve," he said as he dropped items in her handbag. "What have you been doing with yourself?"

"I'm opening a shop."

"Are you?" He snapped her handbag closed and held it up to her, then he retrieved his walking stick and rose. "What sort of shop?"

"A bakery. Right there," she added, turning as if to show him, then she cried out with a pretense of pain. "Oh! I think I twisted my ankle."

Lawrence's amiable face took on a frown of concern. "And it's all my fault," he said, chivalrously taking the blame. "You must come inside, and I'll send for a doctor."

"Come inside?" she repeated, looking around in pretended puzzlement. "Do you live near here?"

"Right there." He pointed to the red door beside them.

"There? Why, you're right next to my shop!" She waved a hand to the doorway behind her. "I've leased those premises."

Lawrence was not only more amiable than his brother, he was also much more trusting. "What an amazing coincidence!" He gestured again to his front door. "Do come in and have a cup of tea and tell me all about it while we wait for the doctor. No, really," he added, overriding her feeble protest, "I insist. Come with me."

She accepted his offered arm and shoulder. As she hobbled to his front steps with quite a convincing show of pain, it occurred to her that if her bakery didn't succeed, she could always take up the stage as a profession. Ten minutes later, she was comfortably ensconced in her neighbor's luxurious drawing room, sipping a cup of tea and pouring out her tale of woe to a very sympathetic listener.

Hawthorne Shipping, Limited, was located in a four-story brick building on Surrey Street, right by the Victoria Embankment. Phillip's corner office on the top floor had a splendid view of the Thames, and through his windows, he could see Waterloo Bridge, Somerset House, and the gardens along the Embankment. It was a fine spring afternoon, with no rain, plenty of sunshine, and a breeze stout enough to clear the London air of its usual coal-induced haze. The first flowers of spring were in bloom, and the sun's rays glittered on the water of the river like the points of diamonds. All this beauty was wasted on Phillip, however, for he was occupied with something far more important than the view from his windows. Business.

"Our engineers and yours have approved the final designs," he said as leaned over his massive mahogany desk, spreading out several large sheets of paper on its polished, plum-colored surface. He glanced at the man who stood opposite him. "Hawthorne Shipping is ready to manufacture three of these luxury liners for Dutton's Neptune Line." He paused, gesturing to the legal documents stacked on one corner of the desk. "With your signature on these contracts, Colonel, I can give our factories the order to proceed."

Colonel William K. Dutton tugged at one end of his snowy white mustache—a mustache that lent the ruthless American millionaire the look of a sleepy walrus. He gave a *harrumph* and sat down, then drummed his fingers on the desk as he stared at the drawings spread out before him.

Phillip also sat down. He leaned back and waited, expressing no impatience as the silence lengthened and the minutes went by. He'd been putting this deal together for over two years. He could wait a little longer.

The Colonel finally looked up. "When could the ships be ready to set sail?"

Phillip smiled at that question. "With three propellers and a pair of four-cylinder steam engines powered by twenty-four boilers, which are fired by one hundred fifty furnaces, a ship nowadays has no need for sails, Colonel."

The other man grinned back at him. "I'm a rag man, myself," he confessed. "Always have been. You young men with your steam engines and boilers—bah! Nothing like the sing and whistle of sails, my lord."

"Believe it or not, I do know what you mean. My own sailing yacht is anchored at Waterloo Pier." He saw no need to tell the other man he hadn't set foot on that ship for about four years.

"Ah." Gratified by this sign of common ground, Colonel Dutton returned his attention to the drawings on the desk, and Phillip told him what he wanted to know.

"If we signed contracts today, we could have the first ship headed across the North Atlantic three years from now." He paused, counted to three, and then said, "Do we have a deal, Colonel?"

There was another long pause. The other man's answer, when it came, was not what he'd been hoping for. "That depends, my lord. That depends."

"Upon what?"

Colonel Dutton sighed and leaned back, looking unhappy. He tugged at his necktie, setting it askew. "Talk to me about your brother."

"Lawrence?" Phillip was a bit taken aback. "I didn't realize he was a consideration in this."

Colonel Dutton lifted a hand. "Now, don't go thinking I'm one to mix business matters with private ones. I'm usually not. But in this case, I'm making an exception. My children mean everything to me. My son, naturally, will take over my business interests in New York. But a daughter's a different matter. When Cynthia marries, I want to be sure her husband is capable of taking care of her in the style she is accustomed to."

Phillip began to get an inkling of where this conversation was going, and it was no surprise to him when Dutton went on, "I'm having some serious reservations about your brother's ability to do that. I don't want my daughter marrying a man who can't pull his weight in the world."

"Lawrence receives a quarterly allowance from the estates, of course, and a share of the profits from Hawthorne Shipping. When he marries, those amounts are to be doubled, and also increased with the birth of each of his children. He is to have the house on Half Moon Street, and the villa in Brighton, and he'll have Rose Park, which is a fine estate in Berkshire. Believe me, should Lawrence and Cynthia decide to make a match, she will be well taken care of."

"With your money."

Americans, he reminded himself, didn't understand the British way of doing things. "Colonel, a British gentleman isn't expected to earn his living. He is often demeaned in society for doing so."

"Yet some do it anyway. You do."

Phillip thought of all the debts he'd inherited upon his father's death and all the work he'd done to rid the family of that burden. Gentleman or not, he'd been forced to become a man of business. He'd never had a choice. "I am, perhaps, an exception."

"If your brother were to marry Cynthia, he would need to be an exception, too. Every man needs an occupation, my lord. It isn't good for a man to be idle, and I don't care what your British gentlemen usually do. When Lawrence first asked my permission to court my daughter nine months ago, I explained that I would not have Cynthia marrying some good-for-nothing who doesn't know the meaning of work. He assured me he was not that sort of man."

"Of course he isn't," Phillip murmured soothingly.

"I'd like to be convinced of that. I understood the reason he decided to return to England after so many years away was to assume his responsibilities within Hawthorne Shipping, and thereby prove himself to my satisfaction. When I suggested accompanying him on this trip, to meet you and conclude this deal, it was his idea that my wife and daughter come as well, so that we could see for ourselves the sort of life Cynthia would have here with him. I've only been here a few weeks, I grant you, but I can't see that your brother does much of anything, except escort my wife and daughter on shopping expeditions."

"That is, perhaps, my fault. As I said, a British gentleman is not expected to work, and I have not been in a hurry to give him his share of responsibility. I confess, I am a man who does not surrender control of things easily, and Lawrence has been away a long time."

"Humph." Dutton did not seem mollified.

Phillip knew that to an American, the sort of lassitude that defined a typical English gentleman's life was regarded as laziness, not as a mark of good breeding. It was plain that without some sort of occupation, Lawrence would not be marrying Cynthia, and he hastily delegated one of his own many duties. "Now that he is home, Lawrence shall be in charge of all my family's charitable activities. We are quite concerned with the welfare of those less fortunate than ourselves, and sponsor many charity events. Lawrence is to manage those."

"That's something, I guess," Dutton muttered. "But running a bunch of charities doesn't sound like much of a living. He gave me the impression he would have more responsibility than that."

"Lawrence is very eager to take on more," Phillip assured the older man, hoping rather than believing that to be true. "As I said, I haven't handed control over to him as quickly as he'd like. I intend to bring him along gradually, teach him and guide him."

"Hmm. Are you going to teach him how to make decisions, too, my lord?"

"I cannot imagine what you mean."

"Why hasn't he proposed to Cynthia?" the Colonel demanded. "He's been courting her for nine months now. When he stayed with us in Newport last summer, he couldn't be dragged from her side. Over the winter, he spent quite a bit of time at our home on Park Avenue, though not as much as he had in Newport."

Phillip wasn't surprised, but it wouldn't do to mention Lawrence's tendency to find the opening phase of anything, including courtship, to be the most interesting.

"Cynthia loves him, and he has assured me he loves her. You've given him a job. So what's he waiting for? Why hasn't he proposed? When I met my wife, I knew within fifteen minutes I was going to marry her. When you find the woman you want, you make her your own, and you don't let go. I don't understand all this dithering."

"Again, sir, I think we see the situation differently because we are of different nationalities. Love is important, of course, but in Britain, an engagement is a matter not only of mutual affection, but also—"

Dutton's fist slammed down on the desk, interrupting this rather insipid explanation. "Damn it, man, does he intend to marry Cynthia or not? If he's trifling with my little girl—"

"I'm sure that is not the case, Colonel. My brother is a gentleman. He would never trifle with a young lady's affections." Though he couldn't begin to count the number of times Lawrence had done that very thing, Phillip hoped with all his heart that this time his brother's feelings ran deeper. "My brother says he loves your daughter, and I know he has every intention of asking her to be his wife."

"Then why doesn't he do it? What's holding him back?"

"Perhaps his reticence is due to how little time Cynthia has spent in England. It's possible Lawrence desires Cynthia to be sure she will be suited to the life here before proceeding to an engagement."

The Colonel did not seem convinced. "Perhaps that's so. We'll see over the next few months, I suppose. But if your brother can't work up the nerve to propose to my daughter by then, I doubt he's got the gumption to take care of her. Until I'm convinced he's sincere and responsible, I won't be signing any agreements with Hawthorne Shipping."

Phillip studied the older man's determined countenance, and he knew that there was no point in further discussion. "I appreciate your reservations, sir. We shall wait and hope that Lawrence and Miss Dutton come to an understanding soon."

Both men stood up, and Phillip added, "My brother and I shall still have the pleasure of seeing you at dinner tonight, I trust?"

"Of course, of course. The Savoy's quite a place, I hear."

"I only wish I was in a position to entertain you at my own home in Park Lane. But these renovations are taking forever."

"Yes, yes, but once all the work is done, you'll be glad of electric lighting and hot water faucets. We've had them for years, but you all don't seem as open to modern conveniences as we Americans are."

"We are much more traditional on this side of the Atlantic," Phillip agreed as he escorted Dutton out of his office. "Still, the house on Half Moon Street was renovated quite some time ago, and I am quickly coming around to your American point of view. Electricity is a marvelous thing."

The two men continued to discuss the wonders of electricity as they went down the stairs.

"I look forward to seeing you this evening," Phillip said as they reached the main foyer of the building and paused by the front doors. "Good day, Colonel."

After Dutton had departed, Phillip had his carriage brought around. As he returned home, he went over his conversation with the American millionaire, and despite Lawrence's dillydallying, he was more convinced than ever of the rightness of his brother marrying Dutton's daughter. Cynthia was a levelheaded, sensible girl. She was also pretty, rich, and—most of all—forgiving. In other words, she was the best thing that had ever happened to his brother, and Phillip intended to remind Lawrence of that fact as soon as possible.

The face of a pretty blonde with big hazel eyes and soft pink lips came into his mind, but he shoved the image out again at once. By tomorrow Maria Martingale would be gone, and Lawrence would never have to know that for one week his first love had been living right next door.

At Half Moon Street, he paused in the foyer, and his butler came bustling forward to take his hat and stick. "Where is my brother?" he asked as he handed them over.

"Mr. Hawthorne is in the drawing room, sir, having tea."

"Thank you, Danvers," Phillip answered and started for the stairs. Somehow, he thought as he went up to the drawing room, he had to make his brother see sense. That was never an easy thing to do, but when he entered the drawing room Phillip got an inkling of just how hard it was going to be this time. Seated beside Lawrence on the plum velvet settee, sipping tea and looking as deceptively sweet as the angel atop one's Christmas tree, was Maria Martingale.

Chapter 4

There's rosemary, that's for remembrance.
William Shakespeare

*H*e should have known. Phillip paused in the doorway, glaring at the troublesome bit of skirt sitting in his drawing room, and berated himself for his own slow wits. He should have known Maria would come crying to Lawrence the moment his back was turned. She had no scruples about breaking her word, so of course she'd have no scruples about how blatantly she broke it.

He should have anticipated this and guarded against it, but now it was too late. He didn't often make a strategic blunder, and it was even more galling to think it was Maria Martingale who had outmaneuvered him.

"Phillip!" His brother jumped up, and it did not escape his notice that Lawrence bore the abashed look of a boy caught snatching sweets. "Look who I've been visiting with. Can you believe it?"

Striving to display a neutrality he was far from feeling, Phillip came into the room. "Miss Martingale," he said, bowing to her as she set aside her teacup and rose from her seat.

"Lord Kayne," she greeted with a curtsy, smiling and looking ever so pleased with herself. "A pleasure to see you again."

"Look at him, Maria," Lawrence put in, laughing, as she sat back down. "Didn't turn a hair when he saw you. That's our Phillip all over, isn't it? Never shows his hand. You'd think it had only been a day since he'd seen you last, not twelve years."

Startled, Phillip glanced at his brother, then back again. It seemed she hadn't yet told Lawrence of their altercation, and he found her reticence puzzling. What was the baggage up to now? "Twelve years?" he murmured as he crossed the room and took the chair opposite. "Has it been that long?"

Perhaps she hadn't yet had sufficient time to cry on his brother's shoulder about her misfortunes and condemn him as a bully and a cad. But no, he decided, studying her face. If he'd interrupted her before she'd had a chance to play on Lawrence's sympathy, she wouldn't be looking like a kitten in the cream. Whatever plan she'd concocted, she'd already put it into play.

"Really, Phillip, sometimes you're the most aggravating fellow," Lawrence said as he resumed his seat beside Maria. "I'd have thought even you would show a bit of surprise to find Maria in our drawing room. Awfully unsporting of you, old chap, to be so unflappable all the time."

"Your brother has always been a difficult man to take by surprise," Maria said, reaching for her cup and saucer from the tea table in front of her. "That's why he's so good at chess, you know. He's always one step ahead of the rest of us."

"Not ahead of you, it seems," he murmured.

The inflection of irony in his voice was lost on Lawrence, but not on her. Her smile widened as she leaned back in her seat. "Perhaps not," she agreed, her hazel eyes filled with amusement.

He felt an answering smile tug at the corners of his own mouth, an amazing thing, since he also felt the desire to wring her neck. "Still," he added, his smile widening, "if memory serves, you haven't managed to defeat me yet."

She straightened in her seat, looking at him in pretended bewilderment. "I can't imagine what you mean."

"Chess," he said, though they both knew that wasn't what he meant at all.

Lawrence groaned. "Don't let's talk about chess. You two were mad about that game when we were children. Always going at it, for hours and hours, I remember."

Phillip remembered, too. He'd been about thirteen, she eleven, when he'd first taught her to play. He could still see her sitting across from him at her father's worktable in the kitchens at Kayne Hall, her elbows on the table and her chin propped on her fists, studying the board with fierce concentration as she tried to find ways to outwit him. She'd been a deuced good player—tenacious, bold, clever, and so, so angry with herself when she lost, always vowing that one day she'd defeat him.

"He only taught me the game because you refused to play," Maria reminded Lawrence, keeping her gaze on Phillip. "Isn't that so, my lord?"

"Yes," he admitted, "but you were a good player. You had a talent for strategy." Looking at her now, sitting far too close to Lawrence on the settee, he wished he'd remembered her talent for strategy before this moment. "I think if we were to play chess today, you would give me a very difficult time of it."

"I always gave you a difficult time of it," she countered at once. "The only difference nowadays is that I'd win."

Lawrence's laughter interrupted any dispute of that Phillip might have made. "Scarce two minutes in the same room, and you two are squabbling already. Some things never change."

He didn't want to squabble with Maria. He wanted to find out just what she'd been up to, then he wanted her gone. "What brings you to call on us, Miss Martingale?" he asked, deciding to take a direct approach, though he didn't expect her to answer with the truth.

"Oh, but Maria didn't come to pay a social call," Lawrence said before she could offer a reply. "She and I actually bumped into each other on the sidewalk outside."

"Did you?" Phillip murmured, leaning forward to pour himself a cup of tea as he gave the woman across from him a hard stare. "What an extraordinary coincidence."

"Yes, isn't it?" Lawrence agreed, blissfully unaware of any tension. "Though it was a bit of a painful one. She twisted her ankle during our collision. All my fault, of course."

"Indeed? You sent for a doctor, I hope?"

"I wanted to, but Maria said she didn't need a doctor. She's being very brave about it."

"Oh, very brave," he agreed, his voice so dry that even Maria couldn't help grimacing a bit, but she recovered her poise at once.

"After a cup of tea, and sitting here for a bit, my ankle's much better," she assured.

"Amazing." He leaned back with his tea, looking at her in feigned admiration. "To recover from an injury so quickly."

"Maria always was a brick," Lawrence said. "But we must talk about her problem."

Here it comes, he thought. "Problem?" he repeated with a pretense of solicitous concern. "Do you have a problem, Miss Martingale?"

"I do." She set aside her tea and clasped her hands together, looking so much the pretty and helpless female that Phillip almost wanted to laugh. "I am in a dreadful hole."

"And you require our assistance?"

"Yes. Terribly forward of me to ask, I know," she added sweetly, "since we all went our separate ways years ago. But after bumping into your brother in such an extraordinary fashion, I cannot help but feel divine Providence has purposely brought us together again."

"How fortunate for you that God is so obliging," Phillip murmured.

She didn't even have the good grace to blink. "Yes, isn't it?" She paused a moment, then added, "The problem is in regard to my shop."

"Maria has leased the premises on the corner," Lawrence put in. "Can you believe it? Small world, eh, what? She's opening a bakery. At least that was her intention, but there's been some sort of muddle, and she's received an eviction notice."

She reached into her skirt pocket and pulled out a folded sheet of paper. It was wrinkled and stained, no doubt from having been crumpled into a ball during a fit of pique and thrown away. "I am being evicted for misrepresenting myself as a woman of good character," she said with a tiny, unamused laugh as she unfolded the letter. "I cannot imagine how they came to conclude this about me," she went on, the letter making a rustling sound as she tucked it back in her pocket. "I am a woman of the staunchest morality."

"Of course you are!" Lawrence said so heartily that Phillip didn't know which of them surprised him more—Maria for the brass to claim a moral character, or Lawrence for agreeing with her. Women of staunch moral character didn't go galloping off to Gretna Green with gentleman far above their station, nor did they break their promises, nor commit deceit to get their way.

"It's clear there's been some sort of mix-up at Millbury," Lawrence went on and turned to Phillip. "I explained to Maria that Millbury Investments is one of our companies, and that we actually own the building. She was stunned."

"You could have knocked me over with a feather," she said with such solemnity that this time Phillip simply couldn't suppress a dry chuckle, but he choked it back and took a sip of tea.

"So," Lawrence went on, "I promised her we'd set everything to rights." Taking up her hand, he gave it a reassuring squeeze. "No one's evicting her, and she needn't worry about a thing."

Phillip sat up in his chair with a jerk, his amusement vanishing at once. "Lawrence," he began, then stopped, watching as his brother's fingers entwined with Maria's in a protective manner that did not bode well.

He tore his gaze from their joined hands and forced himself to speak. "Of course we shall investigate the matter, Miss Martingale," he told her. After all, what else could he say? "But for now, I must beg you to pardon us." Rising to his feet, he gestured to the clock on the mantel. "We have a dinner engagement this evening."

"The Savoy!" Lawrence cried. "Deuce take it, in the excitement of seeing Maria again, I'd forgotten all about it."

Phillip studied the soft pink mouth of the woman on the settee and he was not surprised. Maria had always been a damnable distraction. "We are expected at seven," he said and looked into her eyes. "Miss Dutton," he said with emphasis, "would be so disappointed if we were late."

"Then I mustn't keep you," Maria said, taking the hint. She pulled her hand from Lawrence's, reached for her handbag, and stood up. "I appreciate any assistance you can offer."

"Not at all," Lawrence said. Rising, he offered her his arm. "Allow me to walk you down."

"Thank you." She curtsied to Phillip. "Good day, my lord."

"Miss Martingale." He bowed, and as Lawrence escorted her out of the drawing room, he watched them go with deepening concern.

Does he intend to marry Cynthia or not?

Dutton's frustrated words echoed back to him, and Phillip knew he had to make his brother see that it was time to settle down, take on commitments, be responsible. It was time for Lawrence to grow up, and Miss Dutton was his best chance to do so. Phillip had no intention of letting Maria get in the way.

"That was a delightful surprise," Lawrence said, breaking into his thoughts as he reentered the room. "Bumping into Maria Martingale, of all people. Right outside the door, too! Astonishing coincidence, eh?"

"Yes," he agreed, though what he found astonishing was how his brother could be so easily taken in. Anyone but Lawrence would have seen at once there was nothing coincidental about the encounter. But then, Lawrence had always been a fool for Maria. "But it isn't proper for her to be calling on an unmarried man."

"She didn't call on me. I told you, we bumped into each other outside the door, and her ankle was hurt."

Hurt ankle, my eye, he thought, but he decided to change the subject. "I've been thinking what to do with you now that you're home, and I've decided to put you in charge of all our family's charity work."

Lawrence was instantly diverted. "You have? But you've always hated giving up any sort of control."

"And it's been quite wrong of me. Every man needs a purpose to his life, a fact which was pointed out to me only a short while ago by Colonel Dutton."

"Phillip, I don't know what to say. When I think of all the times I've written, asking you to give me an occupation so that I might prove myself . . ." He paused, shaking his head in disbelief. "I never thought you would agree to do so. Not after all the messes I've made in the past—"

"That's all forgotten," he cut him off, not wanting to rehash any of the scrapes Lawrence had been in over the years. "Consider coming home a fresh start, and taking on the family's charitable efforts is a good way to begin. Come to Hawthorne Shipping and see my secretary, Mr. Fortescue. I'll have him prepare a dossier of all the charity events we're sponsoring this season. The first is the May Day Ball, of course, to raise funds for London orphanages."

"I'll see Fortescue tomorrow."

"Excellent. Now, since it is after six o'clock, we'd best change for dinner."

"Right." Lawrence started to head for the door, then stopped. "I say, Phillip?"

"Yes?"

"Speaking of tomorrow, you will talk to Gainsborough first thing, won't you?"

"Talk to Gainsborough?" he repeated, pretending not to understand as he walked to the fireplace and began stirring the hot coals with a poker. "What about?"

"About Maria, of course! He still runs things at Millbury, doesn't he?"

"He does. But I tend to give him a free hand with matters involving the tenants." Though there were exceptions, for he had taken quite a hand in evicting one particular tenant. With that thought, a hint of guilt stabbed at him, but he did his best to ignore it.

"Still," Lawrence said, intruding into his thoughts, "in this case, you must intervene. Somehow, Gainsborough's got it into his head that Maria isn't of a good character, so you'll have to set him right about that and see she stays."

Phillip sighed, knowing there was nothing for it but the truth. He set the poker back in its place and turned around. "I can hardly allow her to stay, since I am the one who arranged for her to go."

"What?" Lawrence stared at him across the room. "You knew about this? You had her evicted?"

"I did." He folded his arms, leaned his back

against the mantel, and met his brother's gaze. "She didn't tell you my part in the matter, obviously."

"She wouldn't! Maria's no tattletale, and you know it." Lawrence frowned in bewilderment. "But why, in heaven's name, would you have her evicted? And on the basis of her character? Why would you do such a thing to her?"

"After what almost happened between you, how can you ask me that?"

"You mean when we were plotting to run off to Gretna Green and you stopped us?" He gave an incredulous laugh. "That's what this is all about? Why, that was ages ago! We were young and stupid, I daresay, and in hindsight, I realize it was quite right of you to intervene, but what does it matter now?"

Phillip thought of Lawrence holding Maria's hand, and he knew it mattered. He loved his brother, but he was also well aware of his brother's weaknesses. Pretty damsels, particularly those in distress, could play him like a fine violin. And Maria could be a very convincing damsel in distress. He couldn't fault her strategy, however, for it seemed to be working.

"She's all alone in the world," Lawrence reminded him and frowned. "How can you be so heartless?"

The accusation stung, and he stiffened. "I am not being heartless."

"Oh, yes, you are. You should have seen her face when she was telling me about that bakery. So happy, she was lit up like a candle. And you intend to deliberately evict her. It's cruel, Phillip, and I can't let you do it. I let her down once, you know. I can't do it again. And I won't let you do it either. This bakery means everything to her."

"I'm not preventing her from having her damned bakery!" he shot back, feeling defensive all of a sudden. "I just don't want her to have it on the street where we live."

"And all because of that silly elopement business." Lawrence went on as if he hadn't spoken. "I never knew," he murmured, shaking his head in disbelief. "I never knew this side of you existed."

Phillip made a sound of impatience. "I don't understand what you mean."

"I never knew you could be vengeful."

"This isn't about vengeance! It's about . . ."

It's about you being a fool for any pretty little thing in a petticoat.

The words hovered on the tip of his tongue, but he bit them back. He would not be provoked into saying hurtful things to the person he loved more than any other. He set his jaw and turned around, pretending to straighten his necktie in the mirror above the fireplace. "This isn't about vengeance."

"Then what is it about? Is it that you don't trust me?"

When he didn't answer, Lawrence crossed the room to stand beside him. "That's it, isn't it? You don't trust me. What, you don't believe I'll behave like a gentleman?"

"No," he countered. "I'm not sure she'll behave like a lady."

"There are times when I do not understand you, Phillip. This is Maria we're talking about. She isn't just some jumped-up schemer with her eye on the main chance."

That stopped him. His hands stilled, and he met his brother's gaze in the mirror. "Isn't she?"

"No, damn it! And you know it as well as I do. We've known her nearly all our lives. We played together as children. We spent hours in her father's kitchen, remember? You taught her to play chess. I taught her to dance. We helped her learn French. Don't you remember?" Lawrence jabbed a finger at the mirror. "You showed her how to swing a cricket bat. I cannot believe you've forgotten these things."

His mind flashed back to a little girl with blonde braids who couldn't hit a cricket ball to save herself, standing on the village green scowling fiercely at the other children and pretending she didn't give a damn they were laughing at her. He remembered the first time she'd managed to hit the ball and the big, happy smile she'd given him for showing her how to do it. "That was a long time ago," he said and resumed fiddling with his tie. "Things were different when we were children."

Lawrence ignored that. "Remember the plays we'd put on for her father and the other servants? Jolly good fun, that was. I'll never forget when we did *Pirates of Penzance*. She put a manacle over her eye and a fusilier's helmet on her head and sang "Modern Major General." You were accompanying her on the piano, and you laughed so hard, you had to stop playing."

"Yes, yes, I remember, but—"

"And what about when you were twelve and got the influenza? Father was in residence at the time, and he said you didn't need any mollycoddling. So who kept running up from the kitchens to the nursery with hot soup, toast, and tea for you?"

Phillip made a sound of impatience. "Oh, for the love of God—"

"She was just a little bit of a thing, but she carried those heavy trays up four flights of stairs three times a day just for you, sneaking them out of the kitchens right under her father's nose. She could have landed in serious trouble, but she did it anyway. She did it for you. And how do you repay her? By maligning her character and tossing her into the street. Quite unworthy of you, Phillip, and a most ungentlemanly thing to do—"

"All right!" he shouted, provoked beyond bearing by that accusation. "All right! She can stay."

Lawrence clapped him on the back. "Now you're talking sense. I'll go tell her."

"No," he said hastily, "I should be the one to tell her. I'll do so after I've changed my suit. You should change as well. Unless you intend to wear those flannel dittos to the Savoy?"

His brother glanced down at his buff-colored jacket and matching trousers. "Perhaps I should," he said, looking up with a grin. "They'd refuse to let me in. What a sensation that would make."

"It would also make quite an impression on Cynthia, I'm sure, though not the one a man would hope for." Phillip nodded to the door. "We'd best hurry, or we'll be late."

"A grievous sin, indeed!" When he failed to respond, Lawrence gave a sigh of mock sorrow. "You really are impossible to tease, you know. But I don't mind since you've promised to do right by Maria."

He wondered again how that girl could play Lawrence for such a fool. But then his brother gave him a wink, put his hands in his pockets and walked away, throwing over his shoulder, "Guilt works on you every time," and Phillip realized he was the one who'd just been played for a fool.

Maria let herself into her shop by the tradesmen's entrance. She tossed the key onto the long wooden counter closest to the door, and as she pulled off her gloves and hat, she noticed the bread dough she'd left lying on the worktable. She'd best clean up the mess first, she supposed, then she'd have to start packing.

She'd hoped Lawrence would be able to convince his brother to let her stay, but after seeing Phillip's expression in the drawing room, she could hardly dare hope her plan would succeed. Phillip wasn't like Lawrence—he wasn't kind and good-natured and easy to persuade with a bit of feminine helplessness.

Ah, well, she'd played and lost. Maria took a deep breath, laid her gloves on the counter beside the key, hung her bonnet on the hook in the wall beside the door, and crossed the kitchen. She peeled the unusable lump of dough from the floured surface of her worktable and took it to the scullery, along with her stained apron. She tossed the garment and the dough into the dustbin, then donned a fresh apron and returned to her worktable with a whisk broom and dustpan. She started to sweep up the excess flour, but then she stopped. She let go of the tools and slumped back against the counter behind her.

It was so unfair, she thought in frustration, tilting her head back to stare at the gleaming copper pots on the rack above her head. So damned unfair.

That thought had barely crossed her mind before she was forcing it out. There was no point in bemoaning the unfairness of life. It was best to just get on with things. She'd start again, find another kitchen.

Maria straightened away from the counter, but before she could resume her task, a movement through the window beside the door caught her attention. She stiffened as a man's legs came into view, long legs clad in perfectly creased black trousers.

Maria scowled as the door opened and Phillip appeared in the doorway. "What do you want now? Did you come to help me pack?"

His lips twitched, though he did not smile. "I'm afraid not."

She gestured to his impeccable black evening clothes. "Of course not. You might wrinkle your suit."

"That isn't the reason, though I would happily wrinkle all of my suits to speed your departure."

"What a charming sentiment." She sniffed. "So, if you haven't come to help me pack, then why are you here? To gloat, I suppose?"

"Hardly. That would be a most ungentleman-like thing to do."

"Oh, but casting aspersions on a woman's character to have her evicted is perfectly proper behavior for a gentleman."

"No." He expelled a harsh sigh and looked away. "No, it is not."

Maria blinked at this admission, but before she could recover her surprise enough to reply, he looked at her again and went on, "A fact which was pointed out to me with great glee by my brother only moments ago." He paused, then added, "Much to my chagrin."

There were few things in life more satisfying, she decided, than seeing Phillip discomfited, but she couldn't allow herself to enjoy it, for she sensed there was more to come. "So you are here because . . ." She paused and lifted her brows, waiting for the other shoe to drop, but when he didn't speak again, she couldn't resist doing so. "Let me guess. You've come to offer me an apology?"

"Certainly not." He lifted his chin a notch. "I have come to negotiate a truce."

"A truce?" she repeated, and her hopes began to rise again. Perhaps she wouldn't need to go in search of packing crates after all. "What sort of truce?"

He entered the kitchen, shut the door, and crossed the room, pausing on the other side of her worktable. "Did you know that Lawrence was living here when you leased these premises?" he demanded, studying her face. "Tell me the truth, if you can manage it."

She made a sound of irritation. "You really are the most arrogant, pompous—"

"Did you know?"

Maria folded her arms and glared at him, unwilling to make any admission which would weaken her position, but she knew that cool, assessing stare of his missed nothing. It would be pointless to lie. "When I encountered you a week ago, it was purely by chance," she told him. "And when you told me you were living here, it was the greatest surprise to me. Nor was I aware that Lawrence was living with you. In fact, I didn't even know he was back from America."

"The remodeling of my home and the news of Lawrence's return from New York have been exhaustively reported in all the society papers. How could you not have known these things?"

"You might have time to laze about all day long reading the society pages, my lord, but I don't." Before he could respond to that, she went on, "I found out that Lawrence was in London only a few hours after I saw you. The Duchess of St. Cyres, who happens to be my dearest friend, told me of it."

Her mention that her best friend was a duchess didn't seem to impress him. His eyes narrowed. "I don't suppose that once you learned the true facts, you could have chosen to lease premises elsewhere?"

"And give up prime frontage on Piccadilly? Are you mad?"

"So that is your only design in settling here? To open a bakery?"

"A *pâtisserie*," she corrected. "I'm envisioning something along the lines of a Parisian café."

He studied her a moment longer, then gave a curt nod. "All right. I can accept that encountering me was the purest chance."

"A fine concession."

He ignored the sarcasm. "But what of Lawrence? Do you intend to claim that cannoning into him on the very same corner was chance, too?"

"I had to do it! You left me no choice. I'd been searching for months and months, trying to find the right location for my *pâtisserie*. Then I saw this place, and I knew my search was over. I had no intention of letting you stop me from having it."

"And so you made the deliberate choice to break our agreement."

Any shred of patience she had left vanished with those words. "You're damned right I did!" she flared in defiance. "And I wouldn't have cared if the devil himself lived next door. I was not going to let the best kitchen in London get away because of some promise I made to you when I was a silly girl in the throes of heartbreak! This is business, Phillip," she added and slammed her palms down on the table. "This is my livelihood!"

Breathing hard, she stared him down. He stared back. Neither of them spoke. The silence was so long, in fact, that by the time he broke it, she was sure her admission had lost her any chance to stay. But this time, Phillip surprised her.

"Very well, then, I won't evict you," he said, but

before she could even breathe a sigh of relief, he added, "Not yet, at least."

She straightened, frowning at him, feeling wary. "What do you mean, 'not yet'?"

"The term of your lease is one year, but I find that unacceptable. I shall have a new lease drawn for a period of three months, and we shall see how things progress. If I see any sign—any sign at all—that your motives are not purely mercantile, I will have no compunction about evicting you. Every three months, we shall reevaluate the situation."

"You're joking," she said, even though she knew Phillip never made jokes. "I can't establish a business on such an uncertain basis."

"Then I suggest you start packing."

She let out an exasperated sigh. "Oh, all right," she said crossly. "I agree to your terms."

"That I am allowing you to remain does nothing to mitigate the promise you made twelve years ago. You have already violated that promise once, Maria. Violate it again, and I will evict you on the spot, and I won't give a damn how much your character is maligned in the process. Is that clear?"

She set her jaw. "Perfectly clear."

"Good. And remember, I'll be watching every move you make. If you come anywhere near Lawrence, I'll swoop down on you like a peregrine on a field mouse, so watch your step."

With that, he turned away and walked to the door. Maria watched him go, contradictory emotions raging inside her. She was relieved that he'd changed his mind and happy to be keeping this lovely kitchen, but that didn't stop her from wanting to hurl a few eggs at his head as he walked out the door.

Chapter 5

The Queen of Hearts, she made some tarts, all on a summer's day.
English nursery rhyme

Maria was confident she could keep to the bargain she and Phillip had made. She had no desire to see Lawrence, and besides, she had work to do. During the fortnight that followed, she spent every free moment readying her shop to open, with some much-needed help from her friends.

Though their leisure hours were infrequent, all the girl-bachelors from the lodging house in Little Russell Street offered their assistance. Her friend, Miranda, an illustrator, designed the "Martingale's" insignia using Emma's color scheme, and had cards and stationery printed for her. Lucy, who operated an employment agency, dispatched a selection of young women to 88 Piccadilly for Maria to interview, and from among them, she chose two maids and two shop assistants.

In addition to her new staff, she had other, equally valuable assistance. Lucy's sister, Daisy, who was at present a typist for a firm of solicitors by day and an aspiring writer by night, composed advertisements for the bakery and placed them in various London newspapers. Prudence and Emma extolled Maria's baking skills at every opportunity, assuring the ladies of London society that should their own cooks not possess quite as light a hand with pastry as they would wish, Martingale's would soon be able to provide them with the most luscious scones and cakes imaginable.

The help of her friends and her employees enabled Maria to concentrate her efforts on what she did best. From dawn until well past dark, she kneaded dough, tempered chocolate, whipped cream, and cooked icing, meticulously testing each of her recipes on each of her stoves, perfecting her techniques. Even after her assistants had gone home and her maids were fast asleep in their beds upstairs, it was not uncommon for Maria to still be in the kitchens. For when it came time to put her pastries in front of the public, she was determined that they would be the finest it was humanly possible to make.

Because she was so inundated with work, Maria knew avoiding Lawrence would be easy. What she didn't appreciate, however, was that Lawrence had no intention of avoiding her.

Late one night, only a few days before her *pâtisserie* was to open, Maria was staring in bafflement at what was supposed to be a Victoria sponge, but which had turned out to be a heavy sponge flop, when the kitchen door opened and a cheery, familiar voice said, "By Jove, it smells heavenly in here."

She looked up, surprised by the sight of the handsome brown-haired man who stood in the doorway. He had clearly been out about town, for was he wearing evening clothes, cloak and top hat. "Lawrence? What are you doing here?"

Before he could answer, the sound of another male voice, also familiar but much less cheery, floated through the open doorway. "Come away, Lawrence, and stop bothering Miss Martingale. It's clear she's busy and doesn't need us lounging about."

Lawrence winked at her. "Am I bothering you?"

She should say yes, tell him to go away, and save herself the aggravation of arguing with Phillip. "Of course you're not bothering me."

Lawrence took off his hat and leaned back in the doorway, angling his head to see the sidewalk above. "No need to worry, dear brother. She says I'm not bothering her at all."

He returned his attention to Maria. "We're just home from the opera. When we stepped out of the carriage, we noticed you still hard at work, and I suggested we come down and keep you company." Leaning back again, he said, "Do come down, Phillip, there's a good chap. You're standing on that sidewalk as if rooted to the spot."

Probably because he was wishing she and her bakery were thousands of miles away, Maria thought. Nonetheless, she wasn't surprised when she looked through the window by the door and saw him descending the steps. No doubt, he wanted to protect his brother from her, but at least he couldn't say any of this was her fault. She'd been keeping to her end of the bargain.

Lawrence entered the kitchen, but Phillip paused just inside the door. Like his brother, he was formally attired in a black evening suit, and he tucked his black silk top hat into the crook of his arm before giving her a stiff bow. "Good evening, Miss Martingale," he said as he closed the door behind him.

Mimicking his formality, she responded with her deepest, most exaggerated curtsy, then tilted her head to one side and studied him as if puzzled. "Was the opera painful for you, my lord?" she asked after a moment.

"Painful?" He frowned at the word. "Not at all. Why do you ask?"

"You've a grim countenance, so the opera must have been quite an ordeal." She smiled. "Unless coming down here is the cause of your pained expression? You look as if you are paying a visit to the dentist."

Lawrence laughed as he crossed the kitchen to stand on the opposite side of her worktable. "Don't be offended, Maria. You know how he is, with his damnable sense of propriety. He didn't want us to come down. Said it wouldn't do to call on you at this hour."

Phillip shifted his weight from one foot to the other and glanced at the ceiling, looking as if he'd prefer to be anywhere else. "It's after midnight, Lawrence. Not an appropriate time to pay calls."

"Oh, but we've no need to stand on ceremony with Maria," Lawrence said over one shoulder.

Maria didn't miss the impatient glance Phillip gave his brother in return. "This is a respectable neighborhood. Miss Martingale is an unmarried woman. Skulking about down here could hurt her reputation."

"I hadn't thought of that." Lawrence looked at her. "Do you want us to go?"

"Of course not," she answered at once, happy to fly in the face of Phillip's stuffy notions of proper behavior. "The curtains are not drawn, the windows are wide open. Anyone passing by can see us and can hear our conversation. I'd hardly describe it that you're skulking about."

"Bandy the semantics if you wish," Phillip said in his haughtiest tone, "but the fact remains that my brother and I should not be here."

"You're so punctilious, my lord. We've known each other nearly all our lives. It seems a bit absurd to worry about precise rules of etiquette at this late date, doesn't it?" She leaned sideways, looking around Lawrence to give Phillip her most provoking smile. "To my mind, it's a far more grievous offense to avoid old friends, or worse, to pretend they don't exist."

Her shot hit the mark. He stiffened.

"Hear, hear," Lawrence said, interrupting any reply his brother might have made.

"These notions that unmarried men and women can never be unchaperoned under any circumstances are falling by the wayside," she went on. "Women like myself, who have to earn their living and have gone into trade have no reputations to protect, really. It's only ladies who need worry about such niceties."

"Forgive me for being hopelessly old-fashioned," Phillip said with a biting inflection of sarcasm. "But aside from the social ramifications, there was the question of your mood to consider."

This turn in the conversation surprised her. "My mood?"

"Through the windows, we observed you with your hands on your hips, a distinct scowl on your face. I suggested to my brother it might be wiser not to intrude upon you at such a moment."

So now, in addition to being a temptress, she was also a shrew. Maria opened her mouth, but before she could let fly with an equally flattering opinion of him, Lawrence spoke again.

"You did look a bit cross."

"Did I?" She gestured to the flattened layers of sponge cake on the table. "A case of culinary frustration."

He gave the cakes a dubious look. "What are they? Some sort of crepe?"

She sighed. "They were supposed to be a sponge."

"Look a bit flat for a sponge, don't they?"

"Miss Martingale no doubt appreciates your keen observation, Lawrence," Phillip said, but his brother seemed oblivious to the incisive remark.

"What happened to it?" he asked her. "Why would it be flat like that?"

"It's the third oven," she said, waving her hand to one of the stoves behind her. "It's as difficult to gauge as the weather, for I can't seem to bake anything delicate in it."

"Then it ought to be replaced. My brother will talk to Mr. Gainsborough about it, won't you, Phillip?"

Replacing a temperamental oven was well beyond the scope of a landlord's responsibilities, and she didn't wish to be beholden to Phillip in any way. She hastened into speech. "No, no, thank you, but that's not necessary. Every oven has its idiosyncracies. I just have to become accustomed to this one."

"All right, but if it keeps giving you trouble, you'll inform one of us, I hope." He glanced around. "It's turned out quite a nice kitchen, isn't it? Very modern and up to date. Fiona would like it, don't you think, Phillip?"

"Since it was to her design, I believe that's a safe assumption."

"Fiona?" She glanced from Lawrence to his brother and back again. "Are you referring to your aunt Fiona?"

Lawrence nodded. "She was in the midst of opening a tea shop here. She envisioned something along the lines of the ABC's, only more genteel, more ladylike."

"Like Miss Cranston's tea shops in Glasgow?" she asked. "Those are quite fashionable, I understand. London has nothing like them. It would have been a great success. Why didn't she proceed?"

Lawrence began to laugh. "Well, several weeks before she was to open the place, she met Lord Eastland. He's our ambassador to Egypt, or some such. Anyway, they fell madly in love, the dear old fools, but he was returning to Cairo within the week, and couldn't delay his departure, so they decided . . . they . . . umm . . ." He paused and tugged at one ear, still chuckling.

It was Phillip who conveyed the vital point. "They eloped."

"What?" She laughed. "Your Aunt Fiona eloped with an ambassador?"

"Elopements do seem to run in our family," he said coolly, dampening Lawrence's amusement at once.

"I think . . ." Lawrence raised a fist to his mouth and gave a cough, his face reddening. "I think I'll um . . . just have a look about the place, Maria. If you don't mind?"

She waved a hand toward the scullery. "Not at all."

He crossed the room, dropped his cloak and hat on the counter by the stairs, then departed for the back kitchen.

Maria glanced at Phillip, who hadn't moved from his place beside the door. "You aren't standing at the gates of hell, you know," she said with some amusement. "It is safe to come in. After all, I'm not a devil."

"Aren't you?" he murmured, and crossed the room to where his brother had been standing a few moments before. "You have given me cause to wonder about that on more than one occasion."

"Just what is it you fear, my lord?" she asked. "As I said, this isn't hell. I have no evil designs on your brother, no desire to tempt him into sin with the delights of my kitchen."

He nodded at the sponge cakes. "Not with those, certainly." He returned his gaze to her face. "But there are other, more tempting, delights."

Sensation tingled along her spine, a sudden awareness that made the delicate hairs on the nape of her neck stand up. In his voice was an inflection she'd never heard before, a soft note beneath the hauteur that caught her by surprise. On the other hand, perhaps she was imagining things. There was nothing soft in his eyes. In their blue depths was a warning, the flash of anger and something more, something she could not quite identify. She tore her gaze away.

"Don't be absurd," she scoffed. "I don't know why you insist on blaming me for what happened all those years ago." She seized the cooling rack from the table, bent down, and jettisoned the ruined cakes into the rubbish bin. Then she hung the rack on a pair of hooks beneath the table and straightened. "I wasn't attempting to kidnap your brother at gunpoint and force him to Gretna Green."

Footsteps thumped on the floor, and the sound of Lawrence whistling floated through the doorway, preventing any further discussion of the subject.

"If you've finished your explorations, Lawrence," Phillip said as his brother reentered the room and came to stand beside him, "we should be going. It's quite late." He turned as if to leave.

"No need to rush off," she said, her cheerful words stopping him. "I've got a bit of tidying up to do, so I'll be here another half hour at least. Would you like a cup of tea?" Without waiting for an answer, she walked to a nearby cupboard and pulled down the teapot.

"This seems like old times, eh, what?" Lawrence said to his brother while Maria filled the pot with hot water from the boiler tap and added tea. "Remember how, when we were boys, we never wanted our tea in the nursery? We always insisted upon having it down in the kitchens. It drove old Sanders simply wild. 'Gentlemen don't take tea in the kitchens like hall boys!' he used to say. Remember?"

"Yes," Phillip said shortly. "I remember."

She gathered cups, saucers, spoons, and the sugar bowl on a tray, then went to the ice room for milk. "I remember those days, too," she said, returning to the worktable. She set the milk jug on the tray and reached for the teapot. "You two always wanted to sit in the corner of the kitchen by the buttery door," she went on as she poured tea for the three of them.

"To be near you, of course," Lawrence said, smiling as he reached for the silver tongs and added several lumps of sugar to his cup. "You were always using the table in that corner to roll out pastry or pat out scones for your father. You wore a bibbed white apron, I recall, just like the one you're wearing now, and had the same sort of kerchief wrapped around your hair. And you always had tarts waiting for us."

"So I did. Treacle for you and chocolate for Phillip. Every afternoon." She laughed, feeling a pleasurable warmth at the memory of those days. "I can't believe you remember."

"Of course I remember. Those days were—" Lawrence broke off, and the smile vanished from his face. He glanced at his brother, then back at her. He swallowed hard and lifted his cup, looking into her eyes over the rim. "Those were some of the happiest days of my life."

"Mine, too," she admitted.

"And Phillip's as well, though he'd never admit it," Lawrence told her with a wink.

"On the contrary," Phillip contradicted smoothly and took a sip of tea. "Those were happy times for all of us."

"But then we all went off to school." Lawrence set aside his cup and leaned forward to rest his forearms on the table. "Remember when you found out your father was sending you to boarding school in Paris?"

"How could I forget? Father insisted upon it,

saying he hadn't been saving his wages all these years to no purpose. But, oh, I didn't want to go."

"I'll say you didn't! You were so put out about it, you refused to learn French. And to make you learn, Phillip insisted we speak only French for the rest of the summer. How that infuriated you! You finally became so angry with him, you declared you were never going to make him chocolate tarts again."

She glanced at Phillip to find him watching her. He seemed to take no pleasure in these nostalgic recollections, but what else he might be thinking, she couldn't tell. Phillip had always been a difficult person to read. "I remember that," she said, returning her attention to Lawrence. "And he said something back to me, something very snotty, I'm sure, though since it was in French, I didn't understand it. And by the time I learned French, I couldn't remember what it was he'd said."

Phillip stirred. " '*C'est pour le mieux*,' " he quoted under his breath, set down his cup, and turned away from the table.

"For the best, was it?" She considered that, watching his back as he walked away. "I suppose it was, though I hate to admit it." She gave a little laugh. "How like you, Phillip, to know what's best for everyone."

He stopped, and his wide shoulders flexed in his black evening jacket. He started to turn his head as if to reply, but then he changed his mind. Looking away again, he walked to the window by the door. His back to the room, he tilted his head and stared at the gaslit sidewalk above as if yearning to be gone.

"That's our Phillip all over, isn't it?" Lawrence agreed with her. "But he is usually right, you know. That's the infuriating part."

No, the infuriating part is how he meddles in everyone's business, she wanted to say, but she held her tongue. "I have some treacle tarts freshly made today," she said instead. "Would you like some?"

"What a smashing idea! I'm famished."

"You cannot possibly be hungry, Lawrence," Phillip interjected over one shoulder. "Not after a full supper at the Savoy."

"But I've missed Maria's treacle tarts," the younger man answered. "Haven't had them since we were children." He flashed her a look of mock accusation. "After you came home from boarding school, you didn't make them anymore."

"That wasn't my fault," she told him and started for the larder in search of Lawrence's favorite treat. "You can blame my father."

Along with the two treacle tarts, she also brought one of chocolate for Phillip, though she doubted he would eat it. "Papa said I had become a lady then," she went on as she came back to the worktable, "and he wouldn't let me work in the kitchen anymore."

"You did look quite the young lady when you came home," Lawrence agreed. "Pretty as a picture, and all dressed up in ribbons and lace. Phillip and I hardly recognized you." He began to laugh. "Speaking of ribbons, remember that hair ribbon you lost?"

His words sparked her memory. "I do remember. It had belonged to my mother, and Papa gave it to me that summer I came home from France. It was pink, and it had white daisies embroidered on it."

"And when it went missing, you were so terribly upset. Nothing would do but that we had to turn the entire house upside down looking for it." He picked up a tart and turned to his brother. "You remember that, don't you, Phillip?"

"No," he answered without turning around. "I'm afraid not."

"No, I don't suppose you would, since the moment Maria started crying about it, you vanished from sight. I'm the one who had to go combing the grounds with her for hours and hours in search of the blasted thing. We never did find it." He took half the treacle tart in one bite, and gave a groan of satisfaction at the taste. "Deuce take it, Maria, you still make the best tarts in the world. Absolutely smashing."

"Thank you, Lawrence." She glanced his brother. "I have a chocolate one, too, Phillip," she called to him, "if you want it."

She watched him square his shoulders and turn around. "Thank you, Miss Martingale. You are most kind, but I have already dined. And now, I truly must insist my brother and I take our leave. I would not wish our presence here to subject you to any further risk of unwarranted gossip. Lawrence, I am sure, would not wish it either," he added with a pointed glance at his brother.

The younger man gave a heavy sigh and straightened away from the worktable. "Oh, all right," he mumbled, then grabbed the second treacle tart from the plate and ate it as he crossed the room to join his brother by the door. "But Maria said it didn't matter, and if she isn't worried about it, I don't see why—"

"If her reputation isn't a sufficient reason, allow me to remind you Miss Martingale is preparing to open her *pâtisserie* in just a few days." Phillip opened the door and waited for his brother to walk through. "No doubt, she's been inundated with work and is far too tired to stand about all night reminiscing about our childhood."

His desire to be gone was so plain, his intention to keep Lawrence out of her immoral clutches so obvious, she couldn't resist trying to delay their departure a bit longer. "Oh, but I'm not tired at all," she protested as he moved to follow his brother out the door. "Do I look tired, Phillip?"

He turned his head, and his cool blue gaze raked over her as if to determine an answer to her question, but if he formed an opinion about her appearance, he did not offer it.

"Women are so unattractive when they're tired," she went on with merciless sweetness. "We have red, puffy eyes, and haggard lines in our faces." She touched her fingertips to her face with a pretense of concern. "I hope I do not look so awful as that, my lord?"

He opened his mouth, then closed it again. His chin rose a notch. "I did not mean to imply any such insult," he said with dignity.

"Of course he didn't!" Lawrence assured, peeking past his brother's shoulder to look at her. "Why, you're the prettiest girl we know! You always have been."

"The prettiest girl you know?" she echoed, still looking at Phillip. "Indeed?"

His mouth took on a wry curve, making it clear he knew she was twisting his tail. "There are no lines in your face, Miss Martingale," he answered. "As for your eyes, they are neither red nor puffy." He paused, then added, "They are, in fact, quite lovely."

She blinked at this unexpected pronouncement, but before she could truly assimilate that Phillip Hawthorne had just given her a compliment, he went on, "It's true that you have smudges of flour on your face and smears of what look to be dried egg yolks on your apron. There is also a dollop of something on the kerchief over your hair that might perhaps be butter." He turned and followed his brother out the door. "But let me assure you," he added, pausing to give her one last glance as he reached for the door knob, "that you do not, in any way, look haggard."

"Thank you, Phillip," she said as he began to pull the door closed. "You are such a silver-tongued devil."

She was such an impertinent wench.

Phillip stepped out of his bedroom onto the balcony and pulled a slim cheroot and a box of matches from the inside breast pocket of his favorite smoking jacket. What great delight she'd taken in teasing him tonight. But then, he reflected as he lit the cheroot, she always had enjoyed that particular pastime.

He sat down in one of the painted wrought-iron chairs that overlooked the back garden and stared up at the moon, a dim orb amid the thick haze of London coal soot and wood smoke. Her teasing words echoed through his mind.

You look as if you are paying a visit to the dentist.

If that were true, he could hardly be blamed for it. Having Lawrence drag him down through the tradesmen's entrance of a shop at midnight was bad enough, but to do so for the purpose of visiting the very woman he was taking great pains to keep his brother away from made things even worse. Then there were the social ramifications of the situation, which only he'd seemed to consider. Calling upon an unmarried woman who lived alone was unthinkable, and a presumption that, despite her words to the contrary, could not be excused by the fact that she was in trade. No bakery would ever be open at such an hour of the night.

He'd never dreamt Lawrence would make a beeline for her shop the moment they arrived home tonight. His brother had been halfway down the steps to her door before Phillip had even stepped out of the carriage. But, there, that was Lawrence for you, all bounce and go, acting on the impulse of the moment with never a thought to appearances. And Maria was no less careless.

How like you, Phillip, to know what's best for everyone.

The biting undertone in those words quite nettled him. It wasn't that he always knew best. It was that she usually didn't. Maria had always had more sauce than sense.

No doubt she'd been pretending a cavalier disregard for her reputation just to needle him. He took another pull on the cigar in his fingers and exhaled the smoke with a sound of exasperation. Maria never had possessed any regard for propriety.

His mind flashed back twenty-two years, to a pair of big hazel eyes staring down at him—and quite rudely, too—from amid the branches of a weeping willow tree. He'd been alone that afternoon, he remembered, for Lawrence had been confined to the nursery as punishment for stealing a tray of tarts behind the back of the new chef.

He'd settled himself beneath the willow by the pond and had just begun to practice his Latin when a sound had made him glance up. He could still remember exactly how Maria had looked that afternoon—the rays of sunlight that filtered between the leaves and glinted off her long, gold curls, the gray dress and white apron she wore that told him she was a servant, the fat red apple, half eaten, in her hand.

The apple, he reflected, had been quite metaphoric.

"What's *veritas* mean?" she'd asked him, taking a hefty bite of the fruit, making him realize that sound was what had called his attention to her presence. The crunching of an apple.

He'd frowned at her question, rather taken aback. Servants weren't supposed to speak to him unless he spoke to them first. "I beg your pardon?"

"*Veritas,*" she repeated, not seeming to care that her mouth was full. Had the girl no manners at all? She chewed and swallowed, then waved the half-eaten apple toward the book in his hand. "You were saying it out loud. I don't know that word. What's it mean?"

He glanced down at the thick text that was open in his lap, then looked back up at her. "It's Latin for 'truth.' I'm studying Latin."

"Oh." She considered that information for a moment, watching him, then she sunk her teeth into the apple, and with her hands free, she shimmied down the tree. Her descent obligated him to put aside his book and stand up.

She hopped lightly to the ground in front of him and removed the fruit from between her teeth with her left hand. "I'm Maria," she said, thrusting her right hand toward him as if actually expecting him to shake it.

He'd bowed instead. "I am Viscount Leighton, eldest son of the Marquess of Kayne. At your service."

She didn't seem suitably impressed. She didn't even curtsy. She took another taste of her apple, then held the half-eaten piece of fruit out to him. "Want a bite? I'll share."

Even after all these years, the delicate scent of apple under his nose and the sharp sting of saliva in his mouth as he'd taken a bite were still vivid in his mind, for from that moment on, his life had never been the same.

"Studying Latin doesn't sound like much fun," she said as he chewed and swallowed the fruit.

"Wouldn't you rather play? If we had a rope, we could make a swing."

Tempting as that suggestion was, he shook his head. "Thank you, but I have to study." He stood up a little straighter, his shoulders back, feeling quite proud of himself. "I'm going to go to Eton."

"We could tie the rope on that branch," she went on as if he hadn't spoken, turning to indicate a limb that stretched out over the pond.

Curiosity got the better of him. "Why that one?"

"It's over the water, silly. If you swing out from the bank as far as you can and let go of the rope, you fall right into the pond. It'll be great fun."

It sounded like fun, especially on a hot summer afternoon when the alternative was Latin. Resolutely, he shook his head. "Can't. I have to study. Besides, I'm not allowed to play until three o'clock."

"That's all right," she murmured, looking up at him, a smile curving her mouth. "I won't tell on you."

Phillip still remembered that smile. Even then, it had held the power to tempt a fellow into doing things he really, really shouldn't.

He'd capitulated, pulled into forbidden fun by a slip of a maid who shouldn't have even dared to speak to him. The result had been a snapped tree limb that had broken his arm, three weeks of punitive confinement in the nursery, and a sound thrashing from his father.

Phillip smiled ruefully to himself. He'd suspected from the first moment he'd laid eyes on her that Maria Martingale was trouble. He'd known it for sure the summer she came home from France.

He remembered that hair ribbon perfectly, though he'd denied it earlier tonight. A sudden tightness squeezed his chest. He also remembered watching her cry over the blasted thing.

The door on the other side of the tall brick chimneystack opened, and he gave a silent groan into the darkness. *Speak of the devil,* he thought with chagrin.

He straightened in his chair and looked over the low wall that separated his balcony from that of the house next door, confirming that the object of his thoughts had indeed come outside.

She carried a small oil lamp in her hand, and by its soft yellow light, he could see that she no longer wore her kitchen apron. Instead, she was even more informally attired in a long white nightdress and wrapper. She'd also taken off that hideous kerchief, and her curly hair had been caught back into a braid down her back—a long, loosely woven plait of burnished gold that ended at her waist.

She walked to the wrought-iron rail, pausing about half a dozen yards from where he sat. She placed the lamp on the floor nearby, then straightened and turned toward the rail, lifting one hand to her neck.

Phillip tensed in his chair as she slid her fingertips beneath her braid and began to rub the nape of her neck. She was clearly unaware of his presence, and he knew that in such a situation, offering a slight cough was the appropriate thing for a gentleman to do.

He did not do it.

Instead, he remained perfectly still as she tilted her head to one side and began massaging the muscles of her shoulder and the side of her neck.

She groaned, and with that tiny sound, lust washed over him, an inexorable wave of heat and hunger that was so powerful, he could not move.

Between thin, curling ribbons of cigar smoke, he watched her, riveted, as she raised her arms above her head to stretch her aching muscles. The lamplight outlined the shape of her body through the gauzy layers of her nightclothes, and the dark silhouette of her shape called to something inside him that was deeper, darker, and far more primitive than gentlemanly honor.

Look away, he told himself, even as his gaze slid downward over the deep, inward curve of her waist, the undulating outward curve of her hips, the long, lithe shape of her legs. The lust in him deepened and spread, smothering him until he could not breathe.

She let her arms fall to her sides and leaned forward, resting her forearms on the rail. He suspected the faint, anchor-shaped line that defined the shape of her buttocks was merely his fancy, but real or imaginary, it didn't much matter. The effect on his body was the same.

She moved as if to turn around, and he jerked his arm down so that if she looked in his direction, she would not see the glowing tip of his cheroot in the darkened corner, though he was sure this attempt to remain unnoticed would be in vain. The wood smoke and other pollution in the London air masked the scent of his cigar, but surely, she would sense his presence just the same. How could she not? His body burned with lust.

To his surprise, however, she did not seem to perceive him sitting in the shadows. She bent and picked up the lamp, then crossed the balcony and went back into her rooms without even glancing in his direction.

The door closed behind her, but Phillip did not move from his chair, for he knew that if he stood up, he would go after her. Like a compass needle compelled by magnetic force to veer toward true north, he would follow her. He would enter her rooms. He would touch her. He doubted he could stop himself.

The realization that he had so little governance over his own body appalled and angered him.

He closed his eyes, striving to remain where he was, while inside him, honor warred with lust. He sat there, eyes closed, taking slow, deep breaths, waiting for honor to win. He sat there for a very long time.

Chapter 6

Some gave them white bread, and some gave them brown, some gave them plum cake and sent them out of town.

The Lion and the Unicorn

The opening of Martingale's took place on an April morning that was cold and rainy, but the damp weather did not deter people from coming to see Mayfair's newest bakery. Emma and Prudence had done an excellent job piquing the interest of the ladies in the area, for cooks and servants began lining up outside the front door two hours before the shop was due to open. Working since three o'clock, Maria and her maids had seen the women begin to gather along Piccadilly well before six. When Miss Foster and Miss Simms, her shop assistants, pulled back the curtains a few minutes before seven, the queue was halfway down the block.

Maria smiled, peeking between the draperies of the drawing room window at the queue of people that extended nearly the length of the block. She let the curtain fall, feeling a wave of nervous excitement so intense she could hardly breathe. The moment she'd worked so hard to achieve had finally arrived. She continued upstairs to the bedroom and changed into a clean shirtwaist and skirt, donned a fresh apron, patted her hair, and went down to the shop.

For the past half hour, her maids had been bringing up baskets of bread and trays of pastries from the kitchens, and her shop assistants had been arranging them in the display cases on fluffy piles of cream-colored illusion. Maria surveyed the array of cakes, buns, and tarts. Though she made a few changes to the displays—tucking in a fresh camellia here, sprinkling a few rose petals there—she was well pleased with what she saw. Everything was just as she had envisioned one month ago.

She took a final look around to ensure that everything was in readiness, then she unlocked the till of the polished brass cash register and nodded to her shop assistants. Miss Foster and Miss Simms drew back the curtains one by one while Maria watched the faces of people outside as they clamored for a look at her wares. When she saw heads begin nodding with approval, her nervousness eased away into satisfaction and relief.

She ignored the impatient taps on the windows and waited until the big French clock on the wall behind her showed that it was precisely half past seven o'clock, then she beckoned Miss Foster to join her behind the counter and gestured for Miss Simms to unlock the door.

From that moment on, pandemonium ensued.

By ten o'clock, Martingale's had run out of bread. By noon, there wasn't a crumb of cake to be had, and by four, every single tray in the shop was empty.

Maria wrote the words, "All Today's Goods Sold Out. Taking Orders for Tomorrow," on a big sheet of paperboard and hung it in the window nearest the door. For the next two hours, she and her assistants endured grumbles and complaints as they took orders for the morrow, apologizing profusely for the lack of goods available and promising solemnly to plan better in future. By the time the clock struck six, teatime had come and gone, and traffic through the shop had dwindled almost to nothing. All three women were grateful, for they were exhausted.

Maria was just locking the cash register for the night when a voice from the doorway told her that her day wasn't quite over.

"I'd like treacle tarts, please."

She looked up to find Lawrence standing in the doorway grinning at her, one palm flattened against the glass of the front door to prevent Miss Simms from closing it.

She felt a friendly warmth at the sight of him, and she smiled in return. "I should love to provide you with treacle tarts," she told him, "but I'm afraid we've none left." She pointed to the sign in the window. "We've no tarts at all."

"No tarts? Oh, the horror! May I have them for tomorrow, then?"

She turned her attention to Miss Simms, who was waiting by the door, key in hand. "It's all right, Miss Simms. I'll take the gentleman's order and lock the doors. You and Miss Foster must be dead on your feet. You may go home."

Miss Simms looked at her with gratitude and gladly handed over the key. "Thank you, ma'am."

"I shall see you both tomorrow morning at seven o'clock," Maria added, giving Miss Foster a nod of approval. "Excellent work."

Her shop assistants went down to the kitchen to fetch their wraps and umbrellas before departing through the tradesmen's entrance, while Maria turned her attention to her last customer. "Do you really want treacle tarts, or are you just teasing?"

"Of course I want them." Lawrence crossed the room to face her over the counter. "One dozen, if you please."

"A dozen?" She reached for a sheet of notepaper and a lead pencil. "That's a great quantity of tarts for one man to eat. Wouldn't you prefer half of them be chocolate, so Phillip can have some?"

"Hang Phillip!" he answered, making her laugh. "If he wants tarts, he can come fetch them himself."

"He won't, though," she said as she began writing out the order. "I doubt he'd set foot in here. A gentleman doesn't buy his own food. He sends his cook."

"More fool him, then." Lawrence leaned closer to her, resting his forearms on the counter's polished walnut top. "When the baker's as pretty as you, who could stay away?"

It was the sort of compliment Lawrence would give, one he had often given her, and which had made her quite giddy the summer they were seventeen. But now, his words made her uncomfortable. They were all grown up now, well past the silly infatuation they'd felt all those years ago. "You flatter me," she murmured, glancing at the door, "but didn't we both make a promise to your brother we'd keep away from each other?"

"Years ago." He leaned a little closer. "We're much older now."

"And wiser, too," she said sternly, leaning back, knowing it was best to stick to the business at hand. "When would you like your tarts to be ready?"

"Teatime, I suppose."

"I'll have them delivered to your chef just before half past four tomorrow, then."

"Excellent. But that's not the real reason I've come to see you."

"It isn't?"

"No. I've an ulterior motive." His gaze lowered to her mouth, and she felt a pang of alarm. Lord, surely he didn't intend to make advances toward her? She cast a concerned glance at the window, noting the shadows of dusk outside and remembering Phillip's words from a few days earlier.

This is a respectable neighborhood.

Though she hated giving Phillip credit for anything, he might have been right about guarding her reputation. She might not need chaperones, as ladies of the gentry did, but it wouldn't do for her to be thought a loose woman. That would give Phillip the excuse he needed to exercise the morals clause in her lease and have her evicted.

"Lawrence—" she began, but he cut her off.

"I've gotten myself into a bit of a pickle, Maria," he confessed, returning his gaze to hers, "and I need your help."

The idea of Lawrence in a pickle did not surprise her. "You're in some sort of trouble?"

"Not trouble, exactly. But I am in rather deep waters." He straightened away from the counter, spreading his hands in a deprecating gesture. "My own fault, I suppose. You see, I've been feeling rather at loose ends, not knowing what to do with myself, but wanting something to occupy my time. A profession of some sort."

"A profession?" she asked in surprise. "But a gentleman doesn't—"

"Engage in a profession," he finished for her. "Yes, I know. But I'm desperate to avoid being idle." He smiled. "I know I am supposed to do nothing but gamble, visit my club, and go to balls and parties. It's what my friends do, and I enjoyed those pastimes once, too. But they no longer interest me as they once did. I've been feeling more and more the need to settle down and be responsible. That's why I need your assistance."

"I don't understand."

"I've been begging Phillip to give me an occupation in Hawthorne Shipping, but he's been reluctant to do it. You know how he loves being in charge of everything."

Oh, yes. She knew.

"But," Lawrence went on, "He's relented at last and has given me something to do. Our family sponsors dozens of events to raise money for charity, and Phillip's put me in charge of managing them."

She nodded. Clever of Phillip, she had to admit, to give Lawrence something so well suited to his temperament. He had the charm to persuade people to open their purses.

"It's not a position within the company, unfortunately," he went on, "but it's a beginning. My first task is to make the arrangements for our May Day Ball, which benefits London orphanages. I thought a ball would be easy, but I'm discovering just how deuced difficult these things are to arrange, so many little details to be taken care of. I've got the musicians to hire, the flowers to order, hundreds of vouchers and invitations to send out. I didn't know my brother knew that many people! Thank heaven he'd already arranged for a ball-room before the season began, for we'd never be able to secure one now. The house in Park Lane won't do, of course."

His words brought to mind the conversation she'd had with Prudence. "Yes, I heard Phillip is renovating Kayne House."

"He is, and it's a terrible mess at the moment, so he's secured the home of his friend, Lord Avermore, for the ball."

"Avermore?" Maria echoed in surprise. "You don't mean the playwright?"

"That's the one. The earl is in Italy at present, so Phillip is borrowing his home for the event."

"But the man's notorious! I don't read the society papers myself, but even I know Avermore is terribly disreputable. And your brother is friends with him?" She laughed. "I don't believe it, Lawrence. You're having me on."

"I'm not. They've been friends for years."

"How very odd. I'd have thought Phillip far too fastidious to associate with anyone who had a tainted reputation."

"But that's just it! Phillip adores notorious people because he's so upright and honorable himself. His more disreputable friends allow him to flirt with the wild side of life without actually doing anything immoral. But I didn't come here to talk about Phillip's friends. I came to talk with you about the ball. I need your help."

"My help?"

"Yes. I need a menu for the supper."

Maria eyed him with dismay. "But you don't need me for that," she said, desperate to extricate herself. "You've been to a thousand balls in your life, Lawrence. You know what's served. And surely Phillip's chef—"

"No, no, you misunderstand me. Bouchard will handle the gist of things, of course, but he's got enough work to do, poor fellow, just to provide the meats and game. With four hundred expected to attend, we'll have to contract for the other dishes, so I want you to provide the breads and pastries."

"Me?"

"I've no intent to stop there. I want you to be the official *pâtissier* for all of our charity events."

"All of them?" She swallowed hard, not quite able to believe it. The Hawthornes did an enormous amount of philanthropic work, and had always been a very powerful, influential family. Invitations to their charity events were among the most sought after of the season. Even the Prince of Wales had been known to attend their parties on occasion, and if ever there was a man who appreciated good food, it was the Prince of Wales. Oh, to make a dessert that might be eaten by the Prince of Wales! Excitement began rising up inside Maria like champagne bubbles.

"So," Lawrence's voice broke into her thoughts, "will you do it?"

The sound of his voice brought her back to reality. "I can't," she said with a groan. "I can't. Phillip will never allow it."

"Phillip won't mind."

If you come anywhere near Lawrence, I'll swoop down on you like a peregrine on a field mouse.

She remembered those words and Phillip's implacable expression as he'd uttered them. "Oh, yes, he will. He'll mind enormously, believe me."

"He won't even know I've hired you. Not for a while anyway. He's leaving for our shipyards in Plymouth at the end of the week, and he won't be back until just a few days before the May Day Ball."

"Oh, no." She shook her head in adamant refusal. "I have no intention of lying to your brother."

"It isn't lying."

"He always finds out," she went on as if Lawrence hadn't spoken, "and there's always hell to pay. Or have you forgotten that little jaunt to Scotland you and I planned twelve years ago?"

"Oh, but that's all water under the bridge now."

"Not for Phillip. He made me renew my promise to stay away from you. Did you know that?"

"He did?" Lawrence was taken aback. "Whatever for?"

"Isn't it obvious? He's afraid history will repeat itself."

"After all this time? Of all the idiotic notions! Besides, I couldn't begin to hope you'd have me after I was such a cad." He paused, as if waiting for her to protest his self-condemnation, and when she didn't, he gave an embarrassed little cough. "Yes, well, in any case, his fears are groundless. And this is the perfect opportunity to prove that to him."

"He'll have me evicted for breaking my promise."

"No, he won't. Maria, listen to me," he rushed on before she could argue the point. "By the time Phillip returns from Plymouth, it will be too late to find another pastry chef to handle the May Day Ball."

"And after the ball?"

"By then, he'll see that he has nothing to worry about. You and I aren't going to go off and elope."

"He won't let me continue to be *pâtissier* for your charity events, though."

"Oh, yes he will. You'll be such a smashing success, with everyone raving about your wonderful pastries. He won't reward you for that by giving you the sack. But if it will make you feel better, we'll draw up a contract, and I'll sign it."

"What good would that do? Phillip could just revoke it."

"But he won't. I will have given you my word, and Phillip would never force me to go back on it. He's all about doing the right thing."

But what constituted doing the right thing was a debatable point. She didn't think forcing one's brother to break his engagement and abandon the woman he loved had been the right thing, but Phillip hadn't had any compunction about doing that.

Still, how could she refuse the opportunity Lawrence was giving her? To be the *pâtissier* for one of society's most prominent families was the opportunity of a lifetime, every chef's dream. Just thinking of it brought her excitement rushing back with such intensity that she felt dizzy.

She took a deep breath, trying to quell her excitement enough to think. It might be every pastry chef's dream, but it also had the potential for utter disaster. Meticulous planning would be required to handle the work. She would need to hire at least two experienced pastry chefs to work under her, something she hadn't envisioned would happen for at least a year. But those chefs would be necessary, not only to do the work provided by Lawrence, but to assist with the flood of business that would surely follow from other clients.

"I'm a new establishment," she said, as much to remind herself as the man standing opposite her. "Are you sure you want to entrust me with all your charity events?"

"Are you joking? There's nobody I'd trust more. I appreciate that you've only just opened, and if you think you're not ready to take it on, I understand, but—"

"I'd love to do it," she said before she could come to her senses.

He grinned, looking relieved. "You're a brick, Maria."

From Lawrence, that was the highest of compliments, and she smiled back at him. "I'm honored you asked me."

"And don't worry about Phillip. When he finds out, I'll be here to ensure that he doesn't bully you or anything. I'll take all the responsibility." His grin faded. "I promise I won't leave you in the lurch. Not like last time."

Something came into his eyes, a flash of what she'd seen in their blue depths years ago. It felt strangely awkward to see him look at her that way now, awkward and a bit disconcerting. Maria felt a sudden impulse to change her mind. Perhaps it would be best if—

"Right," he said, breaking the silence. "So that's settled?"

She nodded, hoping she wasn't making a huge mistake.

"I'd best be on my way, then," he said and started for the door. "I'm meeting some chaps at my club. I'm their fourth at whist, and they'll have my head if I don't show."

"Wait!" she cried and flipped up the hinged part of the counter top to follow him across the room. "We must meet to discuss the details. What events you have planned, the dates they are to take place, that sort of thing."

He paused, his hand on the doorknob, and turned as she halted beside him. "I'll have my secretary type a dossier with all that information for you."

"That will be perfect. And after I decide on the specific pastry menu for the May Day Ball, you'll need to approve my selections. Oh, and I'll need to know the total number of guests expected."

"It'll be around four hundred, I should think, though I can't give you an exact number until we have all the invitations back. That will take about a fortnight. Where should we meet? Do you have an office?"

"I do." She waved a hand to the room on the

other side of the counter. "But it's likely we'd be interrupted every few minutes by one of my shop assistants, or a tradesman wanting an order, that sort of thing. Still, it's the best place, I suppose. Why don't we meet on a Monday? The shop is closed on Mondays."

"It's all right to meet here on a day the shop is closed? I only ask because Phillip reminded me—and quite rightly—that we need to consider your reputation."

As much as she hated to admit that Phillip was right about anything, she knew she needed to have some degree of care for her respectability, and Lawrence coming and going from here on a day the shop was closed was the sort of thing that could be misinterpreted should anyone see him. "I suppose coming to call on you would be out of the question, too, even though you live right next door," she said with a sigh. "How silly these rules are."

"Rather," he agreed. "We could meet at my office," he suggested a bit dubiously.

"You have an office?"

"Phillip has given me a suite of offices at Hawthorne Shipping. That's in Surrey Street, near Waterloo Bridge."

"I know where it is. Your offices will do nicely." She paused, considering, then added, "If the invitations are all expected to be answered within a fortnight, we could meet on Monday, the fifteenth. That's two weeks from yesterday. Say, two o'clock?"

"Excellent. My secretary will have the details of the other events ready for you at that time as well. All right?"

She nodded, and Lawrence left the shop. After locking the door behind him, she flipped the sign hanging in the transom window above so that customers would know Martingale's was now closed. Dropping back down onto her heels, she watched Lawrence through the window as he walked away down the sidewalk, but she couldn't quite believe he had just put her in charge of the dessert menus for some of the most prominent events of the season. Anyone who counted in London society would taste her pastries. They could praise her . . . or they could condemn her.

Maria's excitement once again vanished, supplanted by a sudden, overwhelming feeling of panic.

She'd just agreed to make desserts for hundreds of people, people of the aristocracy and the gentry, people who were accustomed to eating only the finest cuisine.

Maria pressed a hand to her stomach, feeling suddenly sick. What had she done? She had a skeleton staff, she didn't have even one assistant chef, and she'd only been in business for a day, yet she had to make enough pastries for a ball of four hundred and she had less than a month to prepare? She was out of her mind.

And how would Phillip react when he learned what his brother had done? Despite Lawrence's assurances to the contrary, she was by no means convinced that Phillip would "do the right thing." Not if doing the right thing meant letting her work hand in glove with his brother. No matter what explanations Lawrence gave, Phillip would put the worst possible connotations on it.

Maria took a deep breath and shoved aside any consideration of what Phillip might think. She'd lost his good opinion long ago.

Lawrence had just given her the chance she'd always wanted—the chance to prove herself. Maria crossed her fingers, glanced heavenward, and said a little prayer that Phillip wouldn't toss her out on her ear before she'd had that chance.

He ought to toss her out on her ear.

Phillip paused, one foot on the sidewalk before his house, one foot still on the steps his carriage driver had rolled out, watching the corner as his brother left Maria's shop.

Damn it all, hadn't he extracted a promise from her only three days ago that she would avoid Lawrence at all costs? Even though it was obvious his brother had sought her out, not the other way around, it still exasperated him. What magical quality did she possess that, even after twelve years, Lawrence still found her irresistible?

He pondered that question as he watched his brother halt on the corner. Lawrence must have been quite preoccupied, for as he glanced up and down Half Moon Street for a break in the traffic, he did not even notice Phillip standing by their front door. Instead, he crossed the street in the direction of Piccadilly Circus.

Phillip returned his gaze to Martingale's. It was growing dark, and by the light of the lamps within, he could see her as she walked from window to window, drawing the curtains. She rose on her toes, arms stretched overhead, and he remembered her in a similar pose only a few nights ago.

Instantly, he felt that desire for her stirring once again inside him, a desire that had only been extinguished the other night after a cold bath and many long, sleepless hours, a desire that once again threatened to flare to life because of a mere glimpse of her through a window.

Without thinking, he started toward the front door of her shop, then stopped, realizing—much to his chagrin—that he had the answer to his question.

Maria Martingale was like true north—she possessed a magnetic pull that was almost impossible for a man to resist. Even he was not immune. Phillip prided himself on his self-control, but even he felt an almost unbearable temptation to go to her. No wonder Lawrence, so amiable and easily led, could not stay away. Though he did not know why she was still unmarried at twenty-nine, he suspected she had received a number of offers. He didn't want Lawrence to be her next one.

Phillip muttered a curse under his breath, turned on his heel, and retraced his steps toward his own house. Yes, he ought to toss her out now, before history repeated itself and Lawrence made an irrevocable mistake, a mistake that under these circumstances would be impossible to prevent. Unless . . .

Struck by a sudden notion, Phillip stopped again, and it occurred to him that he must look the veriest fool, dithering on the sidewalk this way. He resumed walking to his own house as he considered the ramifications of his idea.

It was certainly feasible, he thought as he gave an absent-minded nod to the footman who opened the front door for him. Nothing underhanded or dishonorable about it, so Lawrence couldn't play on his guilt over it later. And, most important, it would work to separate his brother from Maria— at least temporarily.

He handed over his hat, gloves, and walking stick to his butler, then went up to his study, preparing to put his idea into motion.

* * *

"You're what?"

Lawrence paused in the act of cutting his beef-steak and stared at his brother across their table in Willis's Restaurant.

"I'm sending you to Plymouth," Phillip repeated, taking a sip from his glass of Bordeaux.

Lawrence's knife and fork hit his plate with a clatter. "But why?"

"Colonel Dutton has expressed a wish to see our shipyards before he commits to ordering any of our ships for his transatlantic line."

"Yes, I know that, but I thought you were taking him to Plymouth yourself."

"I cannot. Other pressing business matters have arisen which compel me to remain here. I want you to escort Colonel Dutton on a tour of our ship-yards in my stead."

Lawrence laughed with the delight of a small boy. "I can't believe you're letting me do this."

"You've been asking for responsibilities in the company." Hoping his brother wouldn't discern the deeper motive for sending him out of town, he went on, "If you are going to settle down and be part of the business, you have to start somewhere. And you were quite right to ask for more respon-sibility, as I acknowledged the other day."

"Yes, yes, but you said you wanted me to take over our philanthropic work."

"So I do. You're more than capable of doing both."

"Not if they conflict. What about the May Day Ball? You also put me in charge of that, in case you've forgotten." Lawrence leaned back in his chair and spread his hands in a gesture of bafflement. "How am I to make the preparations for that and go to Plymouth?"

"I'll take over the May Day Ball. I don't believe there are any other charity events we are sponsoring that can't wait until you return."

"But—"

"And besides," he interrupted, "April is lovely in the country. It's a perfect opportunity to acquaint the Dutton family with the beauty of our English countryside, something they would no doubt appreciate."

"The Dutton family?" Lawrence repeated, looking even happier than before. "Do you mean the colonel's wife and daughter shall make the journey north as well?"

"Unless the Colonel has brought other members of his family with him from New York, then, yes, I mean his wife and daughter." Phillip took another sip of wine. "It might be a nice gesture to show them our estate in Berkshire as well. After all, Rose Park will be yours one day."

"Yes, when I marry." His brother studied him for a moment, and his pleasure faded to a suspicious expression. "Playing matchmaker, are you, Phillip?" he asked, his mouth taking on a rather mutinous curve. "Pushing me toward Cynthia?"

"I have no idea what you mean."

"Of course you don't." Lawrence laughed, his good humor restored as quickly as it had vanished. "That's why your handprints are all over my back."

Phillip did not reply, deciding it was best to leave things at that.

Chapter 7

Out of the frying pan, and into the fire.
Tertullian

$\mathcal{D}$uring the fortnight that followed, Maria discovered that owning a bakery was far more stressful than simply working in one. Especially when that bakery had just agreed to take on some of the most prestigious events of the London season.

She interviewed dozens of apprentice pastry chefs, finally hiring two. During the hours the shop was open, while Miss Simms and Miss Foster waited on customers upstairs, Maria taught her apprentices, Miss Dexter and Miss Hayes, her methods for making the lightest scones, the tenderest puff pastry, and the flakiest strudel. She also kept the account books, paid the tradesmen's bills, and monitored the supplies in and out of the larder with meticulous care.

The contract Lawrence had promised was delivered to her shop by his secretary, but that document did little to banish her apprehension over catering her first significant social event. She focused all her energies on preparation, knowing that was the best way to ensure her success. Late into the night, when the bakery was closed, after her apprentice chefs and her shop assistants had gone home and her kitchen maids were asleep upstairs, Maria kept working, experimenting with her best recipes, trying to improve them, striving for a slate of desserts that would impress even the most jaded aristocrat's palate. She never fell into bed before midnight, but she always rose before dawn to do it all again.

All her efforts proved worthwhile. By the time she arrived at Hawthorne Shipping to meet with Lawrence, she was satisfied that she had a comprehensive selection of unique and elegant desserts from which he could choose.

The central foyer of Hawthorne Shipping was a large room, plainly but elegantly furnished in the modern style. There were several leather Morris chairs, a floor of polished wood with a plain but luxurious rug. There was also a large mahogany desk, its many cubbyholes filled with letters, packages, and documents.

Behind the desk, a stairway led to the upper floors, and to her right was an open doorway, through which she could see mustachioed clerks, with green baize eyeshades on their foreheads and armbands on their shirt sleeves, pouring over stacks of ledgers. The door to her left was closed, but on the other side of it she could hear the distinct tap of typewriting machines.

The clerk who sat behind the desk before her stood up as she approached, giving her an inquiring glance over the pair of gold-framed pince-nez perched on the tip of his nose. "Good day, madam. How may I assist you?"

"My name is Maria Martingale," she said as she paused in front of him. "I am here to see Mr. Lawrence Hawthorne, please." She lifted the leather dispatch case in her hand. "I have an appointment."

The clerk's brows rose, a world of meaning in that simple gesture. "Do you, indeed?"

"Yes. For two o'clock." She glanced at the clock on the wall to her left. "I am several minutes early."

Her punctuality did not seem to cut any ice with the clerk. He folded his hands together and smiled at her with a patient sort of superiority. "I'm afraid you cannot see Mr. Hawthorne."

"But I have an appointment."

"That is impossible."

Confounded, Maria gave a little laugh. "I assure you it is perfectly possible, sir. I am the proprietor of Martingale's *Pâtisserie*, and Mr. Hawthorne has contracted me to prepare the dessert menu for their annual May Day Ball. He requested this meeting."

"That is a strange thing, since Mr. Hawthorne would be unable to attend such a meeting. He is in Plymouth at present on a matter of business."

"Plymouth?" The mention of that city struck a familiar note, but it took her a moment to realize why. "The shipyards!" she exclaimed. "He's gone with his brother to visit the shipyards."

The clerk did not confirm or deny her conclusion, but Maria didn't need him to do so. "This is just the sort of thing Lawrence would do," she said in frustration. "So like him to leave me hanging in the wind and go gallivanting off to Plymouth with his brother, the addlepated nitwit. Why on earth didn't he send me a note to tell me he was leaving town?"

"Since I am not privy to the private thoughts of Mr. Hawthorne, madam, I cannot answer that question."

These words were uttered in such a condescending fashion that Maria was tempted to respond with a mature, well-mannered reply—such as sticking out her tongue—but the clerk's next words enabled her to control that impulse.

"And you are quite mistaken," he informed her with obvious pleasure, "to believe that Mr. Hawthorne accompanied his brother to Plymouth. I know for a fact that the marquess has remained in town," he added loftily, as if by providing this information he was demonstrating that his knowledge of all things involving the Hawthorne family was far superior to hers. "He has sent his brother to Plymouth in his stead."

Maria groaned and pressed her fingers to her forehead, silently cursing Lawrence for being so bloody irresponsible, and cursing herself for forgetting that particular trait in his character. She thought of the hours and hours of preparatory work she'd done, the two apprentice chefs she'd hired, and the additional supplies that filled her larder, supplies for which she had already paid.

She lifted her head. "When is Mr. Hawthorne expected to return?"

"I was not informed of the precise date. However, I believe his schedule dictates a return to London in mid-May."

"This is a fine kettle of fish," she muttered in disgust. "How am I to prepare the dessert menu for the May Day Ball without consulting Mr. Hawthorne? I don't know which pastries he wants me to make, I don't know the quantities . . ." She broke off, too exasperated to continue.

The clerk blinked at her above the pince-nez on his nose, uninterested in her difficulties. Hands folded atop his blotter, that superior little smile still on his lips, he said nothing. He simply waited as if expecting her to scurry away.

Maria had no intention of doing so. She hadn't

done all this work for nothing. "Then I should like to see his secretary."

"Mr. Witherspoon accompanied Mr. Hawthorne to Plymouth," the clerk answered at once with obvious relish. "You cannot see him either."

That meant only one option was left to her. *In for a penny, in for a pound*, she thought, and took a deep breath, hoping she was not about to make a huge mistake.

"Since Mr. Hawthorne and his secretary are both unavailable," she told the clerk, "I should like to see the Marquess of Kayne, if you please."

The smile became even more condescending. "His lordship is fully occupied with important matters of business. He has no time to meet with a . . ." He paused to glance over her person, looking down his nose. "A *cook*."

She stiffened at the snub, but before she could reply, he spoke again.

"You might leave a note for his lordship's secretary and request an appointment," he suggested, sounding as though he doubted that course would accomplish much.

She doubted it, too. But she had no intention of allowing all her hard work go to waste.

"Thank you, but a note won't be necessary," she replied and donned a grave expression. "I can see I must discuss this matter with the

Duchess of St. Cyres. She will determine what is to be done."

The clerk's superior expression vanished. "The Duchess of St. Cyres?"

"Hmm, yes. The duchess had intended to offer a generous contribution to the London orphanages," Maria went on, hoping the lie sounded convincing, "which, as I am sure you know, is the charitable purpose of the marquess's May Day Ball. But—" She paused, shook her head, and gave a heavy sigh. "As the duchess's personal *pâtissier*, I'm afraid I shall have to explain to her grace that I was prevented from meeting with Lord Kayne about the ball's dessert menu because of a . . ." She paused, and it was her turn to look down her nose. "A *clerk*."

He swallowed. "Madam—" he began, but she cut him off.

"This delay could put the entire supper menu in jeopardy, for the ball is only two weeks away. Her grace will withdraw her contribution, of course, and she will feel compelled to explain her reasons for doing so to the marquess." She glanced at the brass nameplate on the clerk's desk. "I have no doubt your name will be mentioned in that conversation, Mr. Jones."

She started to turn away, but the voice of Mr. Jones stopped her. "Perhaps," he said, "it might be best if I escorted you up to his lordship's secretary, Mr. Fortescue?"

Maria turned back around and gave him her prettiest smile. "That would be quite satisfactory. Thank you."

She was ushered up to a suite of offices on the third floor, where Mr. Jones handed her over to an elegant-looking silver-haired gentleman, murmured something to him in a low voice, and departed with obvious relief.

Mr. Fortescue eyed her with disfavor, his manner only slightly less condescending than that of Mr. Jones. He glanced over her plain beige walking suit, straw boater, and leather dispatch case, raised an eyebrow, and said, "You wish to see his lordship, I understand, but you do not have an appointment."

Maria sighed, wondering if she would be forced to endure a repetition of her entire conversation with Mr. Jones. "I had an appointment. It was—"

"And you have been sent by the Duchess of St. Cyres with a message for his lordship regarding the May Day Ball?"

Tired of explanations, Maria decided that one would suffice. "Yes."

"Very well. Wait here, Miss Martingale. I will determine if his lordship is available to see you."

He turned away, knocked at the closed door behind him, and upon hearing a reply, opened the door and went inside. He closed the door behind him, leaving Maria to wait.

She didn't have to wait long. She picked up one of the newspapers lying on a nearby table, but she had barely sat down in one of the leather chairs opposite Mr. Fortescue's desk and opened that day's copy of the *Times* when the door to Phillip's office opened and Mr. Fortescue reappeared. "You may go in."

She set aside the newspaper, picked up her dispatch case, and walked past the secretary into a large room furnished in similar fashion to the foyer downstairs, very modern and masculine, with an oak-paneled dado below a muted wallpaper and uncurtained windows that overlooked the Thames. There was a brass radiator instead of a fireplace, and the lamps were electric, with shades of green-and-amber stained glass.

Phillip rose from his chair behind a large, uncluttered mahogany desk as she came in. He was immaculately dressed, as always, and in his dark blue suit, aubergine waistcoat, and silver-gray necktie, he looked very much the wealthy, successful man of business, while still managing to exude that ineffable quality of hauteur that proclaimed him one of the highest-ranking peers of the realm. "Miss Martingale," he greeted her with a bow. "How do you do?"

"Very well, thank you, my lord," she answered, dipping a curtsy.

"This is an unexpected visit. Please sit down." He waited until she had seated herself in one of the comfortable Morris chairs opposite his desk before resuming his own seat. "My secretary tells me you have come on behalf of the Duchess of St. Cyres, who wishes to make a contribution to the May Day Ball. But I confess, I am somewhat confused as to the reason she would send you on such an errand."

"Well . . ." Maria paused and gave a little cough, finding this much harder than she'd anticipated beneath his cool, discerning gaze. "The duchess didn't exactly send me."

"Indeed? That is a somewhat cryptic reply, Miss Martingale. You have succeeded in arousing my curiosity."

Despite the polite friendliness of his voice, Maria felt a hint of dread as she met his impassive gaze, and she wished she had remembered before this moment how hard it had always been to put anything past Phillip. She plunged into speech. "The duchess will wish to make a contribution to the orphanages. I know she will. I'm sure of it. I mean, she's always happy to do something for orphans—" She broke off and began again. "I had come this afternoon about the May Day Ball, yes, but I hadn't meant to . . . that is, I hadn't expected to . . ." She stopped again, silently cursing her own impulsiveness. She'd insisted upon seeing him, but she had no idea what to say now that she was sitting here. She reminded herself that in time, he would have learned of Lawrence's decision to hire her, and she tried to think how best to phrase the situation in a tactful way. "The duchess is a friend of mine, and she is always willing to donate to a worthy charity."

"I'm very pleased to hear it," he said, sounding amused and somewhat puzzled that such a simple statement had been so difficult to say.

She sighed and gave up any attempt to be tactful. "Oh, I might as well come straight out with it! I came here to see Lawrence."

He didn't even blink. "Forgive me if I'm not surprised. Thought I was out of town, did you?"

"This isn't something sordid, if that's what you're implying. It's perfectly innocent."

"Of course it is."

The very blandness of his voice made her cheeks grow hot. "Damn it, Phillip," she muttered, wriggling in her chair, "it isn't as if I were intending to seduce Lawrence on top of his desk!"

"Then perhaps you should stop stammering and blushing like a schoolgirl caught out past curfew, and tell me straight out why you wanted to see Lawrence."

"Your brother hired me to be the *pâtissier* for all your charity events. Starting with the May Day Ball."

He groaned. "I knew it," he muttered giving her a dismayed stare. "I knew the first time I ever saw you, sitting in that tree talking about rope swings, that you were trouble."

She couldn't help smiling. "I said I was sorry about your arm."

He didn't seem to share her amusement about their childhood adventure. "I should toss you out right now and to hell with it."

Her smile vanished, for this conversation was heading into dangerous territory. "To return to the point, your brother and I set an appointment for today to discuss the details of the ball. The menu, price estimates, that sort of thing. But when I arrived, I learned that you had sent him to Plymouth, and that he had taken his secretary with him. So I asked to see you instead."

"Gave up trying to sneak behind my back?"

"No, I just didn't want all my hard work to be for naught! I've been slaving away for two solid weeks in preparation for this meeting, and now, I find that Lawrence is gone, he's not intending to return until after the ball, and I have no direction and no approval of the menu I conceived. I don't know the quantities to make, nor the theme of the decorations. A job like this can't be thrown together at the last moment. So I am forced to discuss the matter with you."

"It doesn't particularly surprise me that Lawrence hired you. In hindsight, I realize I should have anticipated something like this. Nor am I surprised that my brother left town without informing you of his departure, since he is quite careless about considerations of that kind.

What does surprise me is that you think for one moment I would agree to retain you as my pastry chef."

"I am one of the finest pastry chefs in London, I'll have you know! And it would be deuced difficult to find someone of my skills to do the May Day Ball at this late date. And," she added, "there is the contract, of course."

He frowned. "Contract?"

"I'm afraid so." The glimmer of uneasiness in his face gave her some measure of satisfaction. She set her dispatch case on his desk and unfastened its buckles, then pulled out the document in question. "This contract names me as the official *pâtissier* for all charitable events of the Hawthorne family during the 1895 London season." She looked down at the sheet of paper in her hands and began to read. "Martingale's is to provide all breads, cakes, pastries, petit fours, and confections, and any additional desserts required by the *chef de cuisine*. Specific events, number of guests, quantities of goods supplied, detailed menus, prices, and fees to be determined as required, etcetera, etcetera."

"Of all the absurd—" He broke off and reached across the desk, snatching the sheet of paper from her.

"It's even signed," she told him cheerfully, leaning forward in her chair to indicate the place where Lawrence had scrawled his signature. "See? Right there at the bottom. Mr. Lawrence Hawthorne, your dear brother, the man you put in charge of all your charity events."

He lifted his head and looked at her. "Why?" he murmured, shaking his head. "Of all the people in the world who might have leased Aunt Fiona's shop, why did that person have to be you?"

"Because it was your lucky day?"

His gaze hardened. "You realize it would be a simple matter for me to have this so-called contract overturned? You wouldn't have the means or the power to fight me."

"True, but a contract isn't just a binding legal document, is it?" she asked with an attempt at artless naivete, hoping Lawrence's prediction of Phillip's actions proved more accurate than her own. "It's also a matter of honor. It's a . . . a promise, really. And you wouldn't want Lawrence going around breaking his promises, would you?" She smiled. "After all, we both know that you regard a promise as a sacred thing."

"You, however, do not," he countered in a dry voice. "Otherwise, we would not be having this conversation, and you would be making life hell for some other poor sod."

"Your brother came to my shop and asked me to be the *pâtissier*. What would you have had me do?"

"Oh, I don't know. Refuse?"

"Why should I? This is the sort of opportunity no professional pastry chef would ever refuse."

"So your interest in Lawrence is purely professional."

"Damn it, I have no interest in Lawrence, professional or otherwise! How many times do I have to say it? He came to me. I did nothing to encourage him."

"You exist. That's encouragement enough, I fear." He set aside the contract, and leaned back in his chair with a sigh, pinching the bridge of his nose between two fingers as if he had a headache. He muttered something under his breath. It sounded like, "True north."

She frowned, uncomprehending. "I beg your pardon?"

"Nothing." He lowered his hand and straightened in his chair. "You're right," he said, spreading his hands in a gesture of surrender. "I cannot blame you for any of this."

Such easy capitulation was the last thing she'd expected. "You can't?"

"Unfortunately, no. As loathe as I am to admit it, the fact that Lawrence has always had the foolish inclination to follow you around like a panting puppy is not your fault."

So like Phillip to admit she was right even while making it sound like an insult. "What a relief," she said, leaning back and pressing a hand to her heart. "I was worried you might think ill of me and blame me for all this. It's been keeping me up at night."

He didn't respond to the flippancy. Instead, he folded his arms and tilted his head to one side, studying her. "Is the Duchess of St. Cyres truly a friend of yours?"

"You needn't sound so skeptical! I do have friends, you know. You were once one of them."

"A fact which baffles me at the present moment." Before she could fire off a reply to that, he went on, "Now I understand why the duchess was praising your pastries to me at a cotillion the other day. But she made no mention of a contribution to my orphanage fund. Does she really intend to make one?" He paused, and a rueful smile curved one corner of his mouth. "Or was that just a ruse to get past my secretary?"

"It was not a ruse!" She consoled herself for the lie with the knowledge that in addition to having vast wealth, Prudence was a kindhearted person who could easily be prevailed upon to donate money to any worthy charity. "The duchess will make a very generous contribution."

His smile widened with understanding. "Once you ask her to do so."

She made a sound of aggravation. "Why do you always make me feel as if you can see right through me?"

"Perhaps because you're as transparent as glass?"

"You'll have the duchess's donation by the end of the week," she assured. "But only," she added, mirroring his smile with one of her own, "if I remain your *pâtissier*. If you sack me, Prudence won't donate a penny."

"Broken promises, a few lies, and a spot of extortion all in one day. That's a bit much, isn't it, even for you?"

"It's not extortion," she protested, indignant. "She's my friend, after all."

He studied her for a moment longer, then he gave a curt nod. "Very well," he said, picked up the contract and handed it to her across the desk. "Because the London orphanages are always full and always in desperate need of funds, and because the Duchess of St. Cyres is known to be a very rich woman, I won't override Lawrence's decision. Provided you keep to your word. And—"

It was his turn to pause. Leaning back in his chair, he subjected her to a hard stare. "And provided you have the necessary skills. You are an accomplished *pâtissier*, I trust, capable of more elaborate pastries than a few tarts?"

This was one thing about which she did not ever have to lie. "I am one of the best pastry chefs in England, I'll have you know. I worked not only under my father, but I also trained for almost twelve years under the great chef André Chauvin, even working under him at the Clarendon Hotel."

"Were you the Clarendon's *pâtissier*, then?"

"Not in name. André allowed me the duties of that position, but he could not give me the title of it. As a woman," she added with a hint of resentment, "I was not considered worthy of such a responsibility by the owners of the hotel. It's an axiom of my profession that only men have the talent to be great chefs. A false axiom, but many believe it. That is why I decided to strike out on my own. To prove myself. Why these questions about my bona fides?" She gave him a provoking grin. "Don't you trust me?"

"Not for a moment," he said with an unflattering lack of hesitation.

"But you're not going to give me the sack? And you're not going to evict me?" As he shook his head, she studied him in bewilderment. "I was sure you would."

"As my brother pointed out to me not long ago, forcing you out would be an action unworthy of a gentleman. I tried to buy you off with money, but you refused it. I offered to move you to other quarters, but again you refused. If I wish to be rid of you, this seems the only course I have left. I should thank Lawrence for providing it."

This made no sense, and the only conclusion she could draw was that he was having her on. "Phillip," she said in some surprise, "you've learned how to tease."

"Alas, no, I have not. My character is still deficient in that regard, Miss Martingale. I am quite serious."

"But how does my prosperity compel me to leave?"

"The kitchens you have now are large enough for your present needs, but if you become prosperous enough, you'll find them insufficient, and that will compel you to relocate your bakery elsewhere. Since Lawrence intends to make Half Moon Street his London residence, it's in my best interests to see that you succeed—and move to larger quarters—as quickly as possible. In the interim, if you are the *pâtissier* for all my social events, you'll be far too busy, and too tired, for midnight flirtations with my brother."

She knew telling him again that she had no designs on Lawrence would be a waste of breath. "So killing me with kindness is your strategy?"

"Just so."

She had to admire his ingenuity, but she'd die before acknowledging it out loud. Instead, she sighed, feigning disappointment. "And I'd dared to hope you were making this most generous offer because of your deep and abiding affection for me."

"Affection?" His gaze raked over her in a perusal that was anything but flattering. "Affection," he said, his voice harsh as he returned his gaze to her face, "is not the word I would use, Miss Martingale."

His disdain could not be plainer, and it angered Maria that his low opinion of her still had the power to sting.

"What happened to you?" she asked before she could stop herself. "You were different after your father died. When I came home from France, I noticed how inheriting the title had changed you. It was not a change for the better."

His chin lifted, a sure sign she'd flicked him on the raw. "That is a gross impertinence," he snapped. "Tread carefully, Maria."

She had no intention of doing so. "When we were children, we were friends, you and I. Remember? But once you became the marquess, shallow, stupid things like class distinctions and who's the right sort of people became more important to you than my friendship. Lawrence still treated me as a friend and as an equal, but you did not."

"We are not equals!" he said with such savagery that she was startled. "That is a fact of our lives. With my title and my position to consider, we could no longer be friends." He looked away, adding under his breath, "We should never have been friends in the first place."

"And Lawrence? He wasn't a marquess. Yet you still felt it necessary to take him away from me as well."

"You were planning to elope with him." He looked at her again, his gaze implacable. "A gentleman cannot marry the daughter of a chef."

"God, Phillip," she choked, shaking her head, "you are such a snob."

"It is not snobbery to face facts. Marrying outside one's class never answers. People are not made happy by it in the long run."

"Lawrence and I loved each other."

"Love?" He made a sound of disdain. "You two weren't in love. You were infatuated!"

"Lawrence loved me."

"He had a poor way of demonstrating it, don't you think?"

Those words stung, and she sucked in a sharp breath. It was several moments before she could speak. "The blame for that lies with you."

"I gave him a choice."

"A Hobson's choice! Me or his inheritance. If he'd chosen me, he would have lost not only his living, but also your respect and affection. He could never have borne that. How could you have been so cruel to us?"

"Cruel? I used my influence to save my brother from making a disastrous marriage."

"And to hell with the fact that our hearts were broken in the process!"

His expression did not soften. "A broken heart mends. A poor marriage choice is irreversible."

"And what of our friendship, Phillip? Did you think how much it hurt me to lose your friendship? Or did you just not care?"

He stood up so abruptly, his chair skidded backward, but when he spoke, his voice was icy. "My secretary will send you the details of the events for which I will require your services and arrange the appropriate appointments. Good day, Miss Martingale."

The servant was now dismissed, it seemed. She picked up her dispatch case, rose from her chair, and started toward the door. His voice followed her.

"Maria?"

She paused with her hand on the door knob, but she did not turn around.

"I cared," he said behind her. "But as I said, we should never have been friends. Friendship is not possible between a marquess and the daughter of the family chef. That is the world we live in."

She forced herself to look at him over her shoulder. "No, Phillip. That's the world *you* live in."

"So does Lawrence, and that is why I did all I could to prevent him from marrying you. An elopement always engenders talk, but between people of such disparate classes as my brother and yourself, it would have been far worse than a few titters behind your backs. Many families would have refused to receive either of you. Many of Lawrence's friends would have been obligated to distance themselves from him, at least in public. If you'd had a dowry, money to bring to the marriage, people could perhaps have overlooked your lack of breeding and your lack of connections, but the poor daughter of a chef? No."

"Do you think I care what people say in whispers behind my back?"

"Perhaps not, but Lawrence does. He cares a great deal. He would have felt the social stigma of your marriage far more keenly than you, for he finds losing anyone's good opinion almost unbearable. I love my brother, but I also recognize his flaws. Lawrence has never been good at facing up to unpleasant realities. The social snubs, the dwindling invitations, the gossip, would have eaten away at him, bit by bit, destroying him and you and any love that might have been between you."

The sureness with which he spoke infuriated her. "And all's well that ends well," she shot back. "How convenient life must be for you, to always be able to bend people to your will and justify it because it's for their own good."

She departed without waiting for a reply. Outside the building, she walked along the Embankment, breathing deeply of the dank air coming off the river, trying to banish the anger she felt.

It was a blustery spring day with a chilly wind. A cab slowed invitingly, and Maria hesitated with a glance at the sky. It looked like rain, but even though she had forgotten her umbrella, she did not lift her arm to wave the hansom down. She felt like walking.

He was always so complacent, she thought in frustration, as she strode along the Embankment. So sure of himself. Who was he to meddle in other people's affairs? Who was he to decide what was best for everyone else? Why did he always have to assume he was right about everything? He'd always been like this, and it had always been the most infuriating thing about him.

Maria paused and turned toward the river. She rested her forearms on the rail of the balustrade, staring at the ships going by, but in her mind's eye, all she could see was Phillip's countenance. How much harder he seemed than the boy she'd first met, the boy with the serious face who'd looked up at her sitting in the willow tree that day twenty-two years ago with a frowning, doubtful face, as if she were a woodland sprite or water nymph, or some other creature he'd never encountered before.

She'd been the cause, really, of his broken arm, but he'd taken a beating rather than tell his father she'd been the instigator of the rope swing. Phillip had taught her cricket so she wouldn't be laughed at anymore. Phillip, not Lawrence, had been the one to insist she be allowed in their tree house, and that it was all right for a girl to learn how to fish and play football. Phillip had been the one whose laugh she'd always wanted to hear, the one whose approval she had craved, the one she'd really baked tarts for every day.

She'd forgotten all that. She'd forgotten him, and how much she'd adored him when she was a little girl, forgotten how it had hurt when he'd allowed position and class to come between them and ruin their friendship.

Her mind flashed back to the summer she turned fifteen, of how she'd come home from France to find that only one of her two best friends was glad to see her. She felt again the pain and bewilderment she'd felt then, the pain she'd felt whenever Phillip had turned away, whenever he'd refused to speak to her, whenever he'd seen her coming and walked in the other direction, the pain of a snubbed fifteen-year-old girl who could not understand why the boy she adored would no longer speak to her. Phillip might not know it, but he'd broken her heart long before his brother had.

And wasn't that, really, part of the reason eloping with Lawrence two years later had seemed so appealing? Maria made a sound of self-reproach. Galling to look back as a woman and see how silly she had been as a girl.

Two summers after her return from France, her father had died, and she had wanted Phillip's reassuring presence, but he hadn't been there. The marquess by then, he'd been touring his estates, too caught up in his own affairs to even send her a letter of sympathy. But Lawrence had been home for the summer, and it was to him she had turned instead. He'd been terribly attractive that summer and his offer of marriage had seemed like the answer to a prayer, and she'd fancied herself in love with him. But now, looking back, she could see that she hadn't really loved Lawrence. And he hadn't loved her, for if he had, he wouldn't have abandoned her. No, they had not shared a lasting love, but a fleeting, adolescent infatuation, spurred on by her girlish insecurities and her underlying fear—the fear of being penniless and alone that had been eating away at her since her father's death. Galling as it was to admit, Phillip had been right again.

Maria sighed and turned around, staring up at the carved stone lions of Somerset House. It began to rain, but she scarcely noticed, for she was still caught in the past. Her first flat when she'd come to London had been only a few blocks from here, she remembered, a nice parlor flat all her own off Tavistock Street, far more comfortable than her room below stairs at Kayne Hall. Because of the money Phillip had given her, she'd been able to afford the expense, but she'd been so lonely living by herself. So young and desolate and alone.

She squeezed her eyes shut, those early days in

London echoing back to her with a poignancy she hadn't felt for years. The Hawthorne brothers and all the pain they'd caused her were in the past, but it seemed the past still had the power to hurt.

She took a deep breath and forced herself to look on the bright side. If all those things hadn't happened to her, she wouldn't have ended up in London working for the great chef André, who'd been a friend of her father. Without André, she wouldn't have been serving supper at the ball where she'd met Prudence, who'd been working as a seamstress mending the ladies' ball gowns. Without Pru, she wouldn't have moved into the lodging house in Little Russell Street to share a flat, and she wouldn't have found a whole new set of friends. Most important, she would never have carved out this life for herself, a life that enabled her to fulfill the dream she'd had since she was three and she'd made her first pat-a-cake out of mud.

The rain stopped, and the sun came out. With it, her melancholy mood vanished. She straightened away from the balustrade, shaking off the past as she went down to the Temple underground railway stop to begin the journey home. She was halfway to Mayfair before she realized that she and Phillip had never discussed the details of the May Day Ball.

Chapter 8

God sends meat, and the devil sends cooks.
John Taylor

*N*othing has changed, Phillip thought, watching her through the window of his office as she walked away along the Embankment. All the frustration and desire he'd felt that night on the balcony came roaring back, so hot that it was almost like physical pain, and just as he had done that night two weeks ago, he fought against the desperate, aching desire to follow her.

Though he'd always tried to pretend otherwise, he had never been any less immune to her charms than his brother. Both of them had been wont to tag after her like panting puppies. The fact that he still had that foolish inclination was a galling thing to acknowledge.

She stopped walking and as she turned to stare out over the river, he tried to recall just when this stupid need to be near her had begun, but he could not pinpoint an exact moment. Perhaps it had always been there, from the moment he'd first seen those big hazel eyes staring down at him from amid the fronds of a weeping willow, or perhaps when she'd batted at that cricket ball and missed, much to the amusement of the other children on the village green. In those days, of course, it had all been so simple and innocent—just the desire to be with a girl who had a pretty smile and was jolly good fun, who played a decent game of chess and could make him laugh.

The summer he was seventeen, it had become something far less innocent. His father had died the year before, and he'd come down after finishing at Eton to spend the holidays at Kayne Hall and tour the estate before going on to Oxford. Upon his arrival, he'd found that Maria was also home for the summer, a very different Maria from the one who'd left for France four years before. A magical transformation had taken place while she'd been away, and the gawky, reed-thin girl he'd always known was gone, replaced by a luminous creature with satiny skin, soft pink lips, and a pair of perfect breasts.

That was when he'd begun to dream about her, dreams of kissing her and touching her. He'd woken up many a night that summer to find his body on fire with need—and with shame, too, for even at seventeen, he'd known the rules. A gentleman did not shag the daughters of the servants.

When Lawrence, also home from school, had admitted to having similar thoughts about her, he'd laid his younger brother out with a blow to the jaw that had shocked and bruised them both. They'd never discussed it again.

You were different after your father died.

She was wrong, of course. It was true that he'd changed toward her, but she had misinterpreted the cause. It wasn't his father's death and his ascension to the title the year before that caused him to shut her out the summer she came home and treat her as a servant rather than a friend. It was the fact that being friends with her had ceased to be enough, and anything more had never been possible.

He'd taken it for granted that Lawrence understood that, too, but two years later, Phillip had come home from his annual tour of the estates to discover how wrong he'd been.

Having graduated from Eton, Lawrence was home from school for the summer holidays, and when Phillip arrived a month later, it hadn't taken long to realize his brother was more infatuated with Maria than ever before. He'd seen the pair of them flirting in the rose arbor and exchanging glances and whispers too intimate for their disparate positions. Desperately trying to stay away from her himself, Phillip had kept busy with estate matters and tried to deny that anything more than a mild flirtation was going on. But when he'd discovered, through a tattling servant, their plans to elope, he'd been forced to recognize his own willful blindness. And as the Marquess of Kayne, he'd known what his duty demanded.

By the Embankment below, she stirred, bringing his attention back to the present, and he watched as she turned away from the river. She leaned against the balustrade behind her, and when she tilted her head back, he tensed, thinking for a moment she could see him observing her through the window. But no, he realized, she was looking at Somerset House, and he relaxed again, his mind returning to the events of the past.

Odd, he thought, closing his eyes, how everything that day at Kayne Hall was a blur except those few brief moments alone with her in his study. He could barely remember confronting Lawrence, but he could recall every detail of being with her. How she'd looked standing in his study that afternoon with the summer sun through the window glinting off her hair so bright it made him blink. The tears streaming down her face as he'd told her of Lawrence's decision to part from her. His own voice, cold and detached to mask the rage seething through him, as he'd extracted that fatal promise from her. Her shaking hand as she'd taken the bank draft from his outstretched fingers.

With a violent effort, he shoved the past out of his mind and opened his eyes to find she was still standing by the Embankment. He reached out as if to touch her face, and his fingertips hit the window glass. Damn it all, why was she standing down there in the rain with no coat and no umbrella? Didn't she have a shred of sense? He wanted to go down there and pull her back inside where it was warm and dry, but he could not do it. He would not. Where she went, what she did, were not his concerns.

His palm flattened against the glass, and he closed his eyes again, imagining that it was her warm, silken skin he touched rather than the hard, cool pane of the window, giving in for a few brief moments to what had never been anything but fantasy.

This time when he opened his eyes, she was gone. He turned away from the window, reminding himself that fantasy was all it could ever be.

As Phillip had promised, Maria received a typewritten dossier the following day, which included the details of the upcoming ball and a list of the other charity events for which she would be *pâtissier*. In addition to the May Day affair, there was to

be one other ball of similar size at the end of the
season, and between the two, a luncheon, a cotillion, and a garden fête would also take place. Mr.
Fortescue had also provided the date and time of
each event, but he had forgotten to mention when
Phillip wished to meet with her to discuss further
details.

She sent one of her maids next door with a
note for him requesting an appointment as soon
as possible to approve her dessert selections for
the May Day Ball and to discuss the quantities
required. The next morning, she received a reply
from his secretary, informing her that in regard
to the selection, she had his permission to serve
anything she liked. His lordship, she was told,
implicitly trusted her judgment on such matters, and a personal appointment would not be
necessary.

A free hand was all well and good, Maria
thought, but Phillip was so damned exacting, and
she had no intention of proceeding without some
understanding of what he expected. She needed
more information—the theme of the event, the
other dishes to be served, the cost allowance she
was to be given. She sent him another note, point-
ing out her lack of knowledge on these matters,
and informing him she would appreciate further
direction.

This time, her response was delivered by a footman on behalf of Monsieur Bouchard, his lord-

ship's chef, who, the note informed her, would be happy to discuss all menu arrangements with Mademoiselle Martingale, and would be pleased to receive her in his kitchen at half past eight o'clock the following morning.

Phillip, it was clear, wanted as little to do with her as possible, and was handing her off to his staff. That was perfectly fine with her. Until she met Monsieur Bouchard. Then everything went to hell.

The chef, a stout, balding little man with an enormous black mustache and an even more enormous opinion of his own culinary brilliance, would be pleased to accept the help of mademoiselle with all preparatory work, of course. Even a commonplace English girl, he was sure, could create a decent *gâteau* and an acceptable *pâte à choux*—*parbleu!*—but as for the rest, he would make his own arrangements.

Maria studied Monsieur Bouchard's complacent smirk for a moment, and wondered for perhaps the thousandth time why head chefs were always so full of themselves. "So, that is all I am to do, Monsieur? Make sponge cake and cream puff shells?"

He beamed at her as a tutor would to a particularly bright pupil. "The baguettes would be most welcome, too, mademoiselle. And perhaps the bread and cake crumbs. You shall send them here as I need them, *s'il vous plaît*. You may be assured, I will use them to create the finest desserts imaginable."

In other words, she was to do the unappreciated work, and he was to receive all the praise.

"I don't think so," she said with her sweetest smile. "It's clear you have not been apprised of the arrangements, so allow me to explain them. His lordship has named me as *pâtissier* for this ball, and it is I who shall make the desserts, monsieur." Her smile vanished. "All of them."

"You?" He looked her up and down and began to laugh. He glanced around and the members of his staff began to laugh, too, following his lead. "*C'est impossible, ma petite,*" he said indulgently. "You are a child."

With that, he flicked his wrist in a gesture of dismissal and turned away, adding over his shoulder that she would receive an order for the quantities of bread and cake his staff would need within the week.

Maria studied his back for a moment and thought of André, who'd hurled a plate at her head, called her an imbecile, and fired her the first time he'd seen her making *profiteroles* because he'd thought them too small, only to rehire her a few moments later, after she'd called him an impossible old goat and shoved one of the tiny kirsch-flavored cream puffs into his mouth. She knew that with temperamental chefs, there was only one way to gain respect and achieve mutual understanding.

"A child, you say?" She slammed her hands down on the worktable in front of her hard enough to rattle the crocks and bowls that rested on it. "My father was a protégé of the great Soyeur!" she roared, watching as Bouchard turned back around to face her and his staff began to slowly step away, retreating to the far corners of the room. "I have trained in Paris! I have been a *pâtissier* to André Chauvin!" She was now shouting at the top of her lungs. "I have made *croquembouche* for the Duc d'Orleans and *tarte Tatin* for Prime Minister Gladstone! Yet, I am to bow down to a puffed up little Frenchman with delusions of grandeur? *Non!*" She slammed her hands down on the table again with a fervor worthy of any Gallic chef. "It shall not be so!"

Bouchard was now giving her an assessing stare, and there was a glimmer of respect in his expression. But it was clear he had no intention of relinquishing control so easily. "*Sacré tonnerre!*" he shouted back, striding toward her. "Such impudence from a child is not to be borne. I am *chef de cuisine* to the marquess and I supervise the chefs for the marquess's ball! You are accountable to me, mademoiselle!"

"I am accountable to no one!"

"You will use my recipes." Hands on his hips, he leaned toward her across the worktable. "You will work under my direction and perform only the tasks I give you."

"The hell I will!" She leaned forward as well, until she and the little Frenchman were almost nose to nose across the table. "I am not your kitchen maid, monsieur! I am an independent *pâtissier*, with my own establishment. I will use my recipes, and my staff will make them."

He let fly with a stream of French invective, and she matched it with a few choice insults of her own. But when a third voice entered the argument, it was loud enough to override both of them.

"What in blazes in going on down here?"

Both she and Bouchard turned to find Phillip standing in the doorway to the kitchens, informally clad in a white shirt, claret-red dressing gown, and black trousers. He was frowning like thunder.

"My lord, thank the good God you have come." Bouchard turned toward his employer, his arms stretched out in an imploring gesture. "Who is this girl who comes to me and declares herself *pâtissier*? It cannot be so, that such a waif shall—"

"Waif?" she interrupted and also stepped toward Phillip. "This man of yours who calls himself a chef has done nothing but demean and insult me from the moment I walked in!"

"It is I who have been insulted!" Bouchard cried. "I who have been demeaned."

Phillip held up his hands. "Yes, yes, I've heard

enough. From both of you," he added, glancing from the chef to her and back again. "Monsieur Bouchard, I take it you do not wish Miss Martingale to be pastry chef for the ball," he said in the tone of one trying to handle the situation in a calm and rational manner. "What, precisely, is your objection?"

"The cuisine, my lord, it is to be French." Bouchard spread his arms wide with an exaggerated shrug. "Yet I am sent an English girl to make the pastries? Impossible! It is not the simple bread and butter pudding we are to serve. Mademoiselle, she is English. She cannot make the complicated French pastry. And," he added with a derisive glance in her direction, "She is too young. I must have a *pâtissier* with experience." He returned his attention to Phillip and lapsed into French, slapping the back of one hand against the palm of the other to punctuate each syllable as he went on, *"Il faut mettre la main à la pâte."*

"I've been putting my 'hand to the dough' since I was three years old, I'll have you know!" she cried. "And I've been a professional *pâtissier* for nearly twelve years. I have worked with some of the finest chefs in Europe."

"Bah!" Bouchard scoffed. "Twelve years only? That is not enough to work under me."

"That's good," she shot back, "because I will not be working *under* you!"

The Frenchman started to speak again, but Phillip stopped him. "That will do, Monsieur Bouchard," he said, causing Maria to give the chef a triumphant glance.

"Now, Miss Martingale," Phillip said, bringing her attention back to him, "would you care to tell me what you've done to infuriate my chef?"

"He's just angry because he didn't get a *pâtissier* of his own choosing. Meaning one he can bully."

"This is intolerable!" cried Bouchard. "I am head chef. Never will she work with me. Never. She must go."

"Monsieur," Phillip began, but Maria interrupted.

"I'm not going anywhere until I have settled the pastry menu," she declared, folding her arms. "A menu which my staff will prepare under my supervision, using my recipes and my methods."

"Your methods?" echoed Bouchard. "There is no method to the English pastry cook."

"Why, of all the—"

"Enough!" Phillip roared, cutting her off. He leaned forward and grabbed her by the arm. "Come with me."

"Why?" She pulled against the hold Phillip had on her arm, but she was no match for his superior strength. "Where are you taking me?"

"Out of here, before my kitchen staff declares a

mutiny." He pulled her out of the kitchen, and as she was forced to depart, she shot a glance over her shoulder and saw Bouchard waving farewell to her, a triumphant smile on his face.

"Now look what you've done!" she cried in exasperation as Phillip began propelling her up the stairs. "I had the situation well in hand."

"Of course you did."

"I did! Until you arrived."

He didn't bother to argue with her. They reached the ground floor, turned on the landing and went up another flight of stairs. A few moments later, they were in his drawing room. "What was that all about?" he demanded, closing the door.

"You instructed me to see Monsieur Bouchard and arrange the details of the menu for the ball. So I was."

"You call that shouting match arranging things?"

"Yes, and it was all coming along famously until you interfered."

"Oh, yes. Famously."

She made a sound of impatience. "You don't understand. Bouchard and his staff cannot handle the entire supper for a ball with over four hundred guests, which is why your brother hired me in the first place. Bouchard needs a *pâtissier* to assist, but his pride is stung that he was not allowed to choose his own. And when he sees that I am young and I am female, it is a further blow to his pride. In front of his staff, he must swagger a bit and exert his authority as head chef."

"Then why in heaven's name didn't you just let him do so?"

"Because I would be the one to suffer for it! If I had given in, we would be doing his pastry recipes his way, and my establishment would be nothing more than an extension of his kitchen, supplying him with loaves of bread and trays of lady fingers, and I would be little more than a servant running back and forth at his beck and call. For us to work together as colleagues, I have to stand up for myself."

"Not when I am having my breakfast right overhead, you don't!"

"I couldn't allow that pompous Frenchman to believe for one moment that he is in charge of me or my staff."

"That pompous Frenchman happens to be one of the finest chefs in London."

"As am I. Which was the point of the entire argument. He threw down the gauntlet by insulting me, and I responded in kind. I know it flies in the face of all your notions of proper behavior, Phillip, but to do anything less would have been a great disappointment to him."

Phillip was staring at her in disbelief. "You mean he wanted you to rail and shout at him?"

"Of course. He wouldn't have a shred of respect

for me otherwise. My theatrics tell him I am a culinary artist, that I am worthy to work with a chef of his talent and ability. I have a temperament. I have pride in my work. I will not make his recipes, but my own. I am arrogant. These are things Bouchard understands and admires. Don't you see?"

He didn't. "All I see is that you take great delight in showing off your histrionic talent at every opportunity. You should be on the stage."

"The point is that I was well on my way to convincing him of my abilities when you dragged me out of there!" She frowned in aggravation, looking at him as if he was the one who'd done something wrong.

"I was having a serene, peaceful meal this morning," he informed her, feeling quite testy, "when war began erupting below stairs." He looked her up and down, shaking his head. "I might have known you would be the cause. I shall be fortunate if I do not receive a resignation letter from my chef before the day is out."

"Don't be silly," she said and turned away. "He won't resign."

"Where are you going?"

"To finish what I started," she told him over one shoulder as she started toward the door.

"Oh, no," he said and grabbed her wrist. "You are not going back down there."

She stopped in his hold with an impatient sigh.

"For heaven's sake, Phillip, let go of me," she said over her shoulder. "I'm going back to my shop to make pastries for that impossible little man. One taste of my *ganache*, and he'll think he's found the nectar of the gods."

Phillip let her go, though he was doubtful that even the nectar of the gods would prevent his chef from resigning. That evening, however, as he was preparing to go out, he found he had underestimated the powerful effects of a fine *ganache*.

He was in the foyer waiting for his carriage to be brought around when his butler informed him that Monsieur Bouchard would like a moment of his time. He agreed somewhat unwillingly, wondering what Maria might have done to further agitate the little Frenchman, but the chef was all smiles as he came bustling into the foyer.

"Ah, my lord," Bouchard said, lifting his hands in a flamboyant gesture as he approached, "the *petite mademoiselle* may be English, but she is not the little miss of milk and water. *Non*, not that one."

Phillip raised an eyebrow. "Are you speaking of Miss Martingale?" he asked, the other man's benignant expression making him a bit doubtful on that point.

"But, of course! She throws the tantrum this morning and boasts to me that she is worthy to be *pâtissier* for your lordship's ball, but I look her up and down and I am not so sure, despite her pretty shop next door. And when you drag her out of my kitchen, I think, ah-ha, that is the end of this little one. But then, she brings the plate of pastries, slams them down before me, and storms away. I look at the little cakes she has brought, and I think they are pretty enough, but this does not signify. After all—how do you English say?—the pudding is proved when it is eaten, no? So I taste them with much trepidation."

"And," Phillip said, feeling rather as if he were about to enter a burning house with an armful of dynamite, "did you like them?"

Bouchard clasped his hands together with a blissful sigh. "*Magnifique,*" he breathed with reverence. "Her *mille-feuille* is crisp but tender. Her *profiteroles* are sublime. And her *ganache* . . ." He pressed his fingertips to his lips and made a smacking sound. "Perfection itself."

He couldn't help feeling relieved that there would be no more vociferous battles below stairs. A man wanted peace in his home. "So you are now willing to work with her?"

"*Mais oui*! She is a *pâtissier* of the first excellence! My lord is brilliant to have found her." He pulled a folded sheet of paper from his apron pocket and handed it to Phillip. "This is Bouchard's menu for the ball supper. If you approve, I shall present it to *la petite mademoiselle* so that she is able to choose and prepare the proper pastries to accompany." With that, he nodded happily and departed.

Phillip put the folded sheet in the breast pocket of his jacket as he watched his chef bustle away, and he shook his head in bafflement. Cooks, he decided, were the very devil.

Chapter 9

Ice cream is exquisite. Too bad it isn't illegal.
Voltaire

*A*fter giving Monsieur Bouchard some of her best culinary masterpieces to taste, Maria spent the afternoon paying bills and reckoning up her accounts, leaving her apprentices to work without her for the remainder of the day. When she returned to the kitchens that evening, she found Miss Dexter had done fine without her. Miss Hayes, however, had run into difficulties.

Maria stared at the pair of flat, dark brown discs on the worktable, then glanced at the younger woman across from her. "Third oven?" she guessed.

Miss Hayes gave an unhappy nod. "Yes, ma'am. I don't know why, but it just doesn't circulate heat as well as the others."

Miss Dexter turned from the counter where she was filling tins with the shortbread and fat rascals she had baked in preparation for the following day. "It does all right for some pastries, if you watch them close. But cakes don't do well."

"I'm so sorry, ma'am," Miss Hayes said, sounding almost tearful. "I know you told me not to bake cakes in that oven, but I forgot." She gave a sigh. "Half a pound of butter and a good bit of chocolate wasted. If you need to deduct the expense from my wages, I understand."

Maria thought of all the times she'd had her wages garnished for culinary mishaps, and she put a hand on the girl's arm. "I won't do any such thing, Miss Hayes. Anyone can make a mistake, especially at the end of a long day. Just remember, no cakes in that oven." She glanced at the watch pinned to the bib of her apron. "Why don't the two of you go home? It's seven o'clock. After nearly fourteen hours here, you two must be exhausted."

The weary faces of her apprentice chefs brightened considerably, and several minutes later, the two young women had slipped into their mackintoshes and departed for home.

Maria grabbed a Cornish pasty and an apple out of the larder and went upstairs. She ate her makeshift meal as she ran water from the taps for a bath. After washing away a day's worth of flour, sugar, sweat, and coal dust, she braided back her damp hair and changed into her nightclothes. As on every night, Maria was asleep by eight o'clock and awake and downstairs ready to work by half past three the following morning.

The shop and kitchens were quiet, for her maids would not be stirring for another two hours, and it would be another thirty minutes after that before her apprentices returned to begin their day, but Maria didn't mind the solitude. Here, before the making of the day's breads and cakes began, before she found her time taken up with the daily rush, was her opportunity to indulge her creative instincts. All her best recipes had come to her in the wee small hours before dawn.

She stoked the fire in one stove to life, then put a cross bun from the day before on the warming board and made herself a cup of tea and a soft-boiled egg. The maids, she noted as she ate her breakfast, had left something on the central worktable. Curious, Maria pulled up one corner of the cheesecloth and found Miss Hayes's chocolate torte. Perhaps the maids had thought to keep the torte for breakfast. Maria broke off a corner of one layer and popped it into her mouth. As she tasted the dense, underdone cake, she was intrigued by its chewy texture and powerful chocolate flavor. Struck by an idea, she knew the maids would have to find something else for their morning meal.

She straightened away from the table and set down her cup, then she ventured into the larder and the ice room. An hour later, she was piping thin lines of green royal icing onto a row of tiny, chocolate-encased squares.

Preoccupied with this painstaking task, she did not hear footsteps coming down the steps outside, and when the tradesman's door opened, she jumped, sending an unintended stream of icing across the petit four she was decorating. She was even more surprised by the identity of the tall man in the doorway.

"Phillip!" she gasped. "How you startled me! What are you doing roaming about at this hour?"

"I might ask you the same question. Don't you ever sleep?"

She smiled at that. "The work in a bakery always begins early," she told him and bent again over the row of petit fours. Skipping the one she'd ruined, she moved on to the next, piping on two crossed ribbons and a tiny green bow.

"I don't wish to interrupt your work," he said as he entered the kitchen and closed the door behind him.

"You're not." She paused again. "Just coming home, I suppose?" she said, noting his black evening suit.

"Yes." He gave a slight cough. "When the carriage pulled up, I saw that your lights were on."

Thinking of the last time that had happened, she couldn't resist making fun. "Careful," she told him. "People might see you down here and think something scandalous is going on."

He shifted his weight, looking uncomfortable. "I have something to give you, otherwise I would not have come."

"It seems a bit reckless of you, Phillip. After all, you must have a care for your reputation."

"Don't you mean your reputation?"

"Oh, no," she answered without pausing in her task. "I'm a woman in trade. No one would ever think me an innocent miss whose reputation needed protecting. No one would even raise an eyebrow to see you down here. But it's different for you."

"How so?"

"I can see the society pages now. The Marquess of Kayne," she added in a lofty tone as if reading from a society column, "is a man known for his impeccable good manners and his strict observation of the proprieties. But we at *Talk Of The Town* have evidence to the contrary! He has been seen visiting a certain pastry chef in Mayfair before dawn. Oh, the horror! What is society coming to?"

She piped on the last tiny bow and looked up to find him watching her, his mouth curved with a hint of amusement. "Perhaps I was a bit punctilious before," he admitted. "Forgive me for thinking to protect your good name."

"I appreciate your efforts, honestly, but it's quite unnecessary, and would prove futile in any case. I accepted long ago the assumptions some people have about women in shop trade, and I know there is nothing I can do about it."

"One of those assumptions being a lack of virtue?" He didn't wait for an answer, but went on, "Not that it makes a difference, of course, but I truly did have a reason for coming down here."

She formed a bow on the last petit four and set the pastry bag aside. "Something to give me, I think you said?"

"Yes." He set aside his hat and walked toward her. Halting on the other side of her worktable, he pulled a folded sheet of paper out of his jacket pocket and held it out to her.

"Not an eviction notice, I hope?" she said, in a half-joking way as she took the sheet.

"No. It is a menu for the ball from my chef," he told her, coming around to her side of the table and looking over her shoulder as she unfolded the sheet. "You will notice there is no pastry menu. He is allowing you to choose it yourself."

"Is he indeed?" She chuckled. "So Monsieur Bouchard has decided I'm up to the job?"

"You are a pastry chef of the first water, Miss Martingale. You are magnificent. Your pastry is sublime. Your *ganache* is perfection."

"My, my, I am moving up in the world." She smiled, feeling a sense of satisfaction as she glanced over the menu in her hands, noting the usual ball fare for a ball supper: lobster patties, salmon salad, cold tongue, ham and pheasant, fresh fruit—

"Are these what has my chef singing your praises?"

"Hmm?" She looked up, casting a sideways glance at the man beside her, and found that he was studying her newest concoction.

"These? No, I didn't give any of these to Monsieur Bouchard," she answered as she refolded the menu and put it in the pocket of her apron. "I invented this recipe only this morning. The result of an accident. One of my apprentices was attempting a chocolate torte in that third oven and things rather went awry."

"You mean the oven that produced the flat sponge cake?"

"Yes. The result proved the same with chocolate torte, and the texture was a bit more dense and chewy than ordinary cake, but the taste was quite enjoyable, and it seemed a shame to let it go to waste. So, I cut the cakes into squares, topped them with an ice cream I flavored with crème de menthe, wrapped them in dark chocolate fondant and decorated them with mint icing as you see, making a sort of frozen petit four."

"If one can go by appearances, your experiment was a success."

"Appearance is a vital component, to be sure, but taste is what matters most." On impulse, she picked up one of the confections between her thumb and forefinger and turned toward him. "Would you care to be the judge?" she asked and lifted the petit four to his lips.

He hesitated the barest second before taking the petit four into his mouth. As he tasted it, she realized to her surprise that she wanted him to like it. That made no sense, really, for she thought she'd stopped caring what Phillip thought years ago. Nonetheless, she found herself waiting for his opinion with an anxiousness that was all out of proportion. "Well?" she asked, unable to discern anything from his expression. "What do you think?"

"My God," he mumbled around the mouthful of cake and ice cream, and the reverent tone of his voice told its own tale.

She began to laugh, relieved and more pleased than she would have thought possible. "You like them."

He chewed slowly, savoring the bite of chocolate cake and mint flavored ice cream to the fullest extent. "Like them?" he countered after he'd swallowed the treat. "Woman, they are absolutely wicked. Sinful. By law, they shouldn't be allowed. If what you gave my chef is in any way comparable, I'm not surprised you have him in rhapsodies."

Given such lavish praise from a man whose good opinion was so hard to earn, she had to sample her new concoction as well. She picked up one of the treats with great care—for they were starting to soften and melt—and put it into her mouth.

"Not bad," she judged after a moment, and helped herself to another. This time, she considered and judged the contrasting tastes and textures as she chewed and swallowed. "I might make some of these for the ball. Although," she added as she looked down at her hands, "I shall have to put them on a bed of crushed ice unless I want all your guests to have chocolate-covered fingers."

"Not just their fingers."

"What do you mean?" She looked up and found that he was smiling at her, a wide, wholehearted smile that made her breath catch in her throat. She couldn't remember the last time she'd seen Phillip smile like that. As a boy, perhaps, though even then, it had been a rare thing—a grin of approval for a well-played cricket match or a clever chess play. But the smile on his face now was not the smile of the boy she remembered. This was the smile of a devastatingly handsome man, and she felt an unexpected rush of pleasure at the sight of it.

"Why—" For no reason she could identify, her voice failed her. She took a deep breath and tried again. "Why are you smiling like that?"

"You have a smear of chocolate on your face."

"I do?" She reached for a damp rag from the worktable and looked up at him. "Where?"

"Right there." He lifted one hand, lightly touching the tip of his finger to one corner of her mouth to indicate the appropriate spot. But then, his smile vanished, and his palm cupped her cheek.

The rag fluttered from her hand, forgotten, as his thumb grazed her lips to rub away the dab of chocolate. The contact was so unexpected, so intimate, so unlike Phillip, her lips parted in surprise.

His thumb pressed hard against her mouth, as if he expected a protest and was silencing her before she could utter it, but she was so stunned that it never occurred to her to protest.

Phillip was touching her. Phillip, who never did anything improper, who never stepped outside the bounds. Phillip, who thought her a fast little piece and wanted her banished to the farthest corner of the globe. Phillip was touching her. It was so unbelievable, she didn't know what to do.

His fingers curled around the nape of her neck and his thumb pressed the underside of her jaw, lifting her face. His free arm wrapped around her waist, pulling her hard against him. She sucked in a startled breath, but she had no time to react before he bent his head and captured her lips with his.

The kiss was not tender. It was hard and hot, bruising her mouth, and yet, she felt a thrill like nothing she'd ever felt in her life before.

She closed her eyes, and her lips parted beneath the demanding pressure of his. When his tongue entered her mouth, she made a sound of shock, stirring in his hold, but his hand tightened at her neck and his arm tightened around her waist, keeping her body pressed to his as his mouth tasted deeply of her.

She had been kissed before, but not like this, never like this. Her shock began to recede, and she became aware of other things. The strength of his arms like a steel band around her, the scent of bay rum on his skin, the sound of her own heart thudding in her breast, the taste of crème de menthe and chocolate on his tongue.

She flattened her palms against him, and beneath the slick-silken texture of his waistcoat and the crisp starched linen of his shirt, she could feel the hard muscles of his chest, and she wondered if his heart was beating as hard and fast as hers.

The lush taste of his mouth was sending a strange pleasure spreading throughout her body, a thick, dark wave of pleasure that made her body move against his in a way she could not control, a way that must surely be shameless, but it felt so glorious, she didn't care. She wanted this kiss to go on forever.

Without warning, he tore his lips from hers, an abrupt, almost violent withdrawal that forced her to open her eyes.

"Good God." He jerked her arms down from around his neck and shoved her away as if she burned like fire. "What am I doing?"

"I think—" Maria stopped and took a deep breath, trying to get her bearings. "I think you were kissing me," she said and gave a little laugh of surprise.

He stared at her as if appalled. "What is it?" he muttered, raking a hand through his hair. "What is it about you that makes me do such stupid things?"

If he'd grabbed her cup from the table and tossed her tea dregs in her face, he couldn't have more thoroughly ruined the moment. "Well, thank you very much," she shot back, stung, all her exhilaration evaporating. "So kissing me is stupid? Is that what you mean?"

"It's more than stupid." He rubbed his hands over his face. "It's insane. You make me do things that go against my honor, against my reason, even against my will."

"Make you?" she echoed in disbelief. "Of all the absurd, unfair—" She broke off, spluttering with anger, and it was several moments before she could speak again. "I didn't make you kiss me! I was just standing here!"

"Whatever you do, it makes me insane." He glared at her, his resentment palpable. "A few centuries ago, they'd have burned you as a witch."

"Oh, yes, that explains everything. I'm a witch, and I wove a spell over you." She waved her fingers in front of his face in a mocking imitation of hypnotism, then stopped and snapped her fingers. "No, wait, it wasn't a spell. It was the petit fours! In them was my secret, magical love potion."

"Love?" He repeated the word with disdain, his gaze raking over her. "I assure you, Miss Martingale, love has nothing to do with this!"

That contemptuous declaration was the last straw. She pointed to the door. "I want you to leave. Now."

"An excellent idea." He turned away, heading for the door. "I never should have come down here in the first place."

"I couldn't agree more!" she called after him.

He seized his hat and left without a reply, without even a backward glance. Hands on her hips, Maria scowled at the door as it swung shut behind him, feeling more insulted than she'd ever felt in her life.

How dare he imply that any of what had just happened was her fault? He'd come down here, made advances upon her person, and insulted her. And then, he'd had the gall to blame her for his behavior? Of all the nerve.

Love has nothing to do with this.

His words echoed back to her, and with them, she remembered the disdain in his eyes, sparking not only her anger, but also an unmistakable hurt. It hurt, damn it, to know that even after he'd given her the most extraordinary kiss of her life, he still thought her beneath his contempt. Suddenly, she felt as if she were fifteen again, watching him turn his back on her and walk away.

How galling to know that his low opinion of her still had the power to sting. It shouldn't, not after all this time. What did she care what he thought of her? Hell, she didn't even like him anymore. At moments like this, it was hard to remember that she ever had liked him. And despite that wonderful kiss, he didn't like her. He'd made that painfully clear.

Her eyes narrowed on the closed door. So, he thought he was insane for kissing her, did he?

He wasn't insane. He was insufferable.

He was insane. That was the only possible explanation for his unaccountable behavior. Phillip let himself into his house, shoved his latchkey into his pocket, and strode across the foyer, baffled. He was a gentleman, but he had just behaved in a way that violated every notion of what that meant. Always before, whenever his desire for her flared up, he'd been able to control it, suppress it, will it away. Not this time.

He'd only gone down there in the first place to give her the damn menu, he thought as he started up the stairs to his bedroom. Best to do it right then, he'd decided when he'd seen her lamps burning, before he forgot about it altogether and it ended up in the laundry basket.

He knew he should have simply sent a footman, but if he had done that, he wouldn't have been able to see her. Phillip halted on the landing with an aggravated sigh. Why not admit it? The menu was the lame excuse he'd given himself to go to her.

She'd been on his mind all evening. Everything tonight had reminded him of her. Dinner at the Clarendon, her former place of employment, where there had been a bowl of fat red apples on the table and a friend had ordered chocolate tart for dessert. Then later, chess at his club, where he'd lost the match because he'd been thinking of her, remembering all the times they had played, missing those companionable days. A moment in the smoking room, when he'd started to light a cigar, only to change his mind when the image of her on the balcony in her nightdress had come into his mind.

And then, arriving home to find her lamps lit; and like a moth drawn to a flame, like a compass needle veering north, he'd turned toward her door instead of his.

With each step down to her kitchen, he'd known he was making a mistake. He'd known he was pushing his self-restraint to its limits. But he'd done it anyway, almost as if to test his mettle, to prove to himself that he was perfectly capable of resisting her.

How wrong he had been.

The skin of her cheek had been as silky as he'd imagined. Her lips, sticky with chocolate, had been so sweet to taste. Even now, he could still smell the vanilla and cinnamon fragrance of her hair. And her body . . . God. His throat went dry as he remembered the feel of her pressed against him, her breasts against his chest, the deep curve of her waist beneath his arm, the stirring of her hips against his own. It had been beyond anything he'd ever conjured about her in his imagination, beyond the fevered dreams he'd had of her when he was seventeen.

How he'd come to his senses tonight, he still didn't know. The sound of traffic on the street, perhaps, or the chime of a clock upstairs. Something had brought back a vestige of his sanity, enough to remember that they were in a lighted room, visible to anyone passing by, enough to remember that he was a marquess and a gentleman, and that she was a respectable woman now technically in his employ.

If she were a courtesan, he could have her and be done. If she were a lady, he could marry her, have her, and be done. But she was neither, and that was the damnable part of it all.

He felt a wave of frustration. Absurd that he should be so preoccupied with her. Absurd that an ordinary woman—yes, for despite his accusation, she was not a witch, but a perfectly ordinary woman—should be able to get him so stirred up. She was pretty, to be sure, but he'd bedded more beautiful women in his life. She was nowhere near his equal in birth, station, or connection, and therefore unworthy of a more permanent alliance. Which was why, he reminded himself, he'd saved his brother from her all those years ago.

Twelve years, he reminded himself, jerking at his cravat. The idea that she should be able to obsess his thoughts, inflame his desire, and overcome his will even after all this time was humiliating.

Tonight, one taste of her had not slaked his appetite. Quite the opposite, in fact. He wanted her now more than ever before, but what was true years ago was still true today. He could not give in to his desire for her, he reminded himself as he continued upstairs, or he would dishonor them both and disgrace his family name.

Kissing her had been a huge mistake, and he knew he could not repeat it. He had to stay away from her. Far wiser to avoid temptation altogether than to test his ability to resist it. While he prided himself on his strength of will and his self-control, when it came to Maria Martingale, it was best not to push his luck.

Chapter 10

What are little girls made of? Sugar and spice and everything nice.

English nursery rhyme

As the May Day Ball approached, Maria had little time to think of Phillip, but that didn't stop him from stealing into her thoughts, and every time he did, she became aggravated once more, with him and with herself.

It wasn't as if she didn't have plenty to do. Her business was thriving, her apprentices, though coming along, were still in constant need of training, and she was in the midst of preparations for the ball. Yet, during the ten days that followed that kiss, the scorching intensity of it and the infuriating events afterward came back to haunt her at least a dozen times a day.

She'd never known a kiss could be like that, so

hot and provocative, so erotic, and she realized there was far more to Phillip than the cool, impassive composure he displayed on the surface.

The sputtering of air from the now-empty pastry bag in her hands brought her out of her reverie, and Maria reached for the bowl of sponge batter beside her. She refilled the bag, and as she continued piping batter onto a parchment-lined baking tray, her mind returned to something far more fascinating than the making of ladyfingers.

Baffling that a man who had such a low opinion of her could make her feel this way. She'd still been caught up in the euphoric haze of the moment, her lips tingling from the luscious sensation of his mouth on hers, when he'd proceeded to ruin the most passionate moment of her life.

So why, she wondered in aggravation, was she wasting a moment of her time thinking about him and mooning over a kiss that he hadn't even found enjoyable? Why, in the quiet hours before dawn, did she keep glancing at her kitchen door, hoping he would come by? Maybe *she* was the one who was insane.

Maria set down the pastry bag and flexed her cramped hands, glancing about the kitchen and trying to force her mind to something else. The ball was a mere thirty hours away, and things were a bit chaotic in the kitchens. She'd brought in two additional cooks and four kitchen maids from Lucy's agency to help with the final preparations, and all around her, women were hard at work. Across the worktable from her, her apprentices were making truffles, and she watched as Miss Hayes rolled the chocolate balls in cocoa, and Miss Dexter decorated them with pink roses. Maria frowned, thoughts of Phillip vanishing in the wake of more immediate concerns.

"No, Miss Dexter, not roses!" she cried. "These truffles are for the ball. The flavoring in them is lavender, not rose water! The decoration needs to be a lavender flower. For heaven's sake, the menu is right here," she added in exasperation, jabbing a finger at the sheet of paper in the center of the table. "It might behoove you to read it. The ball is tomorrow night, you know."

The room was suddenly silent. Miss Dexter's round, pretty face puckered under the withering criticism she had just received. "I'm sorry, ma'am," she whispered and ducked her head, but not before Maria saw the tears glistening in her eyes.

Maria's conscience smote her. "Oh, hell," she muttered, and pressed four fingers to her forehead. What on earth was wrong with her? She had just humiliated a member of her staff in front of others, and for no good reason. How many times, she wondered, had André berated her in this same obnoxious manner just before a big event? How many times had she vowed that when she had her own establishment, she would never do that to a member of her staff? She took a deep breath and raised her head.

"My apologies, Miss Dexter," she said. "I had no call to speak so sharply. Forgive me."

Relief caused the tears to spill over. "Yes, ma'am. Oh, ma'am, I am sorry. I know the chocolates for the ball need to be just right. I'll do the flowers again."

"That won't be necessary," she answered. "They'll do fine as they are. But if you would be so kind as to finish these ladyfingers for me, I would appreciate it."

"Yes, ma'am."

Maria reached behind her and yanked at her apron strings. "I shall be back in a short while," she said and gave the two younger women a smile. "As out of sorts as I am today, it's obvious I need to take a few moments away from the kitchens. Once again, Miss Dexter, my apologies."

She went up to the shop and verified with Miss Simms and Miss Foster that everything there was in good order. "I'll be upstairs if you need me," she said, and went to her rooms, thinking she might take a short nap, for it wasn't likely she'd get any other opportunities for sleep until the ball was over. But when she reached her bedroom, she noticed through the doorway to the adjoining bath that one of her maids had laid out fresh towels and soap.

She glanced down and noted that she was covered in sugar, flour, and sweat, as usual. She glanced back up, staring at the porcelain bath. Stupid to have a bath now, she told herself, for she'd only get dirty and sweaty again when she returned to the kitchens. And a full bath would empty one of her boilers, leaving the maids with less hot water in the scullery. But that newfangled bathtub proved an irresistible temptation, and fifteen minutes later, she was sinking blissfully into a tub of warm water.

Afterward, she put on fresh undergarments and sat down before her dressing table to comb out her damp hair. It was a long process, for her hair was thick, unruly and came to her waist, and as she untangled the strands, her mind inevitably drifted back to what had been preoccupying her for days and days.

Why did that kiss fascinate her so? It wasn't as if she'd never been kissed before. Lawrence had been the first, of course. She smiled a little at the memory. What a naive, awkward thing it had been—a quick, timid press of lips behind the hedgerows when they were fifteen. Another kiss in the rose arbor after they'd agreed to elope, less awkward than the first—warm, tender, quite sweet, really—but still far too short to get one stirred up. And during the eleven years she'd lived at Little Russell Street, she'd been fortunate enough to have several genuine suitors, and unfortunate enough to wait tables and work the kitchen with a few lecherous footmen whose faces she'd had to slap. But not a single man who'd ever kissed her made her feel as if she were on fire.

She set aside the comb and plunked her elbows on the dressing table, staring ruefully at her reflection. Of all the men in the world, why did it have to be Phillip whose kiss was so exciting?

Maria reached for her comb. She finished untangling the long strands of her hair, then wove them into a fat, single braid. Holding the ends in one hand, she pulled open the drawer of her dressing table with the other, and reached for a strip of scrap muslin to tie the braid. But when her eye caught on a ribbon of pale blue silk, she hesitated. It was a pretty falderal, to be sure, but it would be absurd to wear it. Why, it'd be dirty after half an hour down in the bakery. On the other hand, she so seldom wore anything pretty nowadays.

She remembered her father, how he'd always wanted her to be a lady, to wear pretty things and find a husband and occupy her time with ladylike pursuits. He'd wanted her to be like her mother, when what she'd always wanted was to be a great chef like him. Maria stared at the strip of blue silk and wavered, and then, for no practical reason whatsoever, she pulled the ribbon out of the drawer and used it to tie the end of her braid.

She rose from her dressing table and started toward the bed, thinking to have that nap, but as she passed the window, she paused to take a peek between the curtains and changed her mind. The sun was shining, and she decided a stroll in the sun sounded much more refreshing than a nap.

She donned a crisp, clean shirtwaist and a skirt of brown serge, then pulled on her boots and tightened the laces. She opened one of the French doors and stepped out onto her balcony.

This was just what she needed. The sun was warm on her face, but the breeze felt cool and invigorating on her damp hair. She walked to the rail and leaned against the balustrade, noticing that on the balcony across the way, the occupants of the house had begun an herb garden of sorts. She could see pots of thyme, sage, and tarragon.

She might do that, she thought. Rosemary and chives for her herb breads, angelica, lavender, lemon verbena and violets for some of the confections. It would be nice to have her own supply. She could have cases installed in one or two of her windows so she could bring the pots indoors in winter.

A door slammed to her left, breaking into these horticultural speculations. Maria turned her head, and almost groaned at the sight of the very man who'd been on her mind for over a week, the man she was trying so hard to forget. He didn't seem to see her, for he walked straight toward the balustrade in front of him, pulling out a cigar from his jacket pocket as he went. But just before reaching the rail, he glanced sideways, saw her, and came to a halt.

Their eyes met, and her stomach dipped with a strange, quivering sensation. His lashes lowered, and the moment she realized he was looking at her mouth, all the excitement of that kiss came rushing back to torment her again. She almost reached up to touch her tingling lips, but caught herself just in time and shoved her hands into her skirt pockets.

Heaven help her, she realized in horror, she was nervous. It was ridiculous, but at this moment, she felt awkward and uncertain, as if she were a green girl of fifteen rather than a fully mature woman of nearly thirty.

Was he nervous? She scanned his face, searching for any sign of it, but there was none. She couldn't begin to guess what he was thinking, but only the most self-deluded fool would think he looked happy to see her.

"Forgive me," he said with a stiff bow. "I did not mean to intrude upon your privacy."

He turned as if to leave, but before he could walk away, she spoke.

"Don't go," she called after him, and the moment she said it, she wanted to bite her tongue off. Despite that kiss, it was plain as a pikestaff that he didn't want to be anywhere near her. And it wasn't as if she wanted to be near him. She'd been trying to forget about him. And anyway, if he stayed, what on earth were they going to say to each other? "That is," she added in a desperate attempt to retreat to safer ground as he paused and turned back around, "you don't have to leave because of me, my lord. Surely, we can share a balcony in a civil fashion."

"One might hope so," he answered, but though he sounded a bit doubtful on that point, he did not depart. He stood there for what seemed an eternity, and then he began walking toward her.

Maria looked away. She struggled to pretend a dignified indifference as he approached, but by the time he reached her side, her heart was pounding so loud in her chest, she could almost hear it. What on earth was wrong with her?

He halted on the other side of the short wall that separated them and turned to stare at the balconies of the terrace houses opposite, but it was several more moments before he spoke. "Fine day."

"Yes," she agreed at once, latching onto the subject with gratitude. "The sun is shining."

The inanity of that comment made her wince, but she could feel his gaze on her, and she forced herself to look at him. "It's nice to have a bit of sunshine," she added, and managed a smile.

"Yes, indeed," he agreed, gave her a fleeting

smile in return, then turned his attention to the view.

She did the same, but when he stirred beside her, she cast another glance at him to find that he was tucking his cigar into the breast pocket of his jacket.

"Didn't you come out here to smoke?" she asked in surprise.

"Yes."

"Then why are you putting your cigar away? I don't mind if you smoke."

"I do. Smoking in front of a lady is not done. An old-fashioned notion, I know." He looked at her again and lifted his chin a notch. "Laugh if you like."

"I shan't laugh." At those words, she saw a flash of relief in his face. This rare sign of vulnerability disarmed her, for it was unlike Phillip to give any clue as to his inner feelings. "It's a very thoughtful gesture," she said, bemused. "Thank you."

"Not at all." He looked away, and that brief moment of vulnerability was gone. "There's a good, strong breeze today," he said, reverting to their former topic.

She murmured a suitable reply, and although she was certain polite small talk was the appropriate thing to do under these circumstances, she felt vaguely disappointed. This man had given her the most passionate, romantic kiss she'd ever had, and she couldn't help feeling a bit let down that the next time she saw him, they were talking about the weather.

They were talking about the weather. Perfect. A pleasant, safe topic. Phillip felt some of his tension ease away. Discussions of that sort, even with her, were not likely to be particularly arousing.

"A good breeze," he felt compelled to add, "helps clear the air."

"True," she agreed. "A most welcome change. The air in London is usually so foul."

Silence fell again, and it was clear another neutral topic was needed, but as he attempted to think of one, the scent of her floated past him on the breeze—that scent of vanilla and cinnamon that had been plaguing him for days. For God's sake, he wondered with a hint of desperation, did the woman always have to smell like dessert? He could feel his control slip a notch. He scrambled to regain it.

"Preparations for the ball coming along?" he asked.

"Oh, yes. We're inundated with work at the moment, of course, but everything is proceeding smoothly."

"Excellent. No more third-oven disasters?" When she shook her head, he went on, "That's rather a pity."

"How so?"

"Those little chocolate and mint things were extraordinary."

She turned her head, and her smile hit him like a physical force. He sucked in his breath. The oven, he reminded himself. They were talking about the oven. He forced himself to speak again. "Do you want me to replace it? The oven, I mean. I will, if you wish it."

She considered that offer for a moment. "Thank you, but I don't think that's necessary. I rather think it's good training for my apprentices to work with equipment that is less than perfect."

"Very sound. But if you change your mind and want me to replace it, let me know."

"I will."

She turned toward the balustrade, studying the view, and he started to do the same, but a flash of blue caught his attention, and he looked down just in time to see the ribbon that tied the end of her braid slip free and fall to the floor behind her. His mind flashed back fourteen years, to another hair ribbon she'd lost in this same way.

"You've lost your ribbon," he told her and leaned over the wall, bending down to retrieve the bit of silk before the wind could carry it away.

"Thank you," she said, taking it from his outstretched hand. "This is a bit like history repeating itself, isn't it?" she asked as she tied the ribbon around the end of her hair.

He tensed, striving to pretend he didn't know

what she was talking about. "History repeating itself?" he asked, pasting on a puzzled little smile.

"The hair ribbon I lost all those years ago," she reminded. "The pink one that belonged to my mother."

"Ah, yes." He nodded as if enlightened. "The one with—ahem—daisies on it."

"Yes. My mother embroidered those daisies, which was why I was so upset when the ribbon went missing. Oh, how I wish I hadn't lost it. She died when I was six, you see, and that ribbon was one of the few things I had of hers. Papa gave most of her things away when she died."

He felt a glimmer of guilt and forced himself to speak. "We have something in common, Miss Martingale. My mother also died when I was six."

"I don't remember my mother at all. Do you remember yours?"

"Only vaguely. She used to sing to me, I believe. She died of cholera."

"My mother died in childbirth. My father was devastated. He always wanted me to be like her. That's why he saved his wages so carefully and sent me to school. He wanted me to be refined and elegant, ladylike."

"But you preferred climbing trees and learning to play cricket?"

"As you are well aware," she said, laughing. "If

it weren't for you and Lawrence, I fear I would have been forced into lace pinafores and made to embroider daisies. As it was, I always had to fight and plead for him to teach me how to be a chef." She paused and her smile faded. "It was so hard when I came home from France, for everything had changed. Papa would no longer let me help him in the kitchens, and I didn't know what to do with myself. I didn't seem to fit in anywhere. I had the education of a lady, but I was not a lady."

Those lovely hazel eyes looked up at him, and there was a hint of pain in their depths. "And I had somehow lost your friendship on top of everything else. I could not understand why."

It felt as if a fist were twisting his guts, and he turned toward the rail. "I never dreamt I had given you distress," he managed. "I was . . . I was busy. Estate business."

"Of course."

He wasn't looking at her, but he could tell from the tone of her voice that she found that excuse as lame as he did. Suddenly, for some insane reason, he wanted to tell her the truth, but he could not. He had never been good at expressing his feelings. In any case, a gentleman did not speak of his carnal appetites to a woman who was not his mistress. And besides, how could he admit to what he'd felt for her then without it being painfully obvious that he still felt it today?

She straightened away from the rail. "I should

be getting back downstairs. We still have a great deal of work to do before tomorrow."

Relief washed over him. "Yes, of course." He bowed to her. "Good day, Miss Martingale."

She dipped a curtsy and walked away, and he willed himself to turn in the opposite direction.

He went into his rooms and as he closed the door behind him, he caught sight of the dressing table on the other side of the room. He stared at it for a moment, then crossed the room to open one of the drawers. He retrieved an old collar box from the bottom, and removed the lid, then unfolded several layers of yellowed tissue paper and pulled out what he was looking for: a folded, faded strip of pink silk embroidered with white daisies.

The memory of that day fourteen years ago was as vivid in his mind as if it had happened yesterday. He'd seen the ribbon fall from her hair, and he'd picked it up, thinking to hand it back to her, but then he'd caught the fragrance of her hair on it, and he'd shoved it into his pocket instead. He'd never given returning it to her another thought, not even when he learned it had once belonged to her mother. Not even when she and Lawrence had spent days searching for it. Not even when he'd seen her cry.

Slowly, he lifted the ribbon to his nostrils. The scents of vanilla and spice that had once permeated the ribbon were long gone, of course, but it didn't matter. He closed his eyes and breathed deep as the thick, heavy sweetness of his secret desire for her began spreading through his body.

The door to his dressing room opened, breaking into Phillip's reverie, and he dropped the ribbon into the drawer as his valet entered the bedroom and halted just inside the doorway.

"Your bath is drawn, my lord," the servant informed him.

"Thank you, Gaston," he answered over his shoulder. "I'll be there in a moment."

"Very good, sir." The valet bowed and withdrew back into the dressing room.

Phillip lifted the bit of silk to his nostrils, imagining one more time the sweet, spice-laden scent of her hair, then he carefully refolded the ribbon. He started to put it back in the box, then he paused.

She wanted it back. Even after all this time.

Phillip rubbed the strip of silk, the callus on his thumb catching the strands of embroidery, and that damnable guilt nudged him again. He ought to return it, he knew. He could invent a lie to explain why he had it. Found it in an old trunk, or something.

He retrieved his silver card case from the breast pocket of his jacket, tucked the ribbon behind his cards where no one would see it, then laid the case on his dressing table.

He'd return it to her, he told himself as he walked to the dressing room. He would. At the first opportunity.

Chapter 11

If music be the food of love, play on.
William Shakespeare

*C*haos reigned in the kitchens of Avermore House, and if one could set any store by that, the Marquess of Kayne's May Day Ball was proving to be a smashing success.

The noise below stairs was deafening. With Bouchard, his *sous*-chef, and Maria all calling out orders; assistant cooks shouting back answers; scullery maids clattering dishes; and footman rattling trays, Maria couldn't even hear the music, though the ballroom was directly above their heads.

"Wait, wait!" she cried as Miss Dexter, a tray of buttered oranges in her hands, raced past her toward the door leading out of the kitchens. The apprentice stopped, and Maria groaned in dismay at the carved-out orange peels filled with custard that lined the tray. "They have to have some sort of decoration, Miss Dexter."

"Yes, ma'am," the other woman agreed, "but I haven't anything left at my post."

Maria glanced around and seized a bowl of whipped cream, ignoring the shouts of protest from the *saucier*, who had just set aside his whisk. "Oh, don't get your knickers in a twist, Villefort," she said, raising her voice to be heard above the string of French curses being hurled at her. "I'll make you some more."

She pulled a spoon from the worktable. "Set down the tray, Miss Dexter, and go whip some cream for Monsieur Villefort before he takes my head off. I'll finish these and deliver them upstairs."

"Yes, ma'am." The other woman hurried away.

Maria scooped a dollop of the cream onto each orange, impervious to the insults of Villefort, who was still berating her. She handed him back the bowl, added a sprinkle of candied orange peel and a sugared violet to each dessert, then grabbed the tray and headed for the door.

"Fuss, fuss, fuss," she muttered as she backed up against the door to push it wide. Turning around, she shut it behind her with a kick of her heel and started up the servants' staircase. "I don't know why the French chefs are always so touchy."

As she mounted the stairs, she could hear the

lively strains of a polka, but she didn't pause for a glance at the dancers in the ballroom. Instead, she continued down the corridor, her speed slowed more than once by having to flatten herself respectfully against the wall to make way for the pretty debutantes and black-suited gentlemen coming in the opposite direction. She entered the supper room, circling the perimeter to the dessert table at the far end. She set down the buttered oranges, then stacked up the three empty trays that were there, noting which dessert selections needed to be replenished. Trays in hand, she started back the way she had come, but then something caught her eye and she stopped.

Phillip was standing amid a group of acquaintances, smiling, and it was that smile that captured her attention. It was a wide smile, devastating in effect, for it lit his normally grave countenance and made him seem so handsome that Maria's breath caught in her throat and she felt as if she were rooted to the floor. Hugging the trays to her chest, she stared at him, further astonished when he threw back his head and laughed. Facing him, talking in an animated fashion, was a beautiful, dark-haired woman in a luscious *ciel*-blue silk gown. It was she, Maria realized, who was making him laugh and smile, and she felt a sudden, inexplicable pang—the horrible sting of jealousy.

She'd managed to make Phillip laugh at times, years ago when they were children. But then he'd started giving himself airs and acting like she was beneath him, and she'd never managed to make him laugh after that.

Maria told herself she had work to do. She told herself she shouldn't be dithering here, wasting time. Yet she could not seem to move from where she stood. She turned her gaze to the brunette facing him and felt a lurch of dismay. The woman was beautiful. Maria studied her profile—the graceful tilt of her neck, the diamonds in her hair, the dress that must have cost the earth. Then she glanced down at her own drab, serviceable gray skirt and white shirtwaist, noting the stained white apron over them, and she grimaced. Never in her life had she felt more unattractive than she did at this moment.

She looked up again, just in time to see Phillip offer the woman his arm. They turned away and started toward the ballroom. Maria swallowed hard as she watched them go. The gap between his station and hers had never seemed wider.

The pair vanished into the ballroom, and Maria started to retrace her steps. Now that a waltz was playing, the corridor was less crowded, and she was able to go back down the corridor much more quickly than she'd come, but at the doorway to the servants' staircase, she once again saw someone who made her pause.

Prudence was standing about ten yards farther down the corridor, her husband, the Duke of St.

Cyres, beside her. She looked lovely in claret-red velvet and white gloves, with rubies at her throat. Another couple, dressed in equal finery, were conversing with them. Watching Pru, Maria remembered the days when they had shared a flat, barely able to scrape two crowns together. They'd been inseparable then. But now, though Prudence made every effort to bridge the social distance between them, nothing changed the fact that her friend was a duchess. Her inheritance and her marriage into the aristocracy had changed their friendship, put a social chasm between them impossible to bridge. They were no longer in the same class. Prudence was invited to the ball, while Maria served it. She felt another, deeper pang, the pang of isolation and loneliness.

As she watched Prudence, Phillip's words from that day in his office echoed through her mind.

If you'd had a dowry, money to bring to the marriage, people could perhaps have overlooked your lack of breeding and your lack of connections . . .

Maria turned away. She descended the servants' stairs to the kitchens. It seemed like a long walk down.

The rest of the ball was a blur. Because they were so busy, Maria managed to shake off her strange despondency for the rest of the evening, but when the last dance was over, when the musicians had packed up their instruments, the guests were piling into their carriages, and the dishes were stacked in the scullery for the kitchen maids, the glum mood that had come over her earlier in the supper room began echoing back.

Nonetheless, she accepted a glass of the remaining champagne from Monsieur Bouchard to celebrate the evening's success along with the other members of the kitchen staff.

"Monsieurs and mesdemoiselles," Bouchard called out to gain the attention of the servants gathered in the front kitchen. "I have a few words to say to you."

The crowd quieted at once, somewhat apprehensively. But the little chef was all smiles when he raised his glass. "*Épatant!*" he pronounced. "You have done well, and I, Bouchard, salute you."

A round of cheers went up around the room, and Maria drank her champagne along with the others. She had to be dragged, however, to the front of the room a few moments later when Bouchard demanded she say a few words as well. "No modesty now, *ma petite*," he told her, refilling her glass from the bottle in his hand. "Your pastries were exquisite, and you deserve the accolades."

The crowd of servants roared approval, and that made her smile. She waited a moment for them to quiet down, then she spoke. "Ladies and gentlemen," she said, lifting her glass, "my compliments to each and every one of you for your hard work. From start to finish, you were superb."

"I couldn't agree more."

The sound of that male voice at the back of the room not only forestalled any applause, it also caused a hush to fall over the room. Every head turned as the Marquess of Kayne entered the kitchens. The crowd split apart, bowing and making way for him as he advanced to the front. By the time he reached the head chef, the room was silent.

"Monsieur Bouchard," he said, halting in front of the much shorter, much stouter man, "excellent work, as always. The cold pheasant, especially, was very fine."

"My lord is most kind." Beaming with pride, his hands clasped together, Bouchard bowed. *"Merci."*

Phillip turned to her. "Miss Martingale, my compliments to you and your staff." A hint of amusement touched one corner of his mouth, but it wasn't really a smile. Maria thought of the pretty brunette she'd seen him with earlier who had managed to make him smile and laugh, and she felt another pang of jealousy. She shoved it down, reminding herself that she had no right to be jealous.

"I was quite impressed with those little chocolate cakes you made," he went on. "The ones with the mint ice cream inside."

She looked into his face and she knew he was thinking of that night in her kitchen when he'd kissed her. There was something in his expression, something almost like tenderness, and pleasure washed over her, a sweet, soothing balm for the sting of a moment before. Everyone was watching them, and she forced herself to say something. "Thank you, my lord."

He bowed to her, then turned again to his chef. "Bouchard, divide the remaining food and send a portion home with each person here. They deserve it."

A cheer went up, following Phillip as he retraced his steps toward the door. The pleasure of his words still lingering within her, Maria watched him go, hoping he would turn and look at her one last time, but he didn't, and after his departure, she was forced to return her attention to her duties. Even though the ball was over, there was still work to do.

While Bouchard and his sous-chef counted heads and divided the food, Maria gathered her own staff and pulled her money purse out of her skirt pocket. She gave each of the maids and cooks she'd hired from Lucy's agency half a crown for tip and a shilling for cab fare. Then, as those servants joined the queue waiting for a share of the leftovers, she settled with her own employees, giving each a full crown and shilling. "I've arranged for the marquess's footmen to collect our trays and cutlery," she told them. "Once you've received your share of the remaining food, you may go.

And no pocketing that cab fare, thinking to walk home," she added sternly. "It's after three o'clock in the morning, not a time for respectable young women to be walking about London. Is that understood?"

"Yes, ma'am," all six of them said in unison.

"Good. I won't be opening the shop until noon, so I want all of you to have a good rest, and I shall see you in about nine hours."

She dispersed her group, then assisted Bouchard with the division of the food. She was among the very last to leave, and by the time she had reached the cloakroom, even the maids responsible for checking coats had departed. Unfortunately, Maria's coat also had disappeared.

She frowned at the rows of empty pegs on the walls of the room, which now contained only two men's overcoats, one dark wool cape, and one fringed shawl of ivory satin embroidered with yellow rosebuds.

"Oh, bother!" She peeked under the cape and the overcoats, but her long, hooded mackintosh of navy-blue rubber lined with green-and-blue plaid was not hanging beneath them. Someone, whether by accident or design, had walked off with it.

Cursing under her breath, she searched the entire floor, including the water closets, but without success. Her mackintosh was nowhere to be found. As she walked down the back stairs to the servants' entrance, she tried to make the best of

things. London's cabs weren't the warmest of vehicles, but at least it wasn't the midst of winter.
She could make do without a coat. At least, that
was what she thought until she opened the door
to the alley.

It was pouring rain.

Maria halted in the doorway and scowled at the
water coming down in sheets. She'd bet her last
quid this weather was the reason her very warm,
very waterproof mackintosh had been taken.

"Hell's bells!" she cried, now thoroughly vexed.
Avermore House fronted on Wimpole Street, and
there was a cab stand right on the corner, but as
a member of the waitstaff, she was not allowed to
come and go through the front doors of the house.
To reach the cab stand, she'd have to circle all the
way around the house and grounds. She might
find another cab stand along the way, but it hardly
mattered. She'd still be soaked to the skin.

"Move along, miss, move along."

The voice behind her had her glancing over
one shoulder, and she recognized Phillip's butler.
In his hand was a ring of keys, and he was using
the other to button up his mackintosh. Maria
eyed the garment with envy, and it took her a
moment to realize he'd spoken to her. "I beg your
pardon?"

"Out the door you go," he said, keys jangling as
he waved a hand toward the open doorway. "His
lordship has bid me lock all the doors, and I'd like

to be getting on with it. We can't have you stand-ing there dithering all night."

Maria glanced outside again, noting that the downpour had not slackened, and she drew a deep breath. There was nothing for it. She stepped out into the downpour, grimacing at the cold rain that hit her face.

Just as she'd feared, by the time she'd exited the servants' gate and circled around to the front of Avermore House, she was drenched. As she rounded the corner and saw the cab stand, she groaned, watching as the cabriolet parked there jerked into motion and started down the street. Even if she could share with the passengers inside, it would do her no good to run after the vehicle, for cabs only operated from stands; once in motion, they would not be hailed from the sidewalk.

Her steps slowed and she glanced up and down Wimpole Street, but there wasn't another cab in sight. In fact, there were no vehicles at all, except a luxurious brougham and an even more luxurious town coach that were just pulling around from the mews, vehicles that clearly belonged to some lingering guests, but which did her no good at all.

"This is what I get for staying behind and send-ing everyone else home ahead of me with cab fare," she mumbled, rubbing a hand over her face as she started down Wimpole Street, making for a busier intersection where she might have better luck. "Now there's not a cab to be had."

She strode down the street as fast as she could manage, but she was tired, her feet hurt, and she just couldn't summon the energy to run. Preoccupied with her own troubles, she barely noticed the brougham she'd seen earlier, but when the town coach following it came to a stop a few yards ahead, she couldn't help but notice. It was a massive, magnificent vehicle, she thought idly as she hastened past it, black with gold trim, a quartet of fine black mares, and a footman with an open umbrella in his hand, who jumped down from the dummy board at the back.

She banged her elbow on a streetlight, and the collision forced her attention back to the sidewalk ahead of her, but she couldn't help wondering if she could hop up beside the footman when the coach started moving again. A toff with a carriage like that might live nearby, of course, but he was going in her direction for now, and he could be headed for Mayfair or Knightsbridge. There wouldn't be any harm, would there, in—

All of a sudden, she was grabbed from behind, a strong arm wrapping around her waist.

"What the devil—?" she cried as she was lifted off the ground and dragged backward toward the luxurious town coach she had just passed. "What are you doing? Let go of me!"

She kicked and writhed, struggling against the hold of her assailant, but she was hampered by her sodden skirts, and as she heard the carriage door opening behind her, she was overcome by a wave of panic. "Let go of me, damn you!" she cried, struggling harder to free herself. "Let go!"

She was turned toward the doorway, and the danger of the situation hit her as she was shoved forward through the opening. She tried to grip the edges of the doorway, but her cold, numb fingers slipped on the wet surface, and she could not hang on. She was pushed inside the carriage, her knees hit the foot pillow, and she pitched forward, almost ramming her head into the opposite door. She could hear her kidnapper following her into the coach, and she scrambled up, reaching for the door handle before her, thinking to escape that way, but it was locked. Sobbing with panic, she turned, ready to gouge her assailant's eyes out, but her heel caught on the foot pillow, tripping her, and she stumbled, falling onto the luxuriously padded roll-and-tuck leather seat.

She started forward to hurl herself at the stranger who had abducted her, but when she saw his face in the light from the coach lamps behind her, she froze. The man settling himself onto the seat opposite was the last person on earth she would have expected.

"Phillip?" She blinked and sank back down. "What do you think you're doing?"

"I might ask you the same question," he countered. "Why in blazes are you walking home in weather like this? Are you mad?"

"Crikey," she gasped with relief, falling back against the seat. "You frightened me nearly to death! I thought I was being abducted by white slavers or something equally terrifying!"

He folded his arms, glaring at her. "Are you going to answer my question?"

"Why didn't you tell me it was you, for heaven's sake?" she demanded, her voice rising as panic ebbed away. Now that the danger was past, she was angry as hell. She sat up. "I've never been so scared in my life! Why didn't you say something?"

"I'm too damned angry to say much of anything at the moment!" That seemed to be true, for although his voice was low and controlled, his blue eyes seemed to spark in the dim light with a fury she'd never seen before. "And I didn't deem it necessary to identify myself. My monogram is emblazoned on the door of my carriage, and you looked straight at it as you walked by, which was how I knew for certain it was you. You worked in my household for years. How could you fail to recognize my coat of arms?"

She shoved her wet hair out of her face. "I don't know! Maybe because no sleep for two days makes me a bit bleary-eyed. Maybe getting cold and wet makes me less observant. Or maybe because of the rain pouring over my face and soaking me to the skin!"

"That I can see for myself, since you're puddling water all over the floor of my carriage." He looked her over and his frown deepened. "Good God, you don't even have a coat." With a sound of aggravation, he began unfastening the ties of his cloak. "Of all the idiotic, hen-witted—"

"I don't have a coat because someone has made off with it! I had a nice, lovely mackintosh in the cloakroom, I'll have you know, but when I went to get it, it was gone. Someone took it, probably some rich, pampered society girl whose fancy little silk shawl was pretty enough to arrive in but not warm enough to go home in!"

"Why didn't you take a cab, or even better, why didn't you ask me to send you home in my carriage? I was standing in the foyer, talking with an old school friend of mine. I didn't see you, but then, I was occupied. You must have passed right by me in the foyer, and I can't believe you didn't see me. Was the rain in your face then as well?"

She scowled. "Maybe I w–would have seen you if I'd come out through the front, but I c–came out the back, on the alley side."

"The alley behind the grounds?" He stared at her as if she was completely off her onion. "There's no taxi stand off the alley. Why didn't you come out the front?"

"Because servants aren't allowed t–to use the front d–doors, that's why!" she shouted back, forcing the words out despite the fact that her teeth were starting to chatter. "We have t–to use the alley be-because we're not g–good enough for the fr–front! Does that satisfy your c–curiosity, my lord?"

There was a moment of silence, and then he gave a sigh. Moving to her side of the carriage, he draped his heavy cloak around her shoulders. It was incredibly warm from the heat of his body, and she nearly groaned aloud at how good it felt. But that didn't mean she was done giving him a piece of her mind.

"And, I d–don't need this sort of abuse fr–from you!" she went on as he knelt in front of her and pulled off her shoes. "I'm tired, I'm wet, and I'm c–c–cold, so stop b–bullying me!"

He set her feet on the sable foot pillow, and this time she did groan, savoring the heat that radiated from the hot-water bottle beneath the fur. "God, Maria, your feet are like ice." He rose up on his knees. "I didn't realize I was bullying you," he said in a quieter voice as he pulled the edges of the cloak together.

"W–well, you w—were. It's m–most unchiv–iv–ivalrous of you."

"My apologies." He started to fasten the first set of ties, but then, for no reason she could identify, he stopped. His hand slid inside the cloak, but he had barely curled his palm over her clenched fists in her lap before he was yanking his hand back. He tore the cloak away from her shivering body, and ignoring her protests, he tossed it aside. He pushed her feet off the foot pillow and scooped her up in his arms, then sat down and leaned back with her on his lap.

"What are you doing?" she asked, moving to rise, but his arm slid around her waist to hold her in place.

"For once, just once, don't argue with me. Put your feet back on the pillow." He waited until she had done so, then he wrapped his cloak around them both and leaned back against the seat, supporting her in the crook of his arm and shoulder.

She could have pointed out that this was a most improper thing for a gentleman to be doing, but his body was radiating heat like a furnace, and it felt so good, it didn't seem worthwhile to needle him about his lack of manners. She settled herself more comfortably on his lap.

Keeping one arm wrapped around her shoulders, he slipped the other out from beneath his cloak and reached up to tap the roof with his knuckles, and the carriage jerked into motion. He flattened his other hand against her spine and began to massage her back. "Getting warmer?"

"Yes." She hesitated, not wanting him to stop. "A little."

Instead of rubbing more vigorously, he slowed his movements, his palm moving in a circle over her shoulder blades.

She rested her cheek in the dent of his shoulder

with a sigh, wiggling her toes on the fur pillow beneath her feet, savoring the warmth. "Phillip?"

"Hmm?"

"Why did you kiss me?"

His hand stilled. "I don't think that is an appropriate topic for conversation." He resumed massaging her back, and added, "Particularly not at a moment like this."

She caught her breath. "Why not at a moment like this?" she asked, though she knew the answer.

"I think talking about the weather would be better," he said, a hint of irony in his voice. "Safer."

"Safer?" She lifted her head at that choice of word, and turned to grin at him over one shoulder, trying to be flippant. "What's wrong, Phillip? Don't you trust me?"

"I don't—" He stopped and cleared his throat. He tilted his chin down and met her gaze in the dim light. "I don't trust myself."

"I do," she whispered, and before she even realized what she was doing, she turned in his arms and pressed her lips to his.

"Then you're a fool," he muttered against her mouth. His hands gripped her arms as if to push her away, but then, with a groan, he pulled her hard against him.

The cloak fell away from her shoulders as she wrapped her arms around his neck and pressed her body closer to his. Her mouth opened in willing acceptance of his kiss, and her breasts brushed his chest.

The kiss was full, his tongue in her mouth, caressing hers with carnal strokes, sliding deeper, then pulling back, compelling her to do the same. Warmth began flooding through her body, waves of luscious warmth that seemed to penetrate her very bones.

He pulled back, breaking the kiss, and she had time for one gasp for air, then he was kissing her again, slow, soft, drugging kisses that seemed to go on and on. He explored her mouth, probing deep, tasting then gently suckling her lower lip. The warmth in her grew stronger, hotter, seeming to pool in certain places—her breasts, her lower abdomen. She moaned against his mouth.

He broke the kiss again, and dimly, she became aware of his body easing out from beneath hers. Afraid he was stopping, she curled her fingers around the silk facings of his evening jacket to keep him there, an instinctive move, for she hardly knew what she was doing. All she knew was that she did not want these blissful sensations to end. Kneeling on the floor, he hovered above her. He was breathing hard, but he did not move.

She opened her eyes. His face above hers bore a harsh expression, almost as if he were in pain; a frown creased his forehead, drawing his dark brows together, and his glittering gaze pinned her to the seat. "Maria."

It was a hoarse whisper. It was a question. It might have been a plea. Whatever it was, she had no time to respond before his body came over hers, the weight of his much larger frame driving the air from her lungs.

He pressed kisses to her face, and she felt his knuckles brush beneath her chin as he began to unbutton her shirtwaist. Shocked, she went still beneath him, her breath coming in little pants as he lifted himself above her and worked his way down the row of buttons. She didn't know what to do, for a situation this intimate had never come her way. But then he pulled her shirtwaist apart and pressed his lips to the side of her throat, and she gave an involuntary gasp of surprise at the sheer delight of it. Another sort of kiss she'd never had, creating sensations she'd never felt.

When he slid his hand inside her shirtwaist and his fingertips touched her bare skin, she jerked in sharp reaction, for just that light caress sent shards of tingling sensation through her body. When he spread his palm over her breast, shaping it through the layers of her clothing, she arched upward into his hand. "Phillip," she moaned, "Phillip, oh, yes, oh, please, yes."

She was pleading for more. More of what, though, she did not know. She could not even guess.

"Damn," he swore, his lips brushing her skin, his hot breath making her shiver. "Damn, damn, damn."

With each word, he kissed her again, forging a hot trail along the column of her throat. At the same time, he shifted his hand, sliding his fingertips beneath her underclothes to the tip of her breast.

Sharp sensation speared her. It was too much, and she cried out, her hips jerking beneath him, making her suddenly aware of a particular sort of hardness where his body was pressed to hers. Even through the layers of their clothing, its shape was unmistakable, and awareness washed over her. She felt sure she must be blushing from her head to her toes.

She'd grown up in the country, she'd gone to a French boarding school, she'd been cornered by a lecherous footman a time or two. She knew—from visits to the farm as a child, from whispered consultations with other girls after trips to the museums, from learning to put up her knee at the appropriate moment—what that hardness in a man's body meant. She also knew what it could lead to.

Wildly, she tried to grasp at sanity. "Phillip," she gasped. "I've never . . . I'm not that sort . . ." She grasped his wrist.

His hand stilled. His breath was quick and harsh against her ear. "You've never lain with a man at all, have you?"

"Of course I haven't!" Her fingers tightened around his wrist, and she told herself to push his hand away, tell him to stop. She didn't move. "I'm not a woman of easy virtue," she whispered, even as she told herself it didn't matter what he thought of her.

"Of course not," he muttered and kissed her ear. "Why should anything about you ever be easy, Maria Martingale?"

He started to withdraw his hand, but for no reason at all, her fingers tightened to prevent it. He lifted his head, his expression harsh. "What do you want?" he whispered. "What do you want from me?"

"I don't know," she whispered back, but even as she spoke, her hand opened, her palm spread over the back of his hand, pressing him to her breast.

He groaned and buried his face against the side of her neck, as his fingers brushed back and forth across her nipple within the tight confines of her corset. She cried out again, her hips writhing against his in a way that was beyond her will.

He muttered an oath and pulled his hand free. "Tell me to stop," he ordered, his palm sliding down her hip and along her thigh. He lifted his body from hers long enough to yank up her skirt. "For God's sake, tell me to stop, Maria, before it's too late."

She didn't say a word, and when he shifted his weight to one side, she cried out in protest, afraid he was stopping. But then he slid his hand up her leg and spread his palm over her stomach and eased it downward, pushing between her thighs.

"Maria," he ground out through clenched teeth. "For the love of God . . ."

He slipped his fingers inside the opening of her drawers. And then he touched her in her most intimate place, and she cried out at the sharp, piercing pleasure of it.

He began to caress her with the tip of one finger in light circles that seemed like torture. She moaned in protest of this exquisite teasing, and pressed her hips up toward his hand.

"Maria, you are so soft, the softest thing I've ever felt," he murmured against her ear. "I knew you would be. I've always known."

Those words stunned her, but before she could even begin to assimilate their implications, he deepened the caress, sliding his finger up and down between the folds of her feminine opening. Shocked and overwhelmed by these physical feelings she'd never even known existed, she buried her face against his neck, wrapped her arms around his shoulders, and held onto him as tight as she could, for he was the only solid thing in the maelstrom. Each tiny slide of his finger brought another throb of sensation. She wanted more, and then still more, but the more she got, the more she wanted. Her body jerked helplessly against his hand again and again, yet, still it was not enough.

"Yes," he coaxed against her ear. "Yes, yes, you're coming, sweetheart. You're coming for me now."

She didn't know what he meant, but she could hear the tiny cries issuing from her own throat, primitive animal sounds of need and desperation. And then pleasure broke over her in waves. He covered her mouth with his and took her sobbing cries into his mouth, as his fingers continued to caress her in quick, sure movements that sent lingering shards of pleasure through her, until she finally collapsed, panting, against the seat.

He kissed her one more time and pulled his hand from beneath her skirt. She stared up at him in wonder, unable to think, a blissful sort of haze settling over her. She felt him shift his weight on top of her. His knuckles brushed her stomach, and she realized dimly that he was unfastening the buttons of his trousers.

The carriage lurched to a stop.

Phillip's hand stilled, and he lifted his head. "Hell," he muttered. "Damn it all to hell." He shoved away from her and flung himself into the opposite seat. Still swearing under his breath, he began to button his trousers.

Maria sat up, yanking down her skirts and gulping in great breaths of air, as she tried to get her bearings and understand what he had done to her. She'd never felt anything like it. She'd never even imagined anything like it. Phillip knew what it was, though. He'd known just what to do, how to use his mouth, his hands, his words to evoke those exciting, carnal responses inside of her.

Maria stared at him, amazed that Phillip, so proper, so civilized, could make her feel so shameless, so wanton, and yet so luscious and beautiful.

He lifted his head. He looked at her for a moment, his face unreadable. "You'd best button your shirtwaist," he advised in a low, tight voice. "In situations such as this, it's customary for the man to do it, but I . . ." He drew a deep breath and looked away. "I cannot."

There was etiquette for situations such as this?

It seemed so ludicrous, she almost laughed, but looking at his rigid profile, she caught herself just in time. Phillip, she feared, would not share her amusement.

Maria fastened the buttons of her shirtwaist, and when she looked up, he was watching her, but the moment their gazes met, he once again looked away.

Once she was dressed, she gave a little cough, and he pulled back the curtain at the window and reached for his cloak. "Here," he said, handing it to her. "Put this on. It's still pouring."

She complied, and he tapped the window glass. The carriage door opened, and a footman rolled out the steps. Head lowered against the rain, she stepped down and ran for her door, fumbling beneath the big, heavy folds of his cloak to reach the latchkey in her skirt pocket as she descended the steps to her kitchen. She unlocked the door and opened it, glancing over her shoulder, but she found that Phillip had not followed her.

She leaned back in the doorway and rose on her toes just in time to see him running up the steps to his own front door. As he paused on the stoop, he glanced sideways to find her watching him.

Their eyes met for a moment, but then he turned away, entering his own house without a word.

That, she thought as she went inside and locked her door behind her, was probably for the best. After all, after that extraordinary experience, what was there to say?

Chapter 12

There is no sauce like hunger.
Cervantes

For the third night in a row, he could not sleep. How could any man sleep with unrequited lust surging through his body and the sounds of a woman's passion ringing in his ears?

Phillip lay in bed, Maria's soft cries of arousal and release echoing through his mind. Over and over, he relived every moment of that short, tortuous carriage ride. He recalled her silken skin warming to his touch, he imagined the soft, wet taste of her mouth and the slick heat of arousal between her thighs, he felt the deep, purely male, satisfaction at her climax. And even though those memories tormented him beyond bearing, compelling him to bring about his own release, he found no relief, for the following night, the sounds of her pleasure would come harkening back to torment him yet again.

Never had he touched a respectable woman in such intimate ways. Always, he had conducted his affairs in the proper way, with paid mistresses and the occasional courtesan. But now, as he cast a fleeting look back over the other liaisons he'd had in his life, he realized something he never had before. Every woman he'd ever bedded had been a blonde with hazel eyes. Substitutes, he realized now, much to his chagrin. All of them had been substitutes for her.

And he thought he'd forgotten her? During the past twelve years, days, weeks, even months had gone by when she had not crossed his mind, but he hadn't forgotten her at all. This need for her, this hunger, had simply been sleeping within him, waiting to be reawakened.

No doubt about it, he thought with disgust, he was insane.

He could still hear her impassioned pleas, and he groaned. Reaching for a second pillow, he slammed it over his ear and rolled onto his side. Stupid to think he could forget her, stupider still to think he could live next door and resist her, stupidest of all to think a few luscious tastes of her would ever be enough to free him from her spell. Impossible, for he had been her captive in one way or another since he was nine and she was seven, and she'd smiled at him over the top of an apple.

He rolled onto his back and stared at the ceiling, thinking of the summer she'd come home from France, when the innocent affection and friendship of childhood had transmuted into this carnal desire.

He closed his eyes, feeling a hint of despair as he felt that desire for her overtaking his body yet again. How many times had he done this very thing as a youth? How many times had he lain in bed, filled with this hunger for her? How many times had he imagined hot, sweet moments like those in the carriage? Dozens. Hell, probably hundreds. Now he had more than sheer imagination. He'd had a taste of reality, and it was not enough.

He imagined her in her bed. He thought of the balcony they shared, the French doors into her rooms. He could tap on the door. If she let him in . . . oh, God, if she let him in . . .

Perhaps then, this need would be sated at last. This torment would cease. This madness would stop.

I'm not a woman of easy virtue.

Why couldn't she be? Damn it all to hell, why couldn't she be? How much simpler everything would be if she were an unchaste woman.

But she was not unchaste.

Phillip tried to grasp at his honor. He could not violate an innocent woman. It went against everything he believed about the conduct of a gentleman. But at this moment, grasping at his honor was like grasping at handfuls of air. If he could have her, he thought, if he could only have her, surely this terrible need would pass.

Her pleas of arousal echoed through his mind again.

Phillip, Phillip, oh, yes, oh, please, yes. . .

This was intolerable. Three nights of hell was enough. Phillip flung back the sheets with a curse and got out of bed. He lit a lamp, and one glance at the clock on the mantel had him reaching for the bell pull to summon his valet. He knew what he had to do, and since it was now four o'clock in the morning, this was the perfect time to do it.

Maria knew she was in serious trouble. She couldn't think, she couldn't work, she couldn't even seem to do the most mundane task without losing her concentration. Three days had passed since those magical moments with Phillip in his carriage, and every time she recalled them, she felt a euphoric happiness. When she lay in bed at night trying to sleep, she couldn't help remembering the feel of his hands caressing her. When she was in her office staring at the columns of figures in her bankbook, she could only think of the passionate intensity in his eyes. When she was in her kitchen in the early morning hours, she caught herself listening for his step on the stairs, hoping he would come to her, hoping he would touch her again. And every time these thoughts went through her mind, she felt more muddled and dazed than before.

For the fifth time in as many minutes, Maria realized she was daydreaming, and she forced her wayward thoughts back to the bowl of pastry cream before her. It was a good thing it was so early in the morning, she thought as she reached for the bottle of orange liqueur on the worktable. There was no one to see her blush.

She drizzled the orange flavoring into the bowl, trying to keep her thoughts on the new recipe she was inventing, but that was impossible, for there were far more delicious things to think about.

She stopped stirring pastry cream and leaned against her worktable. She hadn't even known such physical sensations were possible. But Phillip had known.

She closed her eyes and felt that hot, shameful excitement she'd felt in the carriage rising up again as she remembered the sureness and skill with which he had drawn those exquisite sensations out of her. He'd known just what to do and just how it would make her feel. Never had she dreamed that Phillip was so . . . so . . . erotic.

The sound of her kitchen door opening jerked Maria out of these delightful contemplations like a splash of cold water. She opened her eyes to find the very man who'd been invading her imagination for three days standing in the doorway.

"Miss Martingale," he said, taking off his hat with a bow. When he stepped inside the kitchen and closed the door behind him, Maria's mind flashed back to the illicit words of passion he'd whispered to her, and she felt color flooding her face.

She ducked her head as she dipped a curtsy, silently cursing her fair complexion, knowing her hot cheeks would give away just what she'd been thinking about. Desperate to attain a measure of self-possession, she turned her back and opened the oven door, pretending to check on something cooking within, hoping he would attribute the color in her cheeks to the heat of the stove. She heard his boot heels tapping on the linoleum floor as he crossed the kitchen toward her, but she could not bring herself to turn around. She closed the oven door and rattled a few of the empty pots on the stove, then, feeling she was in sufficient command of herself, she turned around.

He halted on the other side of her worktable, his gray felt hat in his hands. She looked into his face, and the moment she did, all her efforts to seem nonchalant proved vain, for the moment their gazes met, she blushed all over again. Beneath his intense observation, she felt a painful vulnerability like nothing she'd ever felt before, and she had a sudden, overwhelming desire to run away, but she forced herself to remain where she was.

"I realize I am intruding upon your work," he said, "but I wanted a private meeting with you, one in which we would not be interrupted, and this is the only time of day I could be sure of achieving that objective."

"A private meeting?"

"Yes. What happened between us the other night demands it." He drew a deep breath. "I must accept responsibility for my ungentlemanly behavior."

She remembered that ungentlemanly behavior quite well, and how it had made her feel. Maria bit her lip and lowered her gaze to the table. Her cheeks felt as if they were on fire.

Of course he noticed. "I realize I am causing you embarrassment by discussing such things," he said, "and I regret that, but it cannot be helped." Turning away, he began to move about the kitchen as if too restless to stand still. "First, let me say that in offering you my carriage, my primary concern was your health and safety . . ." He came to a halt and cleared his throat, but he did not look at her. "At least at first."

"I don't think you *offered* your carriage," she felt compelled to point out. "You dragged me inside."

Such precise hair-splitting was ignored. "But these concerns were soon displaced by ones I am ashamed to say were far less honorable. Even now, I cannot fully explain my actions." He looked down at the hat in his hands and gave a short laugh. "Such undisciplined conduct is not at all like me."

She was inclined to agree, but he gave her no opportunity to say so. "A man of my rank," he continued as he resumed pacing, "would demonstrate such amorous inclinations toward his mistress, or perhaps his wife, but not to an innocent woman. You are not a *demimondaine*, nor are we married, and for me to have taken such liberties was unpardonable."

Maria stared at him, dismayed. He had come to apologize for the way he had kissed her and touched her? Perhaps she had a terribly careless disregard for propriety, but the idea that he was about to express regret for something that had seemed to her quite wonderful was rather deflating. "Phillip, there's no need—"

"Miss Martingale, please allow me to finish. I realize that my . . . amorous advances upon your person are without excuse and I shall make none. But I must be allowed to express the deep and impassioned desire I feel for you."

Her lips parted in surprise. That Phillip had developed an inexplicable attraction to her was obvious enough after the events of the other night, but that he would confess to such feelings aloud was astonishing.

"In such circumstances as these," he went on, "you must agree that marriage is the only honorable alternative."

Her astonishment deepened into complete and utter shock. She tried to speak, but the idea that Phillip seemed to be proposing marriage to her was so absurd that any sort of reply proved beyond her.

He seemed to take her silence for acquiescence.

"Since you have no family, we should be married from London, for you do have friends here in town to stand by you. I realize that long engagements are in vogue, but under the present circumstances, such a course is impossible. Three weeks, I believe, is sufficient time for banns, a license, a discreet announcement in the newspapers—"

"Wait, please!" she implored, holding out one hand, palm toward him, rather like a policeman halting traffic. "You want to marry me?"

The moment the words were out of her mouth, she began to laugh. She couldn't help herself, for it was such an outrageous notion.

"I did not realize the offer of my hand would be so amusing to you," he said with dignity.

She pressed a hand over her mouth, forcing herself to regain control, sensing she'd hurt his pride. But really, this was so absurd, how could she take it seriously? When she looked at his face, however, she knew he did not see the matter quite the same way she did. Giving a little cough, she lowered her hand and sternly took command of herself. "Forgive me," she said. "It's just that a proposal of marriage from you was the last thing in the world I expected."

"That is understandable, I daresay. Given my conduct and the difference in our social positions, I'm sure you thought I had come to make a far more unsavory proposal. But regardless of your status or mine, I cannot allow my dishonorable behavior towards you the other night to be without honorable consequence."

She frowned, bewildered. "So you feel compelled to marry me out of a sense of obligation?"

"Yes. No. That is . . ." He broke off. "What I feel for you is something that I fear is out of my control. As much as it pains me to say it, I cannot promise that what happened in the carriage will not happen again. As I said, you are an innocent woman, and I cannot vouchsafe that you will remain innocent should we find ourselves in similar circumstances again."

"You could not allow your brother to marry me twelve years ago, yet you now wish to do so?"

"Yes." His grimace of distaste was hardly flattering. "I have saved him from an imprudent marriage only to fall prey to one myself. There is irony in that, I suppose."

She was uninterested in the irony of it. She was still trying to get over the shock. "So . . . so you are in love with me, then?" Even as she asked the question, she could not credit it, especially given their argument about love the night he'd kissed her in this very room. And yet, she found herself holding her breath as she waited for an answer.

"Love?" He tilted his head toward the ceiling and gave a laugh that did not seem in any way amused. "I believe one might more accurately describe it as a madness."

She felt a keen and inexplicable disappointment, but her pride refused to let him see it. "Yes, I recall that you admitted to a certain mental instability in regard to me a few weeks ago."

"I'm certain it will pass, once it has been . . . has been . . ."

"Sated?" she supplied.

"Yes." He rubbed a hand across his forehead. "God, at least I hope so."

Maria decided she'd heard enough. "Thank you for your explanations regarding the other night. I believe I now fully comprehend your feelings." She met his gaze with a hard one of her own. "What you really mean is that you wish to bed me, and you can't think of any way other than marriage to manage it with your honor intact."

He stiffened at those words, and his face took on an expression she knew quite well, the cool, inscrutable mask of the well-mannered gentleman. "This is not about my *wishes*, Miss Martingale. What I feel for you is something I never wished for, nor did I welcome it when it came over me. Could you expect me to do so?" he added as she made a sound of outrage. "You worked in my family's kitchens as a girl. You are the daughter of a chef, the granddaughter—if I remember your pedigree correctly—of a wine merchant. Your mother was related to a squire, but the connection is so tenuous as to be meaningless."

"Thank you, my lord, for that summary of my bourgeois bloodlines."

"I only point these things out because we are talking about my wishes, and my wish would have been to marry a woman of rank equal to mine, for to marry well is one of the primary duties of my position, and by offering you my hand I am abandoning that duty. Furthermore, by giving in to my desire for you I am subjecting myself and my family to ridicule and social ostracism. And, most galling of all, I am doing this because I cannot master my own passions. Believe me, Miss Martingale, my wishes have nothing to do with this."

"Honor has nothing to do with it either," she shot back. "A marquess doesn't need to marry the kitchen maid in order to bed her."

"Damn it, Maria, I have never, ever, thought of you as a servant! Nor have I ever treated you as one. On the contrary, I have allowed an ease and familiarity between us all our lives that no other man of my position would entertain for a moment. As for the rest—" He swallowed hard. "You force me to admit the carnality of my feelings for you. I wish I could deny it, for it galls me to admit I possess emotions I cannot control, but as a gentleman, I must allow honesty to overcome shame."

"These gentlemanly codes of honor are so romantic. How could a woman not be swept away by them?"

He pressed his lips together, perceiving her sarcasm. "I realize that you might regard this offer of marriage as less than eloquent, but I have never been an eloquent man."

"You underestimate your abilities, my lord. You have expressed your feelings quite well today. I fully comprehend the nature of them. How could such perfect clarity not be eloquent?" She gave him no time to answer that question before she went on, "But it does not necessarily follow that I am persuaded by your skill at self-expression. In fact, I am not."

"Maria, do you not comprehend what almost happened in my carriage? I would like to say your virtue is safe in my company, but it is not. I tried to stay clear of you by evicting you, but as my brother pointed out, that would have been an action unworthy of me. And even if I had done it—" He broke off and made a sound of frustration. "I am sure it would have been futile, for I cannot stay clear of you, no matter how I try. Despite the inferiority of your position, despite the incompatibility of our temperaments, despite how unsuitable a match between us would be, despite the scandal and social disapproval that will no doubt ensue, I know a marriage between us is the only honorable option."

"And that is supposed to persuade me to accept?" she cried. "Do you really believe I would agree to marry a man who feels only lust for me, and even that against his will and the dictates of his conscience? Do you think I would marry a man who had so little consideration for me that he severed our friendship without a thought, and later parted me from the boy I wanted to marry because I wasn't good enough? A boy, I might add, who had a genuine regard for me—"

"Genuine regard?" he interrupted, and made a sound of derision between his teeth. "Lawrence was seventeen. His regard for you was based primarily on the fact that you wore skirts."

"And your regard is based on something deeper?"

His head moved slightly to the side, almost as if she had slapped him. Just now, Maria wished she had.

"I have already admitted my weakness where you are concerned," he said stiffly. "Must you throw it in my teeth? At least I am a mature man of thirty-one, not a boy of seventeen. I know the ramifications of my decision."

"A decision that takes mine for granted!"

"And you think that a conceit? In my defense, I can only remind you of my rank. By marrying me, your future and that of our children would be wholly secure. You would be elevated to a position of wealth, title, and status any woman would envy. Forgive me for being aware of my worth as an eligible *parti*."

"I don't care a fig how many other women want to marry you, Phillip! The point is whether or not I want to marry you. So far, I am not persuaded."

"Because I have not confessed love? Because I have offended your romantic sensibilities?"

"No!" she fired back. "Because you believe me to be beneath you!"

He opened his mouth as if to protest this conclusion, but then, he closed it again, saying nothing.

"I see that you don't deny it," she said, and the words left a bitter taste in her mouth.

"There is no point. You *are* beneath me. Your position is far below mine."

"Oh!" she cried, thoroughly outraged. "There are times when I truly hate you! You are such an arrogant, haughty, condescending snob!"

"What?" He seemed astonished. "Now *that* I can and do deny! I am not a snob!"

"Oh, yes you are. You believe I am inferior to you."

"I do not believe you are inferior to me!" he shouted. "I believe your position is inferior to mine. There is a wealth of difference between the two."

"The reason for your disdain does not make it more palatable to me. With my low position in the world, I wonder that you can think to marry me and sully your family tree!"

"It is not disdain to acknowledge facts. I am a marquess, the seventh Marquess of Kayne. My family has been one of the most prominent in Britain for six hundred years. Every king and every queen of England has dined at Kayne Hall since Henry the Second. Among my ancestors are prime ministers and princesses. I can claim acquaintance with heads of state all over the world. To fulfill my duty to my family, I am expected to marry high—the daughter of a peer, at the very least. You can hardly expect me to be happy that a woman of no consequence inflames my passions, controls my will, and overpowers my reason to such an extent that my only honorable alternative is to marry her?"

"It is not an alternative! Not for me. I have no intention whatsoever of accepting your proposal. Forgive my bourgeois sensibilities, my lord, but I believe people who marry should have mutual respect and affection, and it is clear we have neither. What you offer me is not matrimony. It is enslavement."

He stared at her in disbelief. "I believe I am the one enslaved, madam. And though it has cost me every ounce of pride I possess, I have admitted it to you. The power in this situation rests wholly with you."

"And this . . . this desire to which you confess is

your basis for a permanent union between us? A desire you define as a madness? A fleeting madness, at that? When it cools, what will take its place? Not liking or affection, nor even respect, for though I had those feelings for you when we were children, they are well and truly gone. And though you may be quite proud of your aristocratic position in the world, I have never given a damn about your station, your title, your wealth, or any other measure of your character, except the way you have treated me. And since we are now on that subject, let me say that the way you have treated me has been abominable."

"I have already admitted as much," he muttered. "The other night—"

"For the love of heaven, I'm not talking about what happened in the carriage!" she cried in exasperation. "That night was the most wonderful, romantic thing that has ever happened to me, although why that should be so escapes me at this moment." Her voice cracked at that humiliating admission, and she paused to take a steadying breath. "You are asking me to be your wife, and yet, the only tenderness and affection you have displayed toward me was in that carriage."

"Not only then," he corrected. "What about what happened in this very room? Was that not a display of tenderness, Maria?"

The reminder of the night he had first kissed her only made her more angry. "Based on a desire for me you confess is only physical. In every other respect, you have behaved with no consideration for me whatsoever. You cast aside my friendship, avoided my company, and imparted the worst possible motives to my conduct. You separated me from Lawrence by playing upon the weaknesses of us both. You knew he would cast me aside to keep his income and your regard. And you knew I would take the money, for my father had just died, leaving me nothing. You paid me off as if I were some pregnant, disgraced kitchen maid, and yet you say you've never treated me like a servant? And you never once stopped to think of the pain your actions caused me. You behaved like an utter cad then, and there is no force on heaven or earth that would impel me to marry you now!"

Something crossed his face, a queer spasm that might have been guilt. Or anger. It might even have been pain. But he lowered his head before she could be certain, staring down at the hat in his hands.

"You have complimented my eloquence," he said, "but you, too, have been remarkably eloquent today." He looked at her again, and any pain he might have felt was hidden behind that mask of composure he could don so easily. "I have confessed my feelings, and in return, I have been rewarded with yours. A most enlightening conversation all around."

Breathing hard, she stared at him, too angry to

think of a single thing to say in reply and too hurt to care about anything he might be feeling.

"Since we have both expressed ourselves so well," he added, "there seems to be nothing further to say. I will not impose myself upon you again, although I think it would be wise if we did our utmost to avoid each other from now on. I bid you good morning, Miss Martingale."

He bowed and departed, and she watched him through the window as he began to ascend the steps to the street, and when he had vanished from view, she tried to return to her work, but the moment she picked up her spoon, she slammed it down again and turned away from the work-table.

She began to pace the room, but as she walked back and forth across the kitchen, the things he had said echoed through her mind, and her agitation grew.

Do you honestly think I should be happy that a woman of no consequence inflames my passions, controls my will, and overpowers my reason to such an extent that my only honorable alternative is to marry her?

She stopped, clenching one hand into a fist and grinding it against the palm of her other hand with a sound of fury. To think this morning, she'd been getting all dreamy-eyed about him. What on earth had she been thinking?

By marrying me, your future and that of our children would be wholly secure. You would be elevated to a position of wealth, title, and status any woman would envy. Forgive me for being aware of my worth as an eligible parti.

Maria resumed pacing. There were women, she supposed with a sniff, who would envy her because she had received a marriage proposal from a marquess. Those women would call her a fool for refusing the suit of a man so far above her in station, a man who was also handsome, powerful, and enormously wealthy. Had she accepted, there would have been a scandal, to be sure, and some members of society might never have accepted her, but she would have been the wife of one of the country's highest-ranking peers, with no need to work ever again. She would have had beautiful clothes, beautiful homes, and the ability to move within the same social circle as Pru and Emma, her two closest friends. And she would have been able to have children.

Children. A faint glimmer of regret stopped her in her tracks. As a girl-bachelor, she'd resigned herself to being childless some years ago, knowing by the time a woman passed the age of twenty-five, her chances of ever marrying diminished greatly. Had she accepted Phillip's proposal, she would have had the opportunity to have children, but that possibility was once again lost to her.

Maria forced regret out of her mind. His declaration of passion meant nothing, for there was no love in it. He also had no compunction about insulting her. He was offering to make her his wife, his marchioness, and the mother of his children, but in his eyes, she would never be his equal. Without that, marriage to him was unthinkable.

But I must be allowed to express the deep and impassioned desire I feel for you.

Recalling those words made her pause, for even in their echo, she could hear genuine anguish. Not that it mattered, for desire, especially desire so reluctantly felt, was no basis for a man and a woman to marry. She'd been very wise to refuse him. Very wise.

Then why did she feel so miserable?

With that question, her anger, hurt, and disappointment rose up in a sudden, powerful wave, drowning any of her attempts to apply common sense. Maria sank down on a chair, and much to her mortification, she burst into tears.

Chapter 13

If you are not feeling well, if you have not slept, chocolate will revive you. But you have no chocolate! I think of that again and again. My dear, how will you ever manage?

Marquise de Sévigné

$\mathcal{P}$hillip strode back to his own door, even more frustrated than he had been when he'd left his house half an hour before.

I believe people who marry should have mutual respect and affection, and it is clear we have neither. What you offer me is not matrimony. It is enslavement.

"Yes, it's enslavement to be a marchioness with a thousand quid a month in pin money," he muttered as he marched up the front steps. "Being chained to a stove in a hot kitchen, baking bread twenty hours a day is much more liberating."

He entered the house and barely restrained himself from slamming the door behind him. He'd offered her more than any woman of her background could ever hope to obtain, and for that he'd been rewarded with a heap of scathing condemnations.

The way you have treated me has been abominable.

Abominable? It was abominable to offer a woman marriage? *What should I have offered?* he wondered as he went upstairs. Any other man in his position would have taken advantage of her in that damned carriage and had done with it. No other man would have attempted to right the wrong by offering to marry her.

In his room, he found that his valet had returned to the dressing room and was sound asleep. He supposed he ought to go back to bed as well, but her words continued to pound through his head as he undressed.

A marquess doesn't need to marry the kitchen maid in order to bed her.

He made a sound of derision. If he'd thought of her as a servant, he would never have allowed a friendship to develop between them as children. He would have expected her to speak only when spoken to, and to flatten herself against the wall when he walked by, and to present things to him only on a salver so their hands would not touch. And he wouldn't have cared if the entire village laughed at her for her inability to bat at cricket, and if she'd gone off to boarding school without knowing a single word of French, he wouldn't have given a damn about that either.

He went to bed, but as he lay there staring at the ceiling, her condemnations continued to run through his head.

You have behaved like an utter cad.

He flung back the sheets and got back out of bed. There was no point in trying to sleep now. It was dawn anyway. He yanked back the curtains to let in the feeble early-morning light, then he walked to the washstand, poured water from the pitcher into the basin, and splashed cold water on his face.

He had to get clear of her and regain a semblance of sanity. He'd managed to do that once before, but only because he'd sent her away. That was not a viable course of action this time, for she had refused a bribe to go away already, and despite the accusations she'd hurled at him, he was not a cad. He could not bring himself to evict her in order to be rid of her. Which meant he had only one option available to him.

Phillip turned away from the washstand, went into the dressing room, put a hand on his sleeping valet's shoulder, and gave him a shake.

"Gaston, I need you," he said when the other man opened his eyes. He stepped back and the valet rose from the cot, rubbing his tired eyes.

"Yes, sir?" he said, trying to suppress a yawn.

"Sorry to wake you so early, Gaston, but I've decided to leave for Kayne Hall today, and I want to catch the morning train from Paddington. I'm sure my lack of consideration makes me an utter cad," he added over his shoulder as he started back to his own room. "But it can't be helped."

"Sir?" Gaston asked in bewilderment, following him.

"Never mind."

It was a perfect day for travel. The sun was shining, the temperature was balmy, and once Phillip and his valet were outside of London, the air was fresh and clean. By the time they were halfway to Hampshire, Phillip was already feeling the lift of his spirits.

He had cabled Mr. Jamison from Paddington, informing his butler at Kayne Hall that he would be arriving that afternoon, and instructing the man to send a pair of footmen with a horse cart to the station in Combeacre. But when he arrived in the small Hampshire village, it wasn't only his footmen waiting for him on the platform.

Lawrence laughed at the sight of his face as he disembarked from the train. "When you sent that cable to Jamison, I'll wager you didn't expect I'd be here with the footmen to meet you."

"I did not," Phillip answered. "I didn't even know you had already arrived at Kayne Hall."

"We came three days ago. A bit ahead of schedule, I know. But really, how long does it take to tour the shipyards?"

"I don't suppose you could have cabled me?"

"I was intending to. I was," he insisted as Phillip gave him a skeptical look. "Truly." He glanced at Phillip's valet, who was discussing luggage with the porter and the footmen. "Gaston, there's a cart and driver out front for the trunks. See to everything, will you? I'm taking your master with me."

Gaston glanced at Phillip, who consented with a nod. "We're taking a separate carriage, I assume?" he asked, allowing himself to be led off the platform by his brother.

"Yes, but not one of yours." Lawrence guided him out the front of the small depot and stopped. "We're riding back to the house in mine."

"You bought a carriage?"

"I did." Lawrence gestured to a black gig with yellow wheels that stood in front of the depot. "And when we received your cable this morning, I knew I had to come fetch you from the station myself. What do you think?"

Phillip studied the two-seated gig as they walked toward it. "It seems a fine carriage for the country," he said. "But hardly useful in town. Why not just use one of my carriages when you come to the country?"

"Oh, I don't know," Lawrence murmured as he climbed into the gig and took the reins. "Perhaps because your carriages won't be much use to us since they are in Hampshire and my home will be in Berkshire?"

"Berkshire?" Halfway into the gig, Phillip stopped and glanced at his brother, whose face wore a wide grin. "Are you talking about Rose Park?"

"Yes, brother, Rose Park. We will need our own carriage there, don't you think?"

"We?" Phillip settled himself beside his brother on the seat. "Dare I ask if Miss Dutton is part of this collective we?"

Lawrence laughed. "You know she is."

Phillip couldn't help feeling a wave of relief at having that confirmed. One never knew with Lawrence. "I'm delighted to hear it."

"Delighted, but not really surprised, eh? But then, why should you be?" he added with a chuckle as he released the brake and snapped the reins. "That was what you thought would happen when you put me in charge of taking the colonel and his family on this tour."

He held up his hands, palms out in a gesture of concession. "I hoped it, yes. She's a lovely girl, from a good family, and she seems to make you happy."

"I am happy. You were right to keep me steered in her direction, but that's not surprising," he added, returning his gaze to the road ahead. "Maria had you pegged, didn't she?"

Phillip almost groaned. Damn it all, he'd forgotten about that girl for at least ten straight minutes. Still, now that Lawrence had mentioned her name, thereby ruining his temporary peace of mind, Phillip could not will himself to veer the conversation in another direction. "What do you mean?" he asked, a bit nettled. Maria didn't have him pegged at all, for her scathing condemnations of his character had no basis in fact.

"Don't you remember that night in her kitchen two months ago when she was teasing you about always knowing what's best for everyone? You do, you know. Although it is irritating sometimes, I have to say. There have been times when I've wished you'd come a cropper."

"Have you?" Phillip looked out over the countryside, wondering what Lawrence would say if he learned of the events that had taken place early that morning.

"Well, no, not really," Lawrence conceded, "but dash it all, it is hard having an older brother who always knows what's best, who always does the right thing and never steps outside the bounds. Everyone thinks you're perfect."

Not everyone.

Lawrence gave a short laugh. "How I used to resent you for it."

"I know." Phillip paused a moment, then, striving to keep his voice neutral, he said, "You're referring to that elopement business, I suppose."

"Primarily, yes. Odd, isn't it, how we've never talked about it? Not that we need to, not after all this time." Lawrence shrugged. "I've come to realize you were acting for our benefit. Hers as well as mine. And it's all worked out for the best. You said it would, and it has. You see? You're always right."

Something in the very lightness of Lawrence's voice caused Phillip to give him a searching glance, but he couldn't detect any sign of bitterness in his brother's profile.

As if feeling his gaze, Lawrence turned to look at him. He grinned, and Phillip's moment of uneasiness passed. "Well, it is a bit nauseating, Phillip, really. You being right all the time. Couldn't you fall on your face once in a while?" he asked, returning his attention to the road. "It would make me feel better, and it would be good for you. Keep you from thinking you're better than the rest of us."

He gave a violent start. "I don't think I'm better than everyone else, and I've fallen on my face plenty of times."

"I've never seen it."

"What nonsense. And speaking of Miss Martingale, couldn't you have warned me before you left town that you'd put her in charge of the desserts for the May Day Ball?"

Lawrence groaned and nearly dropped the reins. "Oh, lord, I forgot all about that!"

"Yes, so I gathered—when she arrived at Hawthorne Shipping, marched into my office, and declared that since you weren't available, she was forced to meet with me."

"I'm sorry, old chap. You didn't give her the sack, did you?"

"Why even ask? You know I wouldn't do that after you contracted her for the work," he pointed out dryly.

Lawrence gave a rather shamefaced laugh. "Well, it seems to have come out all right. I mean, we heard the ball was a smashing success, and the two of you didn't kill each other along the way."

With great effort, Phillip kept his voice indifferent. "We managed to restrain ourselves."

"Rough go though, eh?" Without waiting for an answer, he went on, "I do wish I knew what she did to ruffle your feathers, and don't tell me it's because she and I almost eloped, for I shan't believe you. You were down on her for some reason long before that."

"In all this gallivanting around you've been doing," Phillip said, deciding it was best to divert the conversation, "did you manage to convince the colonel to let us build his transatlantic liners?"

Lawrence, however, chose to be tiresome. "Can't you and Maria patch things up? As I said, that elopement business is all water under the bridge now, forgiven and forgotten. There's no reason why we can't all be friends again, is there?"

Friends? Phillip felt a sudden smothering need to get away. He gestured to the side of the road. "Stop the carriage, Lawrence, will you? Drop me off along here."

"Whatever for?"

"Just do it, please."

"I think I touched a nerve," Lawrence murmured as he steered the carriage to the side of the road.

"Not at all," he answered, and invented a reason for stopping. "I . . . um . . . want to have a look at the farm. I didn't have a chance to do that the last time I came up from town."

"I'll drive you."

"No, that's all right. I'd rather walk. I've been cooped up in trains and carriages all morning. I could do with a stretch of the legs. It's only a mile on anyway."

Lawrence still eyed him with doubt, but to Phillip's relief, he didn't pry. "See you for tea, I imagine?"

When he nodded, his brother snapped the reins and went on. Phillip entered the woods by the side of the road and started in the direction of the farms, but as he passed the millpond, he stopped at the sight of the enormous weeping willow on the other side of the water.

If we had a rope, we could make a swing.

Even from here, he could see the jagged wound where the branch over the water had broken, but from this angle, he could not see the fork in the tree where she'd been sitting that first day. Without thinking, he started to circle the pond so that he could see it, but halfway around, he realized what he was doing and came to a halt, forcing himself to remember not the first time he'd been here, but the last.

After he'd learned of Lawrence and Maria's plans to elope, after he'd sent Lawrence on to Oxford, after he'd written her a bank draft and a letter of character and sent her away, he'd stood under that tree for the last time, and when he walked away, he'd vowed he would never stand there again. That he would never feel again the things he had felt that day. That he would forget about her, that he would put it all behind him.

Phillip set his jaw, turned his back on the willow tree, and walked away. He'd forgotten her once. By God, he would do it again.

Sunday in Combeacre's High Street was always crowded. After second service, it was the favorite place among the village residents for a stroll and the exchange of a bit of gossip.

"I can't believe we're doing this," Lawrence declared as they walked along the cobbled street. "It's extraordinary."

Cynthia, who walked beside him, laughed at that comment. "Why do you say that, darling? A walk through the village seems quite a mundane thing to me."

"Mundane?" Lawrence shook his head. "It's clear you're American, Cynthia, for you don't know the first thing about our English village life. A marquess doesn't stroll about the village on Sunday amid the common folk. It isn't done."

Mrs. Dutton, who was walking with her husband at the front of the group, glanced over her shoulder past her future son-in-law to Phillip, who was the last of their party. "But Lawrence, your brother is now doing that very thing," she pointed out.

"And it astonished me when he suggested the idea this morning. It isn't like my brother to do anything on a whim."

"It isn't a whim," Phillip corrected. "I always walk the High Street on Sundays when I'm in residence." He gestured to some of the thatch-roofed cottages further along the street. "After all, many of our tenants live here, and as landlord, I have a responsibility to see that their cottages are well maintained."

"True enough, but I'm still amazed. Father always handed that responsibility over to the land agent. Understandable, I suppose," he added with a laugh. "Father was a snob."

Phillip came to a halt on the sidewalk, another of Maria's accusations echoing back.

You are such an arrogant, haughty, condescending snob!

He turned, staring at his reflection in the window of Parrish's Bookshop. When would that woman's words stop flaying him?

He was not a snob. He had never been a snob. But he *was* a marquess, damn it all, and she was the daughter of a chef. She was not his social equal. And it wasn't as if he was the one who'd decided on all these class distinctions anyway—

"Deuce take it, Phillip, what are you looking at?"

"What?" He turned his head to find his brother beside him. The rest of the party had paused a little further up the street and were looking in the window of Mrs. Woodhouse's dressmaking establishment. Phillip blinked and shook his head. "Sorry, Lawrence. What did you say?"

"I simply wanted to know what has you so fascinated. I called to you three times, but you didn't seem to hear me, and you were staring into Parrish's window as if rooted to the spot." He cupped his hands against the glass and peered into the dusty interior of the bookshop. "Hmm, a text on animal husbandry, a novel by Trollope, and Shakespeare's *Complete Works*. All of these are probably in your library already, so I can't imagine–"

"Do you think I'm a snob?"

"What?" Lawrence turned and looked at him, astonished, whether by the question or the abruptness of it, he didn't know. But an answer suddenly seemed important.

"Do you?" he persisted. "You said a minute ago that Father was a snob. Do you think I'm like him? Snobbish and condescending? That I'm haughty?"

"Well . . ." His brother considered the question, tilting his head to one side. "Yes, I suppose you are. Sorry, old chap," he added at Phillip's sound of consternation, "But you are such a stickler for the proprieties. And whenever you disapprove of something, you have a way of conveying that disapproval without even saying a word. It's rather intimidating, really. And, yes, a bit haughty."

"I see."

"There's the way you walk, too, of course."

"What's wrong with the way I walk, in heaven's name?"

"You move through a crowd as if you fully expect people to make way for you. Which they do, of course," he added. "I mean, you are the marquess, so it's to be expected they would. But watching it's rather amazing. A bit like the Red Sea parting, you know. And everyone bows." He took off his hat and put the hand holding it behind his back, then flattened his other hand across his abdomen and bent deeply from the waist. "Make way, make way for Lord Kayne, master of all he surveys."

"Now you're being absurd."

Lawrence straightened, laughing as he shook

back his hair. "Perhaps I am, but—" He broke off, his attention diverted to something beyond Phillip's shoulder. "Here's Squire Bramley coming up the street. I say, that must be his new mare he's got with him."

Phillip turned and saw that the squire was indeed leading a pretty chestnut mare up the street toward them.

"He came by the day before you arrived, wanting to know when you would be joining us at Kayne Hall, for he wanted to show you a new mare he'd brought over from the States. I forgot to tell you about it. Terribly absentminded of me."

"Rather," he agreed with a glance of good-natured exasperation before he removed his hat and turned his attention to the portly old gentleman and his horse. "Good afternoon, Mr. Bramley."

"Lord Kayne." The squire led the mare to the side of the road where Phillip and Lawrence joined him. "Mr. Hawthorne."

"Squire," Lawrence said, and gestured to the Duttons, who had left off studying the fashions in Mrs. Woodhouse's window and were approaching them from the other direction. "You remember my fiancée, Miss Dutton? And her parents?"

"Yes, of course." The squire bowed to them. "How do you do? But Mr. Hawthorne, I also seem to remember you said your brother wasn't coming up from town any time soon."

"Don't blame Lawrence, Mr. Bramley," Phillip said. "My trip home was unplanned, and the greatest surprise to my brother." He gestured to the horse. "So, you've a new mare, I see."

"Yes, bought her in Kentucky. Saw some fine horses when I was there, I did, indeed."

"Yes, they do breed excellent horseflesh in that part of the world." He smoothed the mare's cheek, chuckling as she nudged his hand with a soft nicker. "Sorry, pet," he told her and opened his palm. "I've no sugar to give you."

The mare seemed quite put out about that. She flung her head back, tossing her mane with an indignant snort and making all of them laugh.

Phillip patted her nose while making a soothing sound, and ran a hand along her withers. "She's a fine animal," he said after several minutes of examination. "Would you sell her? I'm needing some quality broodmares for my stables."

The old man shook his head. "I didn't bring her all the way from Kentucky to sell her, Lord Kayne. I'll be breeding this one myself."

"I'm always willing to pay generously for quality horseflesh, Mr. Bramley," he reminded, but as the squire continued to shake his head, Phillip knew additional persuasion might be required. "I would, of course, give you her first foal out of Alexander."

The mention of a foal sired by his best stallion

made the older man hesitate. "That sweetens the pot a bit," he murmured. "I'm off to London shortly, and while I'm there, I shall consider your offer."

"Excellent. Let me give you my London address." He reached into the breast pocket of his jacket. "I am not residing at my house in Park Lane," he explained as he pulled out his card case, "so let me give you my current address."

He pulled out one of his cards, but when he did, more cards came spilling out, and Maria's hair ribbon tumbled out with them. Cards and ribbon fluttered toward the ground, and he bent down at once to retrieve the ribbon, but his brother was quicker.

"What's this?" Lawrence cried, scooping up the strip of pink silk. The moment he glanced at what was in his fingers, he froze and looked at his brother in astonishment. Phillip stared back in mute agony.

"What is it?" Cynthia asked, coming closer.

Lawrence balled the ribbon up in his fist. "Nothing, darling," he said, opening his hand over his brother's outstretched one and dropping the ribbon into his palm. Then he bent and began to gather Phillip's scattered cards.

With a sigh of relief, Phillip shoved the ribbon into his pocket and returned his attention to Squire Bramley. "Let me know if you wish to discuss selling the mare, Mr. Bramley," he said, handing the card to the older gentleman.

"I'm making no promises to sell her, mind, but I shall consider it."

Phillip forced himself to smile back. "Fair enough."

The squire and his horse went on, and Phillip accepted the stack of calling cards from his brother. He returned them to his case and put the case back in his pocket. They continued along the High Street, but if Phillip had any hope Maria Martingale's hair ribbon was forgotten, that hope was soon dashed. Lawrence fell in step beside him as they walked along the sidewalk. "I say, about that ribbon—" he began, but Phillip cut him off at once.

"We will not discuss it, Lawrence," he said in a savage whisper. "Not now, not ever."

Wide-eyed, his brother nodded, and any conversation on the subject was ended before it began, much to Phillip's relief. When they reached home, he went straight up to his study and pulled her ribbon out of his pocket, thinking to rid himself of this stupid stolen reminder of her, but as he held the bit of embroidered silk over the wastepaper basket, he could not seem to make his fingers drop it.

It wasn't his to throw away. The right thing to do was return it to her.

He didn't know how long he stood there. It felt like hours.

Slowly, ever so slowly, he raised the ribbon and pressed it to his lips, savoring a scent of vanilla and cinnamon that he knew was only imaginary.

After a moment, he returned the ribbon to his card case and left the study, and he knew he would only be over Maria Martingale the day he could give the ribbon back to her.

The weeks of May went by. Phillip discussed the building of ocean liners with Colonel Dutton. He went about estate business, careful to avoid the willow tree, the kitchens, and any other places that reminded him most strongly of her. He called on his neighbors, toured the farms, visited the auctions, and participated in the local affairs of Combeacre, and the fulfillment of those duties served as constant reminders of his position and the responsibilities that came with it.

By the time a month had passed, her scathing words had stopped echoing through his mind, and he began to regain the sense of equilibrium he'd possessed before her reappearance in his life. So, when Lawrence suggested they return to town for the remainder of the season, he decided to go as well. Having left so abruptly, there were many business matters awaiting him in London, including the drawing up of the contracts with Colonel

Dutton and the delegation of additional duties within Hawthorne Shipping to his brother.

The evening before they were to leave, Phillip rode back to the millpond. He stood under the willow and stared at the splintered end of the limb that had held that rope swing so long ago. He felt nothing.

Upon his return to the house, he sent word to the kitchens that he wanted a chocolate tart; when it was ready, he went to the kitchens, and ignoring the furtive, curious stares of his kitchen staff, he sat at the table by the door into the buttery and ate every single bite.

That night, he slept without dreaming of her, and when he woke the next morning, he felt more like himself than he had in months. When he pulled the ribbon out of his card case, he could not conjure the scent of her hair. The madness had passed.

Chapter 14

They are at the end of the gallery; retired to their
tea and scandal, according to their ancient custom.
William Congreve

She missed him.

It was a nauseating admission to make, for
she hadn't felt this way about Phillip since he'd
snubbed her when she was fifteen. And every
time she thought of his proposal, a myriad of
conflicting emotions engulfed her—outrage,
pleasure, excitement, pain—and by the time
four weeks had passed, she felt so muddled and
mixed up, she didn't know if she was on her head
or her heels.

Nonetheless, after spending night after night
lying in bed with his confession of desire ringing
in her ears, after spending endless hours remembering those hot, fevered moments in his carriage

and listening for his step outside her kitchen door, after many discreet enquiries of his servants as to when he would be back in town, Maria was forced to admit the appalling truth. She missed him.

Feeling the need to shake off this strange conflux of emotions, Maria decided what she needed was a day off. Sunday afternoon, she left Miss Simms in charge of the shop and went to her former lodgings in Little Russell Street to have Sunday tea with her friends.

Sunday-afternoon tea was a ritual that had been a part of life for the girl-bachelors of Little Russell Street since long before Maria had come there to share a flat with Prudence eleven years earlier. Most of the ladies worked at jobs—they were typists or shop assistants who labored through the week until Saturday noon, and were then free until Monday. Though Maria's schedule had always been more erratic than that of her fellow girl-bachelors, she had always insisted on carving out a few hours after church on Sunday for tea with her friends. But in the three months since she had opened her *pâtisserie*, she had simply not been able to manage even those few precious hours.

Now, looking at the red brick building that had been her home for so long, with its dark green shutters, potted geraniums, and bobbin-lace curtains, Maria felt a pang of homesickness.

When she'd embarked on owning her own shop, she hadn't bargained for how lonely it would be and how little time she would have for her friends.

Even though she no longer lived in the lodging house, she didn't stand on ceremony. She walked right in. "Hullo, everyone!" she called, pausing in the foyer to remove her hat.

Exclamations of delight followed her greeting, and she'd barely hung her bonnet on the coat rack before Mrs. Morris was emerging from the parlor to greet her. "Maria, my dear! How lovely to see you."

Maria hung her handbag on another hook, then turned to accept a kiss on the cheek from her former landlady.

"This is certainly the day for unexpected guests," Mrs. Morris said, ushering her toward the parlor.

"Unexpected guests?" she echoed, but when she saw Prudence and Emma, there was no need for explanations. Like Maria, the Duchess of St. Cyres and Viscountess Marlowe had lives far removed from their former lodgings in Little Russell Street and were not always able to come to Sunday tea.

The sight of her other friends, however, was not so surprising. Lucy and Daisy Merrick still lived here, and so did Miranda Dickinson. Dear little Mrs. Inkberry hadn't lived at Little Russell Street for many years, but she was here today as well. Since she was Mrs. Morris's oldest friend, Mrs. Inkberry always came for Sunday tea.

Maria smiled at all her dear friends, and opened her arms to hug each one of them. After the greetings had been said, Mrs. Morris settled her beside Daisy on the horsehair settee, and as she took off her gloves, the landlady poured her a cup of tea.

"You look tired, my dear child," Mrs. Morris said, handing her the cup of fragrant Earl Grey. "You'll want a scone and clotted cream, of course?"

"Yes, thank you." Maria placed her filled plate on her lap, then accepted her cup of tea and leaned back against the settee with a sigh.

That sound had Mrs. Inkberry leaning closer to study her face. "She does look peaked, Abigail," she said with a glance at Mrs. Morris before returning her attention to Maria. "I hope you aren't working too hard at that shop of yours."

"I am a bit tired," she confessed, but she did not explain that the reason for her tiredness was a lack of sleep brought on by the most infuriating man in all of Britain. "The bakery has been very busy," she offered as her excuse, and decided to change the subject before the two older ladies could lecture her on that score. "What is the news here?"

"We've be discussing what to do with Daisy, now that Ledbetter and Ghent have given her the sack," Lucy said, her blonde brows knitting in a frown as she glared at her younger sister.

"What?" Maria turned to the girl beside her, who was twisting a loose curl of her fiery red hair and looking guilty as sin. "You lost another post?"

Daisy bit her lip, looking sheepish. She gave a little nod. "Yesterday."

"Really, Daisy," her sister said in aggravation, "if you keep on this way, I'll soon not be able to place you anywhere. Even now, I'm not sure I can gloss over the loss of seven jobs of work in a period of fourteen months, and only one letter of character to show for it all."

Daisy left off twisting her hair and folded her arms, her face taking on a mutinous expression. "But this time it wasn't my fault."

Maria could sense the words *It's never your fault* hovering on Lucy's tongue. So could Emma, evidently, for she spoke up at once. "Perhaps my husband could find Daisy a place at Marlowe Publishing," she suggested. "They always need typists."

"You might end up typing out my husband's manuscripts," Prudence put in, laughing. "That could be fun. Although, perhaps not," she amended. "The duke's handwriting is atrocious."

"What I really want is to be a writer," Daisy said. "Like the duke, with his travel guides. Or like you, Emma, with your shopping manuals and etiquette books."

"My sister writing etiquette books?" Lucy rolled her eyes. "Can you imagine? London society would never be the same."

Daisy wrinkled her freckled nose at her sister. "All right, then, I shall become an actress." She pressed the back of her hand against her forehead, gave a dramatic sigh, and fell against the settee. "'Romeo, Romeo, wherefore art thou Romeo? Deny thy father—'"

"Acting is out of the question," Lucy interrupted. "It's an immoral profession."

Heavens, Maria thought in amusement, *that's just the sort of disapproving thing Phillip would say.* And on the heels of that thought, a sense of aggravation. Couldn't she put that man out of her mind for one afternoon? She forced herself back to the conversation at hand.

"I know being an actress isn't really possible," Daisy was saying. "But it would be such an exciting profession. Like Sarah Bernhardt, you know. Remember, ladies, when we all went to see her at Covent Garden a few years ago in *Pauline Blanchard*? She was divine."

"What about writing plays?" Prudence suggested. "Then Daisy could satisfy both her literary and her histrionic talents."

"But that would still bring her in contact with quite the wrong sort of people," Mrs. Morris said.

"Actors," added Mrs. Inkberry darkly, with a warning glance at the redhead on the settee.

"And everyone knows actors are notorious," Miranda said. "Why, our dear Daisy might receive an illicit proposal!"

"Do you think so?" Daisy cried. "Oh, how exiting that would be. I should love to receive an illicit proposal!"

"I received a proposal," Maria blurted out, then immediately grimaced. Damn it, she was trying to forget about him. Telling her friends about his proposal would hardly help her in that regard.

Exclamations of surprise followed her news, for proposals, illicit or honorable, always engendered a great deal of excitement in Little Russell Street. A series of questions and comments began bombarding Maria from all sides.

"Who is he? Is he handsome?" Miranda wanted to know. "Does he have a horrible reputation?"

"Was it a very wicked offer? Did he offer you a house? Jewels? A carriage?"

"Daisy!" Lucy's shocked reproof followed her sister's eager and wholly inappropriate questions.

"Maria, dear," Mrs. Morris said, "we had no idea you had any . . . um . . . followers of that sort. I hope . . . no, I am certain," she corrected herself at once, "you sent the despicable fellow off with a flea in his ear."

Maria blushed as she realized what they were all thinking. "Oh, but it wasn't—"

"Of course she sent him off, Abigail," Mrs. Inkberry said, overriding Maria's attempt at clarification. "Our Maria is a most respectable young woman." She leaned closer to Maria and patted her knee. "You poor dear, to be subjected to such evils. But one can hardly be surprised, I fear," she went on and settled back in her chair. "We know what men can be, and our Maria is an unmarried woman in trade. These things happen."

"It's foul!" Prudence cried. "Foul for a man to assume that because an unmarried woman is in trade she must be a woman of easy virtue." She looked at Maria in dismay. "Oh, I knew I should have insisted upon giving you a dowry instead of a loan. Emma and I could have introduced you into society. As pretty as you are, you'd have received dozens of honorable offers by now. But it's not too late, is it?" She set aside her cup with a clatter and turned to Emma. "What is your opinion?"

"We could introduce Maria into society, of course," Emma answered. "Her dowry would have to be quite substantial, for she has no connections, and as you said, she has been engaged in trade, but—"

"It wasn't an *illicit* proposal!" Maria cried, interrupting this flood of commentary and discussion. "It was a proposal of marriage."

The room went silent. All her friends stared at her.

"Your shock is not very flattering," she grumbled after a few moments. "I'm know I'm coming on for thirty, and utterly on the shelf, but is it all that surprising I would receive an honorable proposal of marriage?"

"Forgive us, darling," Emma said, looking stricken. "It was only that we'd been discussing proposals of a dishonorable sort. And we didn't know—" She broke off and glanced around. "I think I can speak for all of us when I say we didn't know you had a suitor at present."

Maria made a rueful face. "Neither did I."

"Well?" Daisy prompted when she didn't elaborate. "Who is he?"

"Perhaps it's that Mr. Hawthorne?" Lucy guessed. "Didn't he propose to you years ago? Pru told us he lives next door to the shop."

"It can't be Mr. Hawthorne," Prudence said, shaking her head. "He's engaged to Miss Cynthia Dutton."

"He is?" Maria seized on that in an attempt to divert the conversation, hoping to avoid explanations. "I didn't know that. Lawrence has been out of town for two months with the Dutton family." She forced diffidence into her voice. "I'd heard they were at Kayne Hall with . . . umm . . . with the . . . umm . . . marquess."

"They returned from the country yesterday,"

Prudence told her, "and an announcement of Mr. Hawthorne's engagement was in all the society papers today."

"They've come back from the country? All of them?" She sat up straighter in her chair. "Phillip, too?" The moment she asked that question, she could have bitten her tongue off.

"Phillip?" It was Emma who spoke, making Maria wince, for only Emma could put such a wealth of implication into one little word.

"*Oh là là!*" Daisy cried, laughing. "Look at her blushing! She's pink as a peony."

"Oh, all right," Maria said crossly, setting her cup back into its saucer with a clatter. "You might as well know, for I shall never be able to keep it a secret now. You'll press me at every turn until I tell you." She picked up the plate on her lap and set it on the tea table along with her cup and saucer. Then she took a deep breath. "Phillip asked me to marry him."

The reaction was a moment of stunned silence. Maria couldn't blame them. She'd been quite knocked off her trolley by it as well.

Her fellow girl-bachelors began exchanging bewildered glances and shrugs, but it was Miranda who spoke first. "But who is this Phillip?"

"Phillip is Mr. Hawthorne's brother," Emma told them, eyebrows lifting as she gazed at Maria. "The Marquess of Kayne."

"*Oooooh!*" came a chorus of excitement from the girl-bachelors and matrons alike.

"And," Prudence added, also looking at Maria in surprise, "Maria cannot stand him."

"*Ohhhhhhh.*" This chorus was much more disappointed.

Everyone looked at her again, waiting in obvious expectation of more details. With reluctance she capitulated, conveying the entire infuriating proposal, emphasizing the marquess's admission that love played no part in it. She also conveyed his toplofty sentiments about her inferior background and his admission that their marriage would be just as imprudent a match as the one proposed to her by his brother twelve years earlier. As she related the story, her temper began rising again, and by the time she had finished this recital of the facts, she was once again as resentful and hurt and confused as she had been upon his departure from her kitchen a month earlier. "So," she summed up, "I told him what he could do with his arrogant manner, his ridiculous offer, and his snobbish opinions, and I turned him down flat. So, yes, Mrs. Morris, I sent him off with a flea in his ear!"

With that statement, she sat back in her seat and folded her arms, filled with righteous indignation, waiting for her friends to give their hearty endorsement of her decision and praise her wisdom.

But the other ladies did not seem eager to comment, and she could only conclude that they were too appalled to speak. "I know," she said, nodding, "it's amazing, isn't it, that he could even think I'd marry him. After what he did, separating me from Lawrence, what on earth could make him assume I would agree to have him?"

Mrs. Morris cleared her throat and spoke first. "Yes, but dearest, you said yourself that business with Mr. Hawthorne was over and done with years ago."

"And it was, but you see, Phillip—"

"You're not still in love with Mr. Hawthorne?" asked Lucy.

"Lawrence? Heavens, no! But—"

"The marquess," Mrs. Inkberry interrupted, "is surely a man of substantial wealth and property?"

"Yes, of course, but that hardly signifies—"

"Maria, he offered you *marriage*," Miranda said, emphasizing the last word as if it were the holiest of holies. "You would be a peeress, a marchioness."

"I know that, but—"

"Is he handsome?" asked Daisy.

"No," Maria answered at once, but she was immediately contradicted.

"Very handsome," Prudence said. "I met him at the May Day Ball, and I thought him quite well favored."

Maria's snort of derision was ignored.

"He's tall," Emma put in. "Wide shoulders, dark hair. Blue eyes, if I remember, and a lean, strong face."

"A striking combination," said Lucy. "Although it seems the woman whose opinion counts most doesn't agree. You don't think him handsome, Maria?"

All faces turned toward her again, and she tried to consider the question objectively, but it wasn't possible. Phillip was . . . just Phillip. Tall, cool, and dignified, with those deep blue eyes that seemed to see everything and that proud way of notching up his chin. "I suppose he is handsome," she conceded with reluctance, then sighed. "Oh, of course he is! But really, he oughtn't to be! Men so unbearably stuffy shouldn't be handsome. It's wrong, somehow."

"Oh, Maria!" Prudence cried as all the ladies began to laugh.

She knew it was absurd, but that didn't mean she found it amusing. "I don't see why all of you are laughing. I was right to turn him down. He doesn't love me. He described his feelings as 'a madness,' something marriage to me will cure him of! I ask you, could any woman in her right mind accept such a ridiculous offer?"

"Ah!" Prudence nodded, studying her with a little smile Maria did not like in the least. "Now I understand. You're afraid."

"Afraid?" Maria stared at her in disbelief. "Of what, in heaven's name? I'm not afraid of anything, least of all Phillip Hawthorne!"

Prudence ignored that. "Ladies, I think our Maria might be falling in love."

"What?" She jumped to her feet. "That is the stupidest thing I've ever heard!"

"And," Prudence went on, "she's afraid that if she marries him, he'll tire of her, and she'll be brokenhearted."

"For heaven's sake, haven't you heard a word I've said?" Maria shook her head violently. "I'm not in love with him. I don't even like him. He's a snob. And he's arrogant. How dare he take my consent for granted? As if I should be grateful he deigned to offer for me? Of all the high-handed things to do!"

For some reason, that made Pru's smile widen. "Yes, dearest, I think we all appreciate your opinion of his proposal. No need to ruffle up your feathers like an indignant pigeon."

Maria sat back down. "I don't know why you always have to be so romantic about everything, Pru," she muttered. "In love? It's absurd. No woman with an ounce of sense could be in love with Phillip."

"Oh, I imagine there are quite a few women in love with him," Emma put in.

"Nonsense!"

Emma ignored that and took a sip of her tea. "Why, I know for a fact the Duke of Richland's eldest daughter has been head-over-ears in love with him for years."

Maria stiffened as an image of a woman in a *ciel*-blue silk dress came into her mind. "Does she have dark hair?" she asked, and at once felt the silliest fool. "Never mind," she added. "Why she'd want to marry Phillip escapes me."

"Well, he is a marquess, Maria," Mrs. Inkberry reminded, "and though it's clear that does not impress you, he is a man of no small consequence. There are many women who would be delighted to marry him, I should think."

"And he's handsome," Miranda reminded. "We can trust Emma and Pru's judgment on that. And, oh, Maria, he asked you to marry him!"

"I'm a fool, I daresay," Maria said with sarcasm, "for refusing such a paragon of manly virtues, but there it is. I think he's horrid and haughty, and I'm not the least bit in love with him."

"Methinks she doth protest too much," paraphrased Daisy, laughing.

"Oh, this is ridiculous!' Maria cried, nettled beyond bearing. She again stood up and reached for her gloves. "If you'll excuse me, everyone, I must be on my way," she said as she put them on. "I've a big order of bread and pastries for the Marquess's charity luncheon tomorrow, so there's much to do."

"Oh, dearie-dear." Mrs. Morris's voice, terribly arch and highbrow, followed her toward the door. "The Marquess's charity luncheon, ladies, if you please."

"Perhaps she'll change her tune," Daisy said, her voice loud enough to carry to Maria in the foyer, "when she sees the duke's daughter flirting with the marquess over the sandwiches."

A round of giggles followed that comment, but Maria ignored them as she collected her bonnet and her handbag. "Me in love with Phillip?" she muttered, casting an exasperated glance heavenward as she walked out the front door. Then she paused on the threshold. Leaning back in the doorway, she added, "This is the silliest tea I've ever attended in my life!" loud enough for the others to hear before she walked out the door. For added confirmation of her feelings, she slammed the door behind her.

She didn't hail an omnibus or a hansom to return home. Instead, she walked, for she felt so stirred up that a walk seemed the only thing to do. She marched down Shaftsbury Avenue and onto Piccadilly as the words of her friends kept running through her mind. Prudence's comment, especially, seemed to touch her already raw nerves.

"Afraid?" she muttered in disbelief, earning herself an odd look from a gentleman standing beside her as she waited to cross Dean Street. "I am not afraid of anything."

By the time she had walked back to Mayfair, it was almost six o'clock, but to her surprise, she found someone waiting for her when she arrived at the shop. "Lawrence," she greeted. "I heard you were back in town."

He turned away from the display case by the cash register where he'd been talking to Miss Simms. "Yes, we arrived yesterday. Phillip came, too," he added, as if she cared.

Maria glanced at Miss Simms, who was holding a ring of keys in her hand and looking at her in inquiry. "You may go, Miss Simms," she said. "Leave the keys and I'll lock up."

"Yes, ma'am." The shop assistant set the keys on the counter, gave them both a curtsy, and departed through the back of the shop.

As Maria crossed the room, she didn't miss Lawrence's mischievous grin. She suspected he was up to something, but she ignored that grin and walked past him, flipping up the hinged lid of the counter to stand on the other side.

"I thought you'd be interested to know he's back in town," Lawrence murmured, his grin widening at her exasperated snort.

"I don't care a fig what that man does," she answered, slamming down the counter again, aggravated with him, with her romantic friends, and most of all, with herself. "Why should I?"

He wiped the grin off his face at once. "No reason," he said, but the very blandness of his voice only aggravated her more.

She gave him a withering glance, then bent down to set her handbag on the shelf beneath the cash register. "Did you want any pastries, Lawrence?" she asked as she straightened. "Or did you just come by to talk nonsense?"

"I've come to select some desserts."

She glanced into the display case through the glass on her side. "There isn't much left, I'm afraid. There never is at the end of the day."

"That's all right. I only need a dozen. We are having a small party of friends for dinner, and I wanted some of your cakes for dessert."

She pulled a cream-colored paperboard box from beneath the counter and reached for a set of tongs. "Which ones would you like?"

"Need you ask? I see some treacle tarts, so of course, I must have those. Oh, and I see you have chocolate ones, too, I'll need two of those as well. Phillip would never forgive me if he found out you had chocolate tarts and I didn't bring any home for him."

After everything that had happened, she doubted Phillip would eat her chocolate tarts—or anything else she made—but she didn't say so. She slid the glass door open, and using the tongs, began placing tarts in the box on her hip.

"Sorry I missed our appointment," he went on as she worked. "But Phillip asked me to stand in for him and show Colonel Dutton our shipyards, and I was so astonished that he was putting me in charge of something truly important for a change that I forgot all about our meeting. Not that seeing you wasn't important," he hastened to add. "I didn't mean it that way."

"It's quite all right. I understood what you meant. Would you like some of these éclairs, too?"

"Yes, thank you. I understand the ball went all right without me. You and Phillip rubbed along well, I take it?"

Maria paused, her hand tightening around the tongs in her hand as she remembered that extraordinary carriage ride. She ducked her head, pretending vast interest in the pastries in her display case. "Yes," she managed. "Quite well."

"Good, good. No arguments?"

No. We were too busy kissing.

She bit her lip, deciding it would be wise to veer the topic away from Lawrence's brother. "I believe congratulations are in order," she said as she continued putting pastries in the box. "I heard you are engaged to be married."

"I am. You don't hate me, Maria, do you?" he asked, and a frown of concern crossed his features. "You'd have the right," he added before she could reply. "I mean, I left you hanging all those years ago, and I never wrote you, or explained, or . . . or anything. I left Phillip to do it. You mustn't blame him, by the way. It was all my fault. I lost my nerve, and when he suggested offering you a . . . pension . . ."

He saw her wince at the term, and he hastened to say, "It seemed like the best thing to do. He said he'd make it generous enough that you'd be all right. Taken care of, and . . . and all that." He let out a sigh. "I'm sorry, Maria. I should have said it straight off."

"It was a long time ago, Lawrence. And I accept your apology."

"But you do understand that I was the cad, not Phillip?" Lawrence persisted, seeming oddly anxious to emphasize that point. "He was only looking out for me. He's wanted the best for me, always, and you weren't . . ." He looked away with a sound of exasperation. "Hell."

"I wasn't what was best for you," she finished. "Yes, I know."

He studied her, looking unhappy. "You have every right to hate both of us."

She considered that. "Yes," she said, deciding not to sugarcoat it for him. "I do have that right, and there was a time when I did hate you, and Phillip as well." She did not miss the pain in his face, and she relented. "But I understand why you did what you did. And I don't hate you, Lawrence, not anymore."

"And Phillip? You don't still hate him, do you?"

She told herself she should. "No."

"I'm glad." His frown vanished, and he looked so relieved, it surprised her. Why her good opinion of Phillip should mean so much, she couldn't fathom. Did he know Phillip had proposed?

No, she decided at once. Phillip was far too discreet to tell him.

Maria put the tongs aside, closed the display-case door, and stepped to the cash register. Setting the box on the counter, she started to reach below it for a lid, but a thought struck her, and she stopped. "Lawrence, Miss Dutton doesn't know about what happened all those years ago, does she?"

"God, no! I'd never tell her about that crazy business." The moment the words were out of his mouth, he grimaced, contrite. "Sorry. I didn't mean marrying you would have been crazy. I meant—" He broke off with a rueful sigh. "Damn, I do seem to be blundering this entire conversation."

"No, no, it *was* a crazy business. We were so young. We thought we were in love. It felt like love at the time. But it wasn't, was it? Not really."

"No," he agreed. "It wasn't. But why did you ask me if Cynthia knows what we did?" He shot her a glance of alarm. "You aren't going to tell her about it, are you?"

"Of course not."

His relief was palpable. "You're a brick, Maria."

"But," she went on, "perhaps you should."

He looked at her in obvious dismay. "Surely that's not necessary. I mean, it was so long ago. Why rake it all up again?"

As she studied the man opposite her, Phillip's words came back to her.

I love my brother, but I also recognize his flaws. Lawrence has never been good at facing up to unpleasant realities . . . He can't bear to lose anyone's good opinion.

As usual, Phillip had been right, but strangely enough, she didn't resent the fact. "No purpose at all," she assured Lawrence as she put the lid on the pastries and reached for a length of brown-and-gold ribbons to tie up the box. "Nothing happened, and no harm done. No need to bring it up at this late date."

"Thank you. I knew I could trust you. The secret's safe, then, for we both know Phillip won't breathe a word. And besides, I suspect my brother has more important things on his mind these days than our ancient history."

"Does he?" As she formed the ribbons into a bow, she couldn't help wondering if she was the important thing in question, knowing it shouldn't matter in the least if she were. She finished tying the bow and turned to the cash register. "What's preoccupying him?" she asked, and then wanted to kick herself.

"A lady, of course! Can't be anything else when he goes about carrying tokens of her affection with him."

She froze, her hand poised on the brass keys. A lady's token? She thought of the Duke of Richland's daughter and felt again the inexplicable sting of jealousy.

"It fell out of his card case," Lawrence went on, seeming oblivious to the fact that she had gone still as a statue. "You should have seen his face when I snatched it up." He laughed. "I never imagined my brother was so romantic."

I feel a deep and impassioned desire for you.

Desire wasn't love. It was a madness. He'd told her it would go away. It was clear that it had. Her jealousy deepened into misery. "Did you learn the lady's name?"

"No. He refused to discuss it."

"It doesn't matter. I know who she is."

"Do you, indeed?" He leaned closer. "Who?"

She forced herself to look up. "The Duke of Richland's daughter."

For some inexplicable reason, Lawrence laughed. "Richland's daughter?" He shook his head, still laughing. "Not a chance of it."

She wanted to believe him. "How can you be so certain?"

"Because the token was a hair ribbon," he said

as he straightened away from the counter and put on his hat. "Pink," he added and winked at her. "With white daisies on it."

He glanced down and took the box. "We all know who had a ribbon like that, don't we?" He walked away, whistling, leaving a stunned Maria staring after him.

Chapter 15

Forbidden fruit is the sweetest.
Proverb

He was perfectly well. Shipshape and Bristol fashion.

Phillip stared at the tray of pastries his butler had brought to the table, and he didn't feel a thing. The ribbon in his card case didn't feel as if it were burning a hole in his chest. When Lawrence mentioned that the desserts had come from Maria's shop, he was able to smile and inform his dinner guests in quite a natural manner that Martingale's, located right next door, was a *pâtisserie* of the highest quality and his personal favorite. He ate the chocolate tart and listened to the Duttons and his other guests praise the fine quality of her pastry, and he felt not the slightest pang of pain or anger or lust. Yes, he was cured.

Later that evening, after his guests had departed, he suggested brandy and cigars on the balcony to Lawrence, but his brother refused with a yawn, declaring he intended to seek his bed. Phillip ordered a brandy and cigar be brought to him on the balcony and went upstairs.

His valet nodded to him as he entered his bedroom. "Good evening, sir."

"Good evening, Gaston," he answered as he crossed the room. Opening one of the French doors, he stepped outside and took his usual seat on the wrought-iron chair in the corner. It was a fine, warm June night, and for once the scents of flowers and grass from Green Park seemed to override the perpetual city smells.

He leaned back and closed his eyes, feeling more relaxed and at ease than he'd felt in three months. At last, he thought with satisfaction. At last, he was sane again.

"Sir?"

He turned and looked up to find his footman at his elbow with a tray. "Yes, Dobbs, put it there," he said, nodding to the table beside his chair. "Thank you."

The servant complied with this order, then bowed. "Will there be anything else, sir?"

"No, Dobbs, thank you. Good night."

His footman bowed and departed. He took a sip of the brandy, then started to reach for the cheroot and the cutter from the tray, but something moved, a flash of white in the darkness of the balcony that caught his attention, and he looked up.

It was her. She was standing on her side of the balcony, and he had the strangest sense that she had been waiting for him and had only stepped out of the shadows upon hearing the sound of his voice.

As he stood up, he realized it was the white linen of her shirtwaist that had caught his attention, but it was her hair that transfixed him, for it was loose and shimmered like pale gold in the moonlight. The sight hit him square in the chest.

He watched her as she came closer, and desire washed over him, wiping out in one instant an entire month of determination and resolve. He hated her, suddenly, hated her for the desperate hunger inside himself that he would never be able to master.

With rigid control, he bowed, then he turned to go back inside. But he'd barely taken one step toward the doors to his rooms before she called to him.

"Don't go, Phillip."

At the sound of her voice, he stopped again, but he did not turn around. If he looked at her, he would let this madness have him.

He heard her footsteps bring her closer to him, the tap of her boot heels on the slate floor. She stopped several feet from the wall. "I believe you have something that belongs to me."

She knew. He closed his eyes. His chest tightened. Damn Lawrence.

From long practice, Phillip forced his features into polite, expressionless lines. Only then did he look at her.

In the dim, hazy moonlight, her skin seemed lit with a luminous glow. "You have my hair ribbon."

Was it a statement or an accusation? He could not be sure, but he forced himself to reach into the breast pocket of his jacket. As he pulled out his card case, the action brought pain, as if he were ripping it out of his chest. He opened the case and removed the ribbon. He stared at it for a moment, then he shoved it toward her. "Here. Take it."

She didn't move. "I thought I'd lost it." She looked up at him, her pretty hazel eyes wide. "But you took it, didn't you?"

Tell her you found it after she'd left Kayne Hall, he thought. *Tell her that.*

He didn't say it. He couldn't, for it would be a lie. "Yes."

"Why?"

God, did she really expect him to tell her? To confess that she had owned his heart, body, and soul for fourteen years? He stepped over the wall and crossed the short distance between them. He grasped her wrist, lifted her hand, and slapped the ribbon into her palm. "Take it, damn you."

The instant her fingers closed around it, he shoved her hand away, but he couldn't seem to find the will to leave. He tried to make her do it first. "Go inside, Maria."

She put the slip of pink silk into her skirt pocket, but she still didn't move. "Why did you take it?" she asked again, moving closer. "More important, why did you keep it?"

He could feel the tremors in his body, tremors that were deep down within him. They threatened to shatter the taut, tenuous hold he had on a lifetime of principles. "If one of us doesn't leave now," he said, his voice low and tight, "I'll forget I'm a gentleman."

"I believe I'd like to see that." She moved even closer. Her breasts brushed his chest, burning him through layers of clothing. She touched her lips with her tongue, sending a surge of lust through his body. "I'd like to see the walls of Jericho come tumbling down."

He tried one last time to warn her. "I won't be answerable for my actions."

"I know."

He cupped her face, his thumbs touched her soft, soft mouth. "I'll take your virtue."

"That's all right," she whispered, her lips brushing his thumbs, sending that lust spreading throughout his body. "I won't tell on you."

With those words, his reason dissolved. His honor crumbled. Like a dam breaking, the hungry need for her that he'd held back for so long broke through his resolve and poured through his body like a powerful, raging flood.

He slid his hands into her hair, tangling the long, golden strands in his fists, and he tilted her head back. He kissed her, a deep, hard kiss of total possession. It must have hurt her, for it bruised his own mouth. And yet, despite that, she entwined her arms around his neck and made a low, sweet moan of accord.

He tore his mouth from hers long enough to ask the vital question. "Are your maids asleep?"

"Yes," she gasped, and that was all she had time to say before he claimed her lips again. Tasting deeply of her mouth, he began pushing her backward, guiding them both toward her door. Once there, he reached behind her, turned the handle, and shoved the door wide, then continued guiding her backward into her bedroom. Once they were both inside, he kicked the door shut behind them.

Desire was coursing through him like tidal waves, and he strove to contain it. He had yearned for this moment for so long, and he had no intention of ruining it by being too quick. He wanted to arouse her gradually, build the passionate fire in her bit by bit, until it blazed as hot in her as it did in him, until the pleasure of it consumed them both.

He tore his lips from hers and buried his face in

the curve of her neck, forcing himself to contain his moves and go slowly. His hands left her hair and slid down to her slender waist, and his fingers moved up and down her spine in lazy circles as he trailed kisses along the column of her throat and across her jaw to recapture her mouth with his.

He kissed her, long, slow, deep kisses, as his hands left her waist and came up between them to begin unbuttoning her shirtwaist. He worked his way down, button by button, and he could feel a quiver run through her body with each one he unfastened.

Once his hand reached her waist, he pulled back, looking into her face, watching as she slowly opened her eyes. She'd always had beauty to take his breath away, but he had never seen her look lovelier that she did at this moment, and when she smiled at him, shaking back her beautiful hair, he felt it like a tangible force. And when she breathed his name on a tiny sigh, the sound was like throwing brandy on a fire, igniting the desire he was fighting so hard to contain.

He grasped the edges of her shirtwaist and pulled it back from her shoulders, but that seemed to unnerve her, for she stirred, making a sound of agitation. He left off undressing her for the moment and tilted his head, pressing a kiss to her ear. "It's all right. I want to undress you. Don't be afraid."

She stirred again. "Heavens, Phillip," she whispered back. "I'm not afraid. It's just—" She broke off with a little jerking movement.

"What's wrong?"

"You didn't unbutton my cuffs."

In all the fantasies he'd had of her, he'd never imagined her saying something like that. He began to laugh, a deep, rumbling chuckle that caught him by surprise. Her as well, it seemed, for she pulled back to look at him. "Phillip, you're laughing."

"Sorry. It's just that that isn't the sort of remark a man expects at a time like this," he explained as he unfastened the buttons of her cuffs. Her shirtwaist fell to the floor. He lifted his hands to unbutton her corset cover, but she grasped his wrists, stopping him.

"I like hearing you laugh. I always have. That's why I used to do silly things, you know. Trying to make you laugh."

Smiling, he began slipping buttons free. "Like singing 'The Major-General's Song' with that silly fusilier's helmet on your head and a monocle on your eye?"

"You remember that?"

He paused and looked into her eyes. The tightness in his chest deepened and spread. He wanted to say that he remembered everything—not just that fusilier's helmet that kept falling over her eyes because it was too big, but other things, too. He remembered the white-hot anger he'd felt when the teasing of the village children had made her cry; the lift of his spirits every time a letter in her handwriting had come to him at school, the vanilla scent of her hair; the shimmers of fear when he'd seen Lawrence with her in the rose arbor, making her laugh as he had never been able to do; the bleakness of his days after she was gone.

He couldn't say any of that, for the words seemed stuck in his throat, so he cupped her face and took her mouth in another long kiss. He trailed more kisses along the velvety skin of her cheek to her ear as he unbuttoned her corset cover, more kisses along the column of her throat and across her collarbone as he pulled the garment over her head and tossed it aside, and still more kisses along the soft, white skin of her shoulder as he unfastened the hooks of her corset and let it slip to the floor.

He lifted his head, and when he glanced down, he saw the faint, unmistakable outline of her nipples beneath the thin nainsook of her chemise. His control began slipping away.

Now, he thought, now he'd be able to see what until now he had only been able to imagine. He grasped handfuls of nainsook in his fists and began pulling her chemise out of the waistband of her skirt.

"Phillip?"

He paused, breathing deeply of the luscious scents of vanilla and cinnamon on her skin as he his fists tightened around folds of soft white fabric. "Yes, Maria?"

"I—" She hesitated, then gave a little laugh. "I'm not experienced in these matters, but am I supposed to be the only one whose clothes come off?"

"No."

"Good." She raised her hands to his chest, grasped the lapels of his dinner jacket and began pulling the garment off of his shoulders. He didn't know whether to groan or laugh, but he let her slide the jacket off. She then unfastened the buttons of his shirt and removed his cuff links, and he pulled the shirt over his head.

Shirt and cufflinks hit the floor as she flattened her palms against his chest, and the warm touch of her hands sent his control slipping down another notch. He fought to regain it, but he couldn't stop the groan that escaped him as she began to caress his bare skin.

"Yes," he said, his voice a harsh rasp in his throat. "Touch me, Maria. God, yes."

He tilted his head back, letting her explore him, savoring her curiosity even as he struggled to keep his arousal in check. He allowed her to run her hands over the muscles of his chest, shoulders, arms, and abdomen. But when she reached the waistband of his trousers, he knew his self-control would snap if he let her continue her explorations.

"Enough," he said, grasping her wrists. "That's enough for now."

She started to protest, but he was impervious. "My turn," he said firmly. He reached around her waist to unfasten the three buttons at the back of her skirt, then he sank to his knees, pulling her skirt down with him. "Step out of it," he said, and when she did, he shoved the garment out of the way. He unlaced her boots and pulled them off. They, too, were tossed aside, then his hands curved behind her ankles and moved slowly up her calves to her knees, sliding inside her drawers to the garters that held up her stockings.

His fingers lightly caressed the backs of her knees, and delicious tingles of warmth danced along her spine. She looked down, watching as he pulled the ribbon ties of her garters to unfasten them, then slowly slid her stockings down her legs. When he reached her ankles, he slipped her stockings and garters off her feet, then he slid his hands slowly up again. Even through the muslin of her drawers, his touch seemed scorching hot as his palms skimmed her thighs, then her hips, then lifted to the front of her chemise.

He pulled the edges apart, freeing the tiny satin knots from their loops. Then his hands fell away and he sat back on his heels. His gaze met hers.

"Take off your chemise for me," he said. "I want to watch you take it off."

Mesmerized by the heat of his gaze and the intensity of his command, she obeyed. Reaching for the hem of her chemise, she pulled the garment up her body and over her head, then tossed it over one shoulder and shook back her hair. When she looked at him again, she sucked in a sharp breath, startled. Though his expression was grave, as always, she saw something else in his face, something she had never seen there before. Tenderness.

"Oh, God," he whispered hoarsely. "God, Maria, you're so lovely. Even more lovely than I imagined."

She stared at him, appreciating that he had done this very thing to her countless times in his imagination—undressed her, kissed her, made love to her. All these years, he'd had that ribbon, and he'd thought of this, imagined this. That knowledge sent a feeling through her like nothing she'd ever felt before, a feeling beyond physical sensation, a joy so powerful it was like pain, yet so sweet that it was pleasure, and she knew Prudence had been right. She was in love with this man.

He lifted his hands to cup her breasts, bringing back that aching warmth she'd first felt in the carriage. It seemed to melt her like butter, robbing her of the ability to stand. "Phillip," she moaned, her knees giving way. "Oh, crikey."

He caught her, his hands grasping her hips

to keep her upright, and she thought she heard him laugh under his breath. She watched in fascination as he began to stroke and caress her. He shaped her breasts, toyed with them, brushed his fingers lightly over her hardened nipples, and the warmth in her deepened and spread. She brought her hands up to cradle his head, moaning low in her throat as she pulled to bring him closer.

He came that short distance, straightening on his knees, and she watched in amazement as his lips parted over her breast and he drew her nipple into his mouth.

She gasped with shock at the piercing sweetness of it, tilting her head back and arching toward him, her hands tightening in his hair, her arms cradling his head. She felt him draw her nipple between his teeth, and she squeezed her eyes shut against the sweet excitement of it. He suckled her, his teeth and tongue gently working, while she could only shiver and gasp, holding his head to her breast, clinging to him to keep herself from falling.

He sucked harder. She moaned, and again, her knees gave way, but his arm wrapped around her back, holding her upright. He laid his cheek to the side of her breast as he used his free hand to untie the thin satin drawstring that held up her drawers. He tugged the garment down her hips, and it fell, pooling around her feet.

Then his arm tightened at her back, his other arm curved beneath her knees, and he rose with her in his arms, then he carried her to the bed.

He laid her in the center of the bed, and she opened her eyes to find him watching her as he pulled off his boots. Maria glanced down, watching as he undid the buttons of his trousers and slid them off his hips along with his linen.

Her mattress dipped with his weight as he moved to lie beside her. His weight on one elbow, he gazed down at her for a moment, then reached out to touch her face. His fingertips lightly grazed her cheek, down the column of her throat, over her breast, and lower, tracing light, random patterns across her stomach. She wriggled and gave a hushed squeal at this unbearable teasing, and that made him smile.

"Ah, yes," he murmured. "How could I have forgotten you're ticklish?"

"I'm not," she lied, unable to stop herself from laughing even as she tried to push his hand away. "I don't know why you would think that. Oh, Phillip, don't!" Those last words were a desperate wail.

He relented, but she soon realized he had another, more delicious form of torture in store for her. He pressed a kiss to her stomach that sent quivering tickles of sensation rippling through her, fluttering quivers like the beating of butterflies' wings. She shivered. His tongue touched her navel, then moved lower, and lower still, trailing soft, wet kisses down to the edge of her blonde curls.

He paused, and she caught her breath, waiting in tense anticipation. When she felt his hand ease between her thighs, she thought he was going to touch her as he had in the carriage, but then he surprised her, sliding his other hand between her legs as well. The quivering suspense inside her grew stronger as he began pulling her legs apart.

He eased his body between her legs, sliding his arms beneath her thighs. Shocked, she tensed, realizing in a vague sort of way what he was intending to do. She opened her eyes and lifted her head with a sound of protest.

He paused, lifting his head to look at her. "It's all right," he told her. "Just relax for me."

Relax? Her legs were spread apart, her most intimate place exposed to him. It was unthinkable . . . It was . . . oh, God . . . it was wicked. She felt herself blushing from head to toe, and she shook her head. "I can't, Phillip," she moaned, letting her head fall back, too embarrassed to look at him. "I can't."

"Maria, listen to me." He turned his head and kissed the inside of her thigh. "I want this. I want it badly."

He slid his body down a notch, and she squeezed her legs against his shoulders with a moan. "Don't.

Oh, Phillip, don't!" she moaned as she felt his hot breath against the top of her thigh.

"I want to kiss you here," he said, his lips brushing her curls. "Pleasure you here. Let me do this."

His voice was shaking as he spoke, and she wavered, in an agony of shame and desire. He nuzzled her, and she relented, relaxing her legs.

His tongue touched the folds of her sex, and she cried out at the shocking carnality of it. Her fingers grasped fistfuls of the counterpane and her hips arched upward. His hands tightened, imprisoning her hips as his tongue caressed her sex, lightly at first, then deeper and deeper. The pleasure in her deepened as well, spreading through her body.

Oh, that anything could feel like this. It was wicked and wanton. It was wonderful. That Phillip, whom she'd always thought so proper, should know of such things as this. It amazed her.

The tension of being held prisoner was becoming unbearable, and she jerked her hips in protest. He relaxed his hands to let her body move, and the moment he did, that pleasure she'd felt before came again, surging through her body in thick, pulsing waves, again and again and again. She was whimpering—she could hear herself making the soft sobs she'd made before, sounds she knew now were sounds of release. Her hips lifted one more time and her body arched tightly against his mouth, the pleasure finally shattering in a shower of white-hot sparks. She collapsed, panting, shuddering, against the mattress. He continued to stroke her softly, gently, with his tongue, bringing her a few more lingering surges of that sweet pleasure, before he kissed her one last time.

His body moved, sliding upward over hers with sudden urgency. She could feel his shaft, hard and engorged, rubbing the place he had kissed her moments before. His breathing against her ear was hot and fast. "Maria, I want to take you. I want to be inside you. Do you understand what that means?"

"Yes," she gasped, but when she felt the tip of his shaft pushing between the feminine folds he had stroked with his tongue, she felt a wave of something different. Panic.

"Phillip?"

He heard the apprehension in her questioning voice, and he paused, lifting his body above hers. "It's time, love," he murmured, nuzzling her throat, kissing her ear. "I've waited so long. I can't wait any longer to have you."

He kissed her throat, pushing his shaft into her with a groan. "Yes, love, yes," he murmured, pulling back, then easing deeper into her. "That's it."

His voice was unsteady, excited, and she knew this was giving him the same pleasure he had given her. She wrapped her arms around his back, pulling him down, bringing him even more deeply into her, but with that move came something else—a sudden, searing burn, and she cried out.

He turned his head, capturing the sound of her surprise and pain into his mouth. "It'll be all right, my love," he groaned, shifting his weight to cradle her in his arms as she shuddered with the unexpected sting he had evoked. He lifted his head and his cobalt-blue eyes looked into hers. "It'll be all right, I swear, it will."

He lowered his head, nuzzling her throat again, and he began to move more forcefully. She held on to him, her palms flat against the powerful muscles of his back, as he pushed into her harder, faster.

Beginning to understand this new rhythm, she moved her hips beneath him experimentally, thrusting up to meet him. He groaned again and quickened his pace even more, until his body was pressing hers into the mattress with each thrust, his weight driving the air from her lungs.

Then, suddenly, a violent shudder rocked him, he let out a hoarse cry. He thrust against her one last time, then was still.

Her arms tightened around him and an overpowering tenderness washed over her that was almost as wonderful as the pleasure he had given her. With one hand, she caressed his broad back, and with the other, she toyed with his hair as she felt the tension leave his body and lethargy take its place.

He pressed a kiss to her mouth, then rolled to his side, taking her with him, cradling her in his arms. She rested her cheek in the dent of his shoulder, staring up at the ceiling.

She had lost her innocence. She ought to feel shame, she supposed, if sermons and whispered cautions were anything to go by. Unless a woman was married, virginity was a sacred thing, treasured and preserved. A bit like dried flowers, she thought with a hint of amusement—musty, flat, and lifeless.

But she did not feel like that at all. She felt fresh and alive. Joy bloomed inside her with all the vibrancy of spring. Virginity was all very well, Maria decided, but being a fallen woman was much more beautiful. Smiling, she closed her eyes, and within moments she was asleep.

Chapter 16

Man shall not live by bread alone.
Matthew 4:4

Maria felt him stir beside her, and when he rose from the bed, she opened her eyes. The lamp was still lit, but it was morning, for daylight filtered in between the edges of the draperies at her windows.

She peeked over the counterpane to study him as he moved about the room gathering his clothes. In profile, she could see the defined, muscular contours of his body. It amazed her that he was so strong, and yet had touched her with such sweet tenderness.

She watched as he bent to reach for his trousers, and renewed heat stole through her body at the sight of his sleek, bare bum. When he turned around, he caught her watching, but she still couldn't resist a glance over the rest of his body. She stared for a moment, her blush deepened, and she raised her gaze at once, to find he was smiling at her.

"Good morning," he said, dropped the clothes, and started toward the bed.

She bit her lip and looked away as he approached, feeling strangely shy, and yet happy. When he leaned over the bed, cupped her chin and turned her face to plant a kiss on her lips, her happiness deepened into a joy so intense it was almost painful.

"Good morning," she answered and reached up to caress his cheek. It was roughened with beard stubble, like sandpaper against her fingers. How extraordinary a man was. "What time is it?"

He turned his cheek to kiss her palm. "It's after six."

"Six? Oh, lord." She came out of her romantic daze at once and pushed aside the sheets. He straightened, stepping back to allow her to rise from the bed, but it was only after she had done so that she remembered she was naked. It was one thing to study him covertly as he moved unclothed about the room, but quite another to be the subject of his scrutiny. Still, it was too late to duck back under the covers, and besides, she had no time for prudery.

She was still blushing as she crossed the room, for she could feel his observant gaze studying her back, but when he said, "My God, you're beautiful," her shyness vanished, and only her happiness remained.

She smiled at him over her shoulder, then opened the armoire and pulled out undergarments, a skirt, and a shirtwaist for herself as he began to don his clothes. "I can't believe I slept so late," she said as she pulled a chemise over her head and reached for stockings and garters. "I am usually awake far earlier than this."

"And I am often just coming home," he answered as he sat on the edge of the bed to pull on his boots.

The clock in the corridor struck the quarter hour, and she gave a cry of vexation. "My apprentices have already arrived," she muttered, buttoning her shirtwaist. "I can't think why one of my maids didn't come to fetch me already."

"One of them did."

She stopped, looking up from her buttons. "What?"

"That's what woke me. One of your maids came in. She saw me." He paused, meeting her gaze. "She saw us."

Maria turned away, reaching for her petticoat and skirt, trying to think as she put them on. "It doesn't matter, I suppose," she finally said, knowing she couldn't worry about what her staff might think just now. "I mean, I shall have to face her," she added as she pulled on her boots, "and that will be embarrassing, to say the least, but—"

"Maria, we have to talk."

She shook her head and began lacing her boots. "I have to finish dressing and go down. Heaven only knows what my apprentices have been concocting without me. And we've heaps of work today. There's your charity luncheon to prepare for, for one thing."

"Yes, I know, but we must talk now." He crossed to her side, and as she straightened, he put his hands on her shoulders and turned her toward him. "Your servants will draw the logical conclusion. They will believe you are my mistress."

"Yes, I realize that." She took a deep breath and squared her shoulders. "But there's nothing to be done about that now."

"Yes, there is. You'll marry me."

The happiness inside her at those words was a vastly different feeling from the emotions evoked by his first proposal, but when a door banged down below, and voices could be heard floating up the stairwell, she cast an anxious glance at the door. "Phillip, I have to go. Facing my servants is one thing, but the shop will open in just over an hour, and I have to go down. Your charity luncheon—"

"Will you stop worrying about the luncheon?" He grabbed her hands and kissed them. "I'll have Bouchard find whatever's needed somewhere else."

"Oh, no, you won't. I will not shirk my obligations."

"This particular obligation is to me, and I relieve you of it." He entwined his fingers with hers, pulled her toward him, and kissed her.

"I don't like the idea that some other bakery is receiving even one bit of your business," she grumbled, though she tilted her head to one side so he could kiss her neck.

"My competitive darling," he murmured, laughing against her skin. His hands let go of hers, and his arms slid around her waist. "But what does it matter? Before the season's over, Bouchard shall be using the bakery he used before, or find a new one."

She stiffened in his arms. "Why can't he continue to use mine?"

Phillip drew back, a slight frown knitting his dark brows. "Because you won't have it, of course."

Her blissful mood faded as an inescapable dread began to take its place. "What do you mean? Why won't I have my shop?"

He stared at her as if in astonishment. "Because you'll be my wife. You'll be a marchioness. You can't keep the bakery."

"Can't?" she repeated, bristling at the word. "So you shall dictate to me what I can and cannot do? If you become my husband, you become my master?"

His frown deepened. "A marchioness does not engage in trade. Once we're married, you'll close the shop."

"But owning my own *pâtisserie* has been my dream, what I've been striving for these past twelve years. I've only been open three months. I can't give up a dream of twelve years after only three months."

"But you'll be my wife."

"Will I? I believe the last time you proposed, my answer was no. Yet, you now take it for granted that my answer is yes? You presume a great deal."

"You're damned right I do. I've taken your virtue. I've bedded you. We have to marry now. Any other course of action is unthinkable."

He wanted her to close the shop. She felt a wave of panic. "But we hardly know each other!"

"We've known each other since we were children."

"I know, but—" Frustrated, she broke off, trying to think of how to explain what she meant. "There has been no courtship between us, no time to become reacquainted."

"I know, and it is regrettable. I appreciate that a woman always desires to be courted, but we haven't time for it."

"And what of my livelihood?"

"Darling, once we are married, you'll be a marchioness, with an allowance of a thousand pounds a month. You won't need a livelihood."

"I'm not talking of what I need. My work is important, just as important as your shipping business, your estates—"

"Nonsense. Being a marquess is an enormous responsibility. A bakery is—"

He broke off, but it was too late.

"A bakery is not important. That's what you were about to say." She didn't wait for him to affirm or deny it before she spoke again. "I see no pressing need to give up my life and all I've worked for to go rushing into matrimony."

She tried to pull away from him, but he tightened his grip on her fingers. "But Maria, the need is pressing. You might be carrying a child. My child."

She went still. Heavens, she hadn't even thought about a child. Her panic intensified, but she tried to force it down. "We don't know if there will be a child," she said, trying to sound calm and reasonable. "And if there is . . ." She swallowed hard, forcing the words out past the sick lurch of fear in her stomach. "I know that you will take care of us, even if . . . even if you and I do not marry."

He stared at her, and this time there was no need to guess what he was thinking. Disbelief, shock, and anger were plainly written on his face. "You were an innocent woman. Do you think that I would ruin you and not insist upon doing right by you? Do you think I would subject you to the shame of an illegitimate child? Do you think

I would stand by and watch my child be born a bastard? God, Maria, do you think so little of me that you believe I would allow any of that to happen?"

"And do you think so little of me that you do not consult me before making these decisions about my life and my future?" she shot back, growing angry herself, gripped by an unreasoning fear, a feeling of being trapped. "Once again, you are dictating to me what you think is best for me! You do not ask what life I want, you take it for granted that the life I want is the one you offer."

"And what else should I presume?" he countered. "What other options are there?"

She struggled for an answer, struggled for a compromise. "Why can't we simply be together for now, and be content with that? There are ways . . . I have heard there are ways to prevent pregnancy. We could be lovers."

"What? A man of my position and a woman of yours cannot simply be lovers! You are either my wife or my mistress. Anything in between is not possible."

"Why not? Many couples are lovers who are not married."

"Not married to each other, I grant you. They are each married to someone else, which provides the veneer required to protect a woman's reputation. If we became lovers, your reputation would suffer, just as it would if you were my mistress."

"No one has to find out."

"People always find out. Your servants know. By the end of the day, they'll have told my servants. The society papers watch me tirelessly. How long do you think it will be before they discover that the pastry chef who lives next door, who makes the cakes for my parties, is also very pretty? How long before snide little snippets about you appear in the papers? I'm surprised it hasn't been remarked on already."

His expression hardened. "No. We shall be married. There is nothing more to say."

"There is a great deal more to say!" she cried, rebelling against giving up everything she had worked so hard to attain, refusing to be forced into something just because he thought it best. "Once again, you feel this is all about you. Your desire. Your decision. Your honor."

"By offering you marriage, I believe it is *your* honor I am trying to save!"

"You didn't offer it. You demanded it. There is a difference."

"By suggesting that we be lovers, you are expecting me to abandon a lifetime of principles! You are expecting me to abandon my honor as a man and a gentleman."

"No, what I expect, what I *demand*, is that you treat me as an equal, with equal say in what happens to us."

He made a sound of impatience. "For God's sake, are we back to that again?"

"You're damned right we are!" She met his implacable gaze with a resolute one of her own. "Marriage is a partnership, Phillip, not a feudal kingdom. Until you can accept that I have the right to dictate the course of my own life, I will not marry you. Until you can accept that my wishes and my opinions are just as worthy of consideration as yours, I will not marry you. Until you can accept that what I would give up to be your wife is just as important as what you offer in exchange, I will not marry you."

She could hear her voice breaking, and she could feel the sting of angry tears in her eyes, and she knew she had to leave before she fell completely apart.

She turned away and walked to the door of her bedroom. Hand on the knob, she turned, for there was one more thing she had to say. "And while we are on the subject, until you demonstrate that you possess genuine love and affection for me and some willingness to win my hand rather than demand it, I will not marry you." She opened the door. "Now, if you will excuse me, my lord, I have work to do." With that, she walked out and shut the door behind her.

Phillip strode across the balcony to his own rooms, frustration seething within him, the words of their angry exchange still ringing in his ears.

She was refusing him because she did not want to give up her own life? What on earth did that mean? It was idiotic. A woman's life was marriage, children, everything he had offered her.

He entered his own rooms and slammed the French door behind him, causing Gaston to come running from the adjoining dressing room. The valet, only half dressed himself, in trousers and shirt, halted at the sight of his master's face and disheveled appearance. "Sir?"

Phillip grasped for control. In situations such as this, it was necessary for a gentleman to remain cool, levelheaded, and logical. "Draw me a bath, Gaston, will you?"

"Yes, sir." The valet departed back into the dressing room, and a few minutes later, the sound of water gushing through the taps could be heard from the bathroom beyond.

As Phillip waited for his bath, the things she'd said continued to echo through his mind, and his anger and frustration gave way to bafflement.

Her bakery was her dream, she'd said. A dream she'd had for years, a dream she had no intention of giving up to marry him.

What sort of woman chose a life of hard, backbreaking work over matrimony? A life of servitude over a life of luxury and privilege? It defied common sense.

Matrimony, not business, was a woman's realm.

Not once, but twice, he'd offered her what any other woman would be ecstatic to accept, and twice, she had spurned it.

"Your bath, sir."

He nodded, but as he followed Gaston through the dressing room, his mind remained preoccupied with what Maria had told him. She would rather make pastry than be his wife. *Lovely*, he thought as he stripped out of his clothes and stepped into the steaming water. She was spurning him for sponge cake.

He bathed, dried off, and sat in the reclining shaving chair by the bathtub. As Gaston scraped beard stubble from his face, Phillip closed his eyes and continued to try to comprehend the incomprehensible.

Her work was important, she'd said. Being his marchioness, his wife, the mother of his children evidently was not. She would rather be alone than be his.

That knowledge ripped through his chest, and he made a sound at the pain.

Gaston stopped and pulled back the razor, looking stricken. "Sir?"

"It's all right, Gaston." Phillip took a deep breath. "It's all right. You didn't cut me."

Despite those words, his valet examined his face carefully before proceeding with his task.

Phillip remained still under the razor, striving to regain command of himself. As he dressed, as he ate breakfast, as he ordered his carriage be brought around to take him to his offices, he struggled to tamp down his emotions.

His carriage had not yet pulled up in front of the house, and as he stood in the foyer, there was nothing to do but wait. He pulled out his watch, verified the time, and put it back in his pocket. Pain flickered up from within, and he strove to quell it. He shifted his weight from one foot to the other. He twirled his hat in his fingers. He looked out the front windows. No sign of his carriage.

With an oath, he turned to the gilt-framed mirror on the wall of the foyer. It was not insufferable to offer marriage to the woman whose virtue you had just taken. It was simply right. It was not unreasonable to expect to marry the woman you loved. It was not unreasonable to assume that since she had just given you her virtue, she loved you in return. It was not unreasonable to offer marriage in consequence.

You did not offer it. You demanded it.

He stared at his reflection, and it suddenly seemed as if he were looking at a stranger. The face that stared back at him was not a face he recognized. It was not the cool, inscrutable face of the well-mannered British gentleman. In his reflection was every shred of pain, anger, bewilderment, and love within him, plainly written on his face for anyone to see.

How, he wondered in despair, was he going to attend that luncheon? How was he going to sit at a table with two dozen friends and acquaintances without all of them knowing exactly what he felt? How was he going to watch her coming and going with her breads and cakes, knowing she had chosen them instead of him? If there was a child, how was he to bear watching it come into this world without his name?

Phillip adjusted his perfectly straight tie, pulled an ever-so-slightly deformed petal from the white camellia in his lapel, and brushed an imaginary speck of lint from his charcoal-gray morning jacket. These motions were meaningless to his appearance, he knew, but just now they seemed vital. He could feel the only woman he had ever wanted slipping away for the third time, and he knew that this time, the pain of losing her would annihilate him.

Phillip heard the clatter of carriage wheels on the street outside. He met the eyes of the man in the mirror, and he knew somehow, some way, he had to change her mind. He had no intention of making the same mistake again.

Chapter 17

Your words are my food, your breath my wine. You are everything to me.

Sarah Bernhardt

She'd made the right decision. Maria repeated that fact to herself for perhaps the hundredth time that morning as she stood in the kitchens at Avermore House. She was putting the final touches on the pastries and confections before they were sent to the dining room, but she stared down at the tray of iced lemon cakes before her without interest, her mind elsewhere, her emotions in turmoil.

After leaving Phillip, she'd noticed the speculative, sidelong glances of her maids, apprentices, and shop assistants as they had worked to make the final preparations for this luncheon. She didn't know which one of her maids had seen Phillip in her bed that morning, but it was clear that all her staff knew by now she was an unchaste woman. Still, that was not what was causing her distraction, for she'd never cared much what other people thought of her. She'd always known it was what she thought of herself that mattered.

Nor was it the extraordinary physical experience of lovemaking that preoccupied her today. The things Phillip had done to her had been wonderful, and—truth be told—she still felt a bit dazed and wobbly from the experience. She'd never known the happiness that could come from such an intimate experience. The physical sensations of lovemaking no doubt astonished everyone upon feeling them for the first time. But it was the events afterward that dominated Maria's thoughts and had her vacillating from moment to moment between wanting to kiss him and wanting to kill him.

It was Phillip, only Phillip, who could send her into this sort of emotional turmoil. No other person who'd been important to her life—not any of her friends, not Lawrence, not André, not even her father—had ever been able to enrage her, fascinate her, and wound her as Phillip could do. And it always had been that way, she realized. Always.

Her mind flashed back to the first day she'd ever met him. The serious boy in short pants under a willow tree, reciting Latin as if it were the most important thing in the world, telling her so proudly how he was going to Eton. She hadn't even known what Eton was. She hadn't cared. It was how he'd looked at her when she'd held out her hand to him—puzzled, as if he'd never seen anything quite like her before, a bit appalled, too, for he'd been a stuffy sort of chap even then. His expression had intrigued her, for most boys had thought her rather fun, deeming her not so silly as other girls. But it was when Phillip had broken his arm because of the rope swing she'd talked him into making, when he'd taken all the blame and gotten a beating, when he'd insisted to his father that he'd been alone, making no mention she'd been there—that was when she'd known they would be friends. She'd been sure she could depend on him through thick and thin.

The clatter of a pan hitting the kitchen floor and a curse from Monsieur Bouchard broke into her reverie, and she tried to focus her attention on the task at hand, but when she studied the lemon cakes she had to decorate, she felt no spark of enthusiasm.

Her work had always fascinated her. From the first moment her father had allowed her to help him in the kitchens when she was a tiny girl, she'd wanted to be a chef. A pastry chef. She'd wanted to make cakes for lords and princes. And she had. She'd wanted to own her own *pâtisserie*, and now she did. Maria looked up, staring around the kitchen, where chefs in aprons were scrambling around like ants on an anthill, and suddenly, it all seemed a silly, trivial business.

She'd told Phillip this morning how important her shop was to her. And it was. At least, it had been. Until this morning. Until Phillip had reminded her that there were other important things. She looked down again at the cakes, which would be consumed and forgotten in a matter of minutes.

A child, though. A child was different.

Maria flattened a hand against her abdomen. What if she were to have a child? Ruthlessly, she pulled her hand down. She did not want to marry a man to avoid shame or dishonor. Such things were Phillip's primary concerns, but they were not hers. It wasn't the life she'd envisioned for herself, true enough, but if there was a child, she would have it, and she would keep it, and she would hold her head up. She would not be ashamed, no matter what society had to say. Again, other people's opinions had never mattered to her.

Except for Phillip's.

Oh, how it had hurt when she'd come home from France and watched him snub her. How it had hurt when he would see her coming, stick his chin up, and turn the other way. It had been like a stab in the heart. She wasn't good enough to talk to, once he was the marquess. Despite the fact that her father had scraped together the money for boarding school, despite the fact that she had an education equal to that of any lady, she wasn't good enough. She had never been good enough.

That was what had turned her to Lawrence. Lawrence had been the balm for her wounds. Lawrence had never cared that she'd worked in the kitchens, and while Phillip had spent two summers making it clear he wanted nothing to do with her, Lawrence had made his admiration crystal clear. He'd been the one to hold her hand when her father died. He'd been the one to listen to her sob out her fears because she had no money and didn't know what to do. She'd always thought Phillip was the one she could count on, but it was Lawrence who had stepped up and offered her a solution. To a frightened, grieving girl of seventeen, marriage to a gentleman, a dear and familiar friend, had seemed the answer to everything, the solution to all her difficulties, the banishment of all her worries.

But life wasn't that easy. It wasn't that simple. Marriage didn't solve everything. She knew that now. And yet, even knowing all of that wasn't what had made her refuse Phillip this morning.

She didn't want him to marry her because being a marchioness would make her life easy. She didn't want him to marry her because there might be a child. She wanted him to marry her because he loved her. And though she had received not one, but two, marriage proposals from him, amid all the words about desire and honor, about marriage and children, there had been no words of love. There had been no consideration of what she had worked so hard to earn. No acknowledgment of what she would be giving up to marry him.

The lemon cakes blurred before her, and savagely, she rubbed her eyes with the tips of her fingers. Once again, she tried to focus on her task. She added a tiny sprig of lemon balm and a twist of citrus peels to the top of each cake, but the decoration did not seem to make them any more interesting or meaningful.

Maria glanced around for a member of her staff to take the tray of cakes to the dining room, but since this was merely a luncheon, she'd brought only half her staff with her, leaving the others at the shop, and in the crowd swarming through the kitchen, she did not see Miss Dexter, Miss Simms, or little Molly Ross. Maria gestured to one of Phillip's footmen, who was standing nearby, and when he came to her side, she handed him the cakes. "Take these to the dining room, please," she instructed.

"Very good, miss."

The footman departed, and she moved on to the next tray, but she just couldn't bring herself to care about putting little sugared violets on little chocolate truffles. Maria stared at the tray, heartsick and miserable, and afraid.

Yes, afraid. Why not admit it?

Shrewd of Prudence to see it that day in Little

Russell Street. She was afraid to fall in love with Phillip, for if he did not love and respect her, he would cast her aside, and the idea that she would be abandoned again terrified her. And this morning, when he'd talked about her giving up her shop as if it were a matter of course, as if giving up her dreams and ambitions were a simple matter, all that fear had risen up again. If she gave up the shop and he later abandoned her, she would have nothing.

She thought of the hair ribbon, and though she was touched by the fact that he'd carried it all these years—rather awed by it, actually—it was a far different thing to live with another person, make a life with them day in and day out, than it was to carry a token of them and imagine a fantasy. What if the reality of her did not live up to the fantasy he'd conjured?

She was afraid of that, too.

Maria looked around her, studying the chefs and maids dashing about in a flurry of activity. She thought of her shop, her kitchen.

Yes, she realized suddenly, she could give up the shop. She loved Phillip. If she could be sure he loved her, and not a fantasy of her, she would trade the life she had made alone for a life with him. If she could only be sure . . .

"Miss Martingale?"

She turned, and the footman was standing there with the tray, a horrified look on his face.

"His lordship sent them back."

"What?" She frowned and looked at the cakes, then returned her gaze to that of the footman. "What do you mean, he sent them back?"

"I mean, he sent them back." The servant licked his dry lips and glanced around. Maria followed his gaze, and saw that Bouchard's saucier and sous chef, standing on the other side of the worktable, had heard the footman's words, and they had stopped working. They were staring at her askance.

She sighed, rubbing a hand over her forehead. "What's wrong with them? They look perfectly fine to me."

"His lordship demands that you present yourself immediately to explain this travesty."

"Travesty?" She lifted her head. "He says my lemon cakes are a travesty?"

The room went quiet, and as chefs, maids, and footmen stared at her, Maria realized her raised voice had drawn the attention of everyone working in the kitchen.

"Of all the—" She broke off, and grabbed the tray. She marched up the servants' staircase, wondering what on earth he intended to do. Did he mean to dress her down in front of everyone? Surely not. Phillip would never do such a thing. Still, he had been very, very angry with her this morning, so perhaps he was paying her out for her stubbornness. Yet, that also seemed quite uncharacteristic of him.

Puzzled, and more than a little frustrated, she went down the corridor toward the grand dining room of Avermore House, where she paused just outside the doors. She peeked around the corner and saw Phillip sitting at the head of the long table, looking straight at the doorway as if expecting her. Caught in his sights, she froze, uncertain what to do.

"Ah, Miss Martingale," he called, beckoning her with one hand.

She did not move. "Is there a problem with the lemon cakes, my lord?" she asked, her voice ringing out loud enough for every one in the room to hear.

"Come here, Miss Martingale, if you please."

His words gave her a sinking feeling in the pit of her stomach, but she walked along one side of the long table with her head high, ignoring the whispers and stares. When she drew closer to him, she couldn't help a quick, apprehensive glance down the table. Prudence was there, she noticed, sitting to his right, as the highest-ranking woman in the room. Further down the table was Emma. But the sight of her friends did not soothe her jangled nerves, for they moved in this world. They belonged here now. She did not.

With everyone's eyes on her, she reminded herself again that no matter how angry he might be with her, Phillip was first, last, and always, a gentleman, and a true gentleman did not publicly dress down someone in his employ, especially not in front of her friends.

She took a deep breath and faced him. "My lord?" she inquired, striving to sound cool and businesslike.

Instead of answering, he rose and took the tray from her hands. "Take this, Jervis, if you please," he ordered, giving it to the nearest footman.

The footman obeyed, and Phillip returned his attention to her. When he did, she saw the un-mistakable hint of a smile at one corner of his mouth, and her puzzlement deepened. What on earth was this about? "I regret if my lemon cakes have caused your lordship any distress," she murmured, trying to fathom his intentions.

"Distress? On the contrary, they have caused me no distress."

"I don't understand." She leaned closer to him. "You called them a travesty," she whispered.

"I know," he whispered back and also drew closer to her. "I lied."

She blinked. "What do you mean?"

"I mean, I lied." He reached down and grasped her hands in his. "Insulting your cakes was the only way I could think of to get you to come up here. God knows, ordering you never works."

"Phillip!" she cried before she remembered there were thirty-six sets of eyes on her. She tried to jerk her hands away. "My lord, what are you doing?"

He kept a firm grip on her hands, ignoring

all his guests, his attention fixed on her and her alone. "I wanted you here, Miss Martingale," he said, loud enough for everyone to hear, "because we have some unfinished business to discuss."

"Unfinished business?"

"Yes. About our conversation this morning."

Her cheeks grew hot, and not for the first time, she cursed her fair complexion. "Phillip," she whispered with a frantic glance down the table, "now is hardly the time—"

"On the contrary," he said in a voice far louder than hers, "this is the perfect time. In our discussions this morning, there were certain things I failed to tell you. I intend to remedy that now, in front of all these people."

She tried again to pull her hands away, but he held them fast.

"As everyone in this room knows, I am a gentleman. A gentleman does not declare his feelings in front of others. A gentleman does not reveal his heart to the world. A gentleman doesn't confess to his secret wishes and desires in public."

He paused, and the tenderness in his eyes made her heart twist with a pang.

"But," he went on, "I'm saying these things in front of these people because I want what I feel to be known to all my acquaintances. And yours as well." He paused, gesturing to Prudence and Emma. "I believe the Duchess of St. Cyres and Viscountess Marlowe are friends of yours?"

He spoke with slow, deliberate emphasis, but though she could not quite determine why he was calling attention to her friends, she nodded in confirmation. "Yes. Very dear friends."

"Excellent. Several of my friends are here as well. I want all of them to witness what I am about to declare, Miss Martingale, because a public declaration is the only way I can think of to convince you of the depth and sincerity of my affections."

She stared at him in utter astonishment. Phillip making a public declaration? Of his *feelings?* It was so unlike him, she couldn't quite take it in.

"I don't care about the difference in our backgrounds," he said. "I don't care that I'm a marquess and you're a woman who owns a bakery. And if you want to own that bakery for the rest of our lives . . ." He glanced at the guests lined up and down the table, then returned his gaze to hers. "Do it. I don't care about that either."

"You seemed to feel differently earlier today," she felt compelled to point out.

"And I was wrong. Maria, I don't care that position dictates you can't own a shop. I don't care that in the eyes of society we would be an imprudent match. And I don't care if the world thinks you're not good enough for me. I know you've always believed that's what I think, but it isn't true." His hands tightened around hers. "I have never thought you weren't good enough for me. The fear

I have always had, deep down in my heart, is that I'm not good enough for you."

Murmurs of astonishment rippled through the room, but he didn't seem to notice.

"You see, I was never the one who could make you laugh." He glanced at Lawrence, then back at her. "I was never the one who made coronets of rosebuds for your hair and told you that you were pretty." He swallowed hard, and his chin lifted a notch, telling her as clearly as any words how difficult it was for him to reveal himself this way. "I always wanted to say those things, do those things, but I couldn't, for a gentleman is not supposed to behave that way. A gentleman is not supposed to fall in love with the chef's daughter. But right now, today, I don't give a damn what gentlemen do. I'm just a man, and the only thing I care about is you."

"Then why did you send me away?" she cried, still afraid to believe. "If you loved me, why did you send me away all those years ago?"

"Isn't it obvious?"

"Damn it, Phillip," she cried in vexation, "nothing you do is ever obvious to me."

"I like to think that's part of my charm," he said gravely.

She bit her lip. Her heart hurt. "Don't tease. You never tease. Don't start now."

"Maria, listen to me. I sent you away because I couldn't have borne it any other way." He let her hands go and slid his behind her neck. He leaned close to her as gasps of astonishment rippled down the length of the table, and in his eyes was all the blazing intensity that she'd seen when he had first confessed his desire for her. "I couldn't have borne it," he told her in a savage whisper against her ear, "that my brother would be the one to have you instead of me. I should apologize for sending you away, for separating you from him when you loved him, but I can't. Because I don't regret it. I'm not sorry. I'd do it again. I couldn't have borne having you so near to me, and yet out of my reach." He leaned back to once again look in her eyes. "Don't you see?"

She did. And she understood what it must have cost him to do what he had done. She cupped his face in her hands. "I'm glad you're not sorry," she whispered back. "I'm not sorry either. It was all infatuation, you know. Lawrence and me."

His hands slid away from her neck to once again clasp hers. "My feelings, however, are not. I want you to be my wife," he said, loud enough for everyone to hear, "I want you to be my marchioness, the mother of my children, and my lifelong companion and partner. And if it takes the rest of our lives and seventeen hundred proposals to convince you to marry me, then that's what it takes, and I don't care about that either."

Still holding her hands in his, he sank to one knee in front of her. "I love you, Maria Martingale. I have always loved you, from the very first moment I saw you, and I will love you until the day I die. Will you marry me?"

As she looked at him, she felt the strangest feeling, as if she had just stepped back in time to that day when she'd looked at him, stuck out her hand and introduced herself. The feeling that he was her friend, that she could always depend on him to stand by her. He was asking her to be a part of his world, and though it was a world she'd often sneered at, she knew she had to revise that opinion, for she could not imagine any world, any life, without him.

"Yes, Phillip, I will."

And as she gave her answer, she felt everything in the world shift into place and come right again. Joy welled up inside her—joy so powerful, it hurt.

"I was afraid, you know," she confessed still in a whisper only he could hear. "I was afraid of falling in love with you, because if I did and your feelings were a fleeting infatuation, you would eventually abandon me, as Lawrence had done. Or, worse, you would send me away again. But when I found out about the ribbon, that you'd carried it all these years, I started to understand that your feelings for me were far deeper than I'd ever imagined. And yet, despite even that, I was still afraid. This morning, when you were talking about the shop, you caught me so off guard. You rattled me, for I hadn't been thinking about the shop at all, and it was all happening so fast, I panicked." She took a deep breath. "I still didn't quite believe you."

He smiled tenderly and his hands tightened around hers. "And now?"

"I love you," she said, her voice catching on a sob. "I cannot imagine life without you now. I realize that wherever I go, you will always be beside me. And that's why I shall give up the shop, for I need to always be beside you. You have become everything to me."

His hands freed hers, and he cupped her face. "As you have always been to me."

He tilted her face upward as if he meant to kiss her. Shocked, Maria resisted, glancing toward the people at the table, some of them smiling, some disapproving, some thoroughly appalled. She looked back at him, doubtful. "Does a gentleman kiss a woman in front of other people?"

He tilted her head back. "This one does," he said and captured her lips with his.

Warm up the winter nights
with a sizzling hot read!
With four upcoming
Romance Superleaders
from bestsellers
Elizabeth Boyle, Laura Lee Guhrke,
Kerrelyn Sparks, and Kathryn Caskie,
you won't even feel the cold . . .

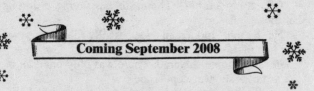

Coming September 2008

Tempted By the Night

An exciting new paranormal romance
by *New York Times* bestselling author

ELIZABETH BOYLE

*Lady Hermione Marlowe has loved the rakish Earl of
Rockhurst from afar forever, defending his scandalous ways
at every turn. One of her greatest desires is to follow after him,
completely unseen, so as to reveal his true noble nature . . .
and then, much to her shock, Hermione finds herself fading
from sight as the sun sets, until she is completely invisible!
Freed of the confines of Society, she recklessly follows the
earl into the temptations of the night and shockingly discov-
ers that his disreputable veneer is merely a cover for his real
duty: safeguarding London as the Paratus, the Protector of
the Realm.*

✳

Thomasin appeared in the same state of shock. "Oh. My.
Goodness," she managed to gasp, her eyes wide with
amazement as she gazed somewhere over Hermione's shoulder. "You are never going to believe this, Minny."

India blinked and tried again to speak, her mouth waver-
ing open and shut as if she couldn't quite find the words to
describe the sight before her.

"What is it?" Hermione asked, glancing over her shoulder
and only seeing the narrow, tall figure of Lord Battersby
behind her. Certainly his arrival wouldn't have India looking like she'd swallowed her aunt's parrot.

"Oh, let me tell her," Thomasin was saying, rising up on her toes.

"No, let me," India said as she finally found her voice. "I saw *him* first."

Him. Hermione shivered. There was only one *him* in the *ton* as far as she was concerned.

Rockhurst.

Oh, but her friends had to be jesting, for the earl would never make an appearance at Almack's. She glanced at both their faces, fully expecting to find some telltale sign of mirth, some twitch of the lips that would give way to a full-blown giggle.

But there were none. Just the same, wide-eyed gaping expression that she now noticed several other guests wore.

Turning around slowly, Hermione's jaw dropped as well.

Nothing in all her years out could have prepared her for the sight of the Earl of Rockhurst arriving at Almack's.

"Jiminy!" she gasped, her hand going immediately to her quaking stomach. Oh, heavens, she shouldn't have had that extra helping of pudding at supper, for now she feared the worst.

And here she thought she'd be safe at Almack's.

"I didn't believe you," she whispered to India.

"I still don't believe it myself," India shot back. "Whatever is he doing here?"

"I don't know, and I don't care," Thomasin replied, "but I'm just glad Mother insisted we come tonight, if only for the crowing rights we will have tomorrow over everyone who isn't here."

"Oh, this is hardly the gown to catch his eye," Hermione groaned. "It is entirely the wrong shade of capucine," she declared, running her hands over the perfectly fashionable, perfectly pretty gown she'd chosen.

Thomasin laughed. "Minny, stop fussing. The three of us could be stark naked and posed like a trio of wood nymphs, and he wouldn't notice us."

"True enough," India agreed. "You have to see that you are too respectable to garner his fancy."

"He fancied Charlotte," Hermione shot back, trying to ignore the little bit of jealousy that niggled in her heart as she said it.

"Oh, I suppose he did for about an hour," India conceded, "but you have to admit, Charlotte was a bit odd the last few weeks. Not herself at all."

Hermione nodded in agreement. There had been something different about Charlotte. Ever since . . . ever since her Great-Aunt Ursula had died and she'd inherited . . . Hermione glanced down at her gloved hand. Inherited the very ring she'd found yesterday . . .

Beneath her glove, she swore the ring warmed, even quivered on her finger, like a trembling bell that foretold of something ominous just out of reach.

"Did you hear of his latest escapade?" Lady Thomasin was whispering. There was no one around them to hear, but some things just couldn't be spoken in anything less than the awed tone of a conspiratorial hush.

India nodded. "About his wager with Lord Kramer—"

"Oh, hardly that," Thomasin scoffed. "Everyone has heard about that. No, I am speaking of his renewed interest in Mrs. Fornett. Apparently she was seen with him at Tattersall's when everyone knows she is under Lord Saunderton's protection." The girl paused, then heaved a sigh. "Of course there will be a duel. There always is in these cases." Lady Thomasin's cousin had once fought a duel, and so she considered herself quite the expert on the subject.

"Pish posh," Hermione declared. "He isn't interested in her."

"I heard Mother telling Lady Gidding, that she'd heard it from Lady Owston, who'd had it directly from Lord Filton that he was at Tatt's with Mrs. Fornett." Thomasin rocked back on her heels, her brows arched and her mouth set as if that was the final word on the subject.

"That may be so, but I heard Lord Delamere tell my brother that he'd seen Rockhurst going into a truly dreadful house in Seven Dials. The sort of place no gentleman would even frequent. With truly awful women inside."

Hermione wrinkled her nose. "And what was Lord Delamere doing outside this sinful den?"

"I daresay driving past it to get to the nearest gaming hell. He's gone quite dice mad and nearly run through his inheritance. Of so my brother likes to say."

"And probably squiffed, I'd wager," Hermione declared, forgetting her admonishment to Viola about using such phrases. "I don't believe any of it. Whatever is the matter with Society these days when all they can get on with is making up gossip about a man who doesn't deserve it?"

"Not deserve it?" Lady Thomasin gaped. "The Earl of Rockhurst is a terrible bounder. Everyone knows it."

"Well, I think differently." Hermione crossed her arms over her chest and stood firm, even as her stomach continued to twist and turn.

"Why you continue to defend him, I know not," India said, glancing over where the earl stood with his cousin, Miss Mary Kendell. "He's wicked and unrepentant."

"I disagree." Hermione straightened and took a measured glance at the man. "I don't believe a word of any of it. The Earl of Rockhurst is a man of honor."

Lady Thomasin snorted. "Oh, next you'll be telling us he spends his nights spooning broth to sickly orphans and bestowing food baskets to poor war widows."

India laughed. "Oh, no, I think he's like the mad earl in that book your mother told us not to read." She shivered and leaned in closer to whisper. "You know the one . . . about the dreadful man who kidnapped all sorts of ladies and kept them in his attic? I'd wager if you were to venture into the earl's attics, you'd find an entire harem!"

"Oh, of all the utter nonsense! How can you say such dreadful things about a man's reputation?" Hermione argued. "The earl is a decent man, I just know it. And I'll not let the Lord Delameres and the Lord Filtons of the world tell me differently."

"Well, the only way to prove such a thing would be to follow him around all night—for apparently only seeing the truth with your own eyes will end this infatuation of yours, Hermione."

She crossed her arms over her chest and set her shoulders. "I just might."

"Yes, and you'd be ruined in the process," Thomasin pointed out. "And don't think he'll marry you to save your reputation, when he cares nothing of his own."

India snapped her fingers, her eyes alight with inspiration. "Too bad you aren't cursed like the poor heroine in that book we borrowed from my cousin. Remember it? *Zoe's Dilemma* . . . No, that's not it. *Zoe's Awful* . . . Oh, I don't remember the rest of the title."

"I do," Lady Thomasin jumped in. "*Zoe or the Moral Loss of a Soul Cursed.*"

India sighed. "Yes, yes, that was it."

Hermione gazed up at the ceiling. Only Thomasin and India would recall such a tale at a time like this. She glanced over at the earl, and then down at her gown. Oh, she should never have settled on this dress. It was too pumpkin and not enough capucine. How would he ever discover her now?

Thomasin continued, "You remember the story, Minny. At sunset, Zoe faded from sight so no one could see her. What I would give to have a night thusly."

"Whatever for?" India asked. "You already know the earl is a bounder."

Their friend got a devilish twinkle in her eye. "If I were unseen for a night, I'd make sure that Miss Lavinia Burke had the worst evening of her life. Why, the next day, every gossip in London would be discussing what a bad case of wind she had, not to mention how clumsy she's become, for I fear I'd be standing on her train every time she took a step."

Hermione chuckled, while India burst out laughing.

"I do think you've considered this before," Hermione said.

Thomasin grinned. "I might have." Then she laughed as well. "If you were so cursed, Hermione, you could follow Rockhurst from sunset to sunrise, and then you'd see everyone is right about him."

India made a more relevant point. "Then you could end this disastrous *tendré* you have for him and discover a more eligible *parti* before the Season ends."

And your chances of a good marriage with them, her statement implied, but being the bosom bow that India was, she wouldn't say such a thing.

Still, Hermione wasn't about to concede so easily. "More likely you would both have to take back every terrible thing you've ever said about him."

"Or listen to your sorry laments over how wretchedly you've been deceived," Thomasin shot back.

Hermione turned toward the earl. Truly no man could be so terribly wicked or so awful.

Oh, if only . . .

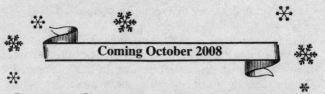

Coming October 2008

Secret Desires of a Gentleman

The final book in the *Girl-Bachelor Chronicles*
by *USA Today* bestselling author

LAURA LEE GUHRKE

Phillip Hawthorne, Marquess of Kayne, has his life mapped out before him. He is a responsible member of the peerage, and rumor has it he may become the next prime minister. And then he runs into Maria Martingale. Twelve years ago, Maria was the cook's daughter, and she fancied herself in love with Lawrence Hawthorne, the marquess's younger brother, but Phillip quickly put an end to that romance. Now Phillip, still as cold and ruthless as he had been all those years ago, is concerned Maria will ruin things for Lawrence and his impending marriage, so he does the only thing he can think of to distract her—seduction.

❋

Maria started down the street, still looking over her shoulder at the shop. "Perfect," she breathed with reverent appreciation. "It's absolutely perfect."

The collision brought her out of her daydreams with painful force. She was knocked off her feet, her handbag went flying, and she stumbled backward, stepping on the hem of her skirt as she tried desperately to right herself. She would have fallen to the pavement, but a pair of strong hands caught her by the arms, and she was hauled upright, pulled hard against what was definitely a man's chest. "Steady on, my girl," a deep voice murmured, a voice that somehow seemed familiar. "Are you all right?"

She inhaled deeply, trying to catch her breath, and as she did, she caught the luscious scents of bay rum and fresh linen. She nodded, her cheek brushing the unmistakable silk of a fine necktie. "I think so, yes," she answered.

Her palms flattened against the soft, rich wool of a gentleman's coat and she pushed back, straightening away from him as she lifted her chin to look into his face. The moment she did, recognition hit her with more force than the collision had done.

Phillip Hawthorne. The Marquess of Kayne.

There was no mistaking those eyes, vivid cobalt blue framed by thick black lashes. Irish eyes, she'd always thought, though if any Irish blood tainted the purity of his oh-so-aristocratic British lineage, he'd never have acknowledged it. Phillip had always been such a dry stick, as unlike his brother, Lawrence, as chalk was from cheese.

Memories came over her like a flood, washing away twelve years in the space of a heartbeat. Suddenly, she was no longer standing on a sidewalk in Mayfair, but in the library at Kayne Hall, and Phillip was standing across the desk from her, holding out a bank draft and looking at her as if she were nothing.

She glanced down, half-expecting to see a slip of pale pink paper in his hand—the bribe to make her leave and never come back, the payment for her promise to keep away from his brother for the rest of her life. The marquess had only been nineteen then, but he'd already managed to put a price on love. It was worth one thousand pounds.

That should be enough, since my brother assures me there is no possibility of a child.

His voice, so cold, echoed back to her from ten years ago, and shaken, she tried to gather her wits. She'd always expected she'd run into Phillip again one day, but she had not expected it to happen so literally, and she felt rather at sixes and sevens. Lawrence she'd never thought to see again, for she'd read in some scandal sheet years ago that he'd gone off to America.

His older brother was a different matter. Phillip was a marquess, he came to London for the season every year, sat in the House of Lords, and mingled with the finest society. Given all the balls and parties where she'd served hors d'oeuvres to aristocrats while working for André, Maria had resigned herself long ago to the inevitable night she would look up while offering a plate of canapés or a tray of champagne glasses and find his cool, haughty gaze on her, but it had never happened. Twelve years of beating the odds only to cannon into him on a street corner. Of all the rotten luck.

Her gaze slid downward. Phillip had always been tall, but standing before her was not the lanky youth she remembered. This man's shoulders were wider, his chest broader, his entire physique exuding such masculine strength and vitality that Maria felt quite aggrieved. If there was any fairness in the world at all, Phillip Hawthorne would have gone to fat and gotten the gout by now. Instead, the Marquess of Kayne was even stronger and more powerful at thirty-one than he'd been at nineteen. How nauseating.

Still, she thought as she returned her gaze to his face, twelve years had left their mark. There were tiny lines at the corners of his eyes and two faint parallel creases across his forehead. The determination and discipline in the line of his jaw was even more pronounced than it had been a dozen years ago, and his mouth, a grave, unsmiling curve that had always been surprisingly beautiful, was harsher now. His entire countenance, in fact, was harder than she remembered it, as if all those notions of duty and responsibility he'd been stuffed with as a boy weighed heavy on him as a man. Maria found some satisfaction in that.

Even more satisfying was the fact that she had changed, too. She was no longer the desperate, forsaken seventeen-year-old girl who'd thought being bought off for one thousand pounds was her only choice. These days, she wasn't without means and she wasn't without friends. Never again would she be intimidated by the likes of Phillip Hawthorne.

"What are you doing here?" she demanded, then grimaced at her lack of eloquence. Over the years, she'd invented an entire repertoire of cutting, clever things to say to him should they ever meet again, and that blunt, stupid query was the best she could do? Maria wanted to kick herself.

"An odd question," he murmured in the well-bred accent she remembered so clearly. "I live here."

"Here?" A knot of dread began forming in the pit of her stomach as his words sank in. "But this is an empty shop."

"Not the shop." He let go of her arms and gestured to the front door of the first town house on Half Moon Street, an elegant red door out of which he must have just come from when they'd collided. "I live there."

She stared at the door in disbelief. *You can't live here*, she wanted to shout. *Not you, not Phillip Hawthorne, not in this house right beside the lovely, perfect shop where I'm going to live.*

She looked at him again. "But that's impossible. Your London house is in Park Lane."

He stiffened, dark brows drawing together in a puzzled frown. "My home in Park Lane is presently being remodeled, though I don't see what business it is of yours."

Before she could reply, he glanced at the ground and spoke again. "You've spilled your things."

"I didn't spill them," she corrected, bristling a bit. "You did."

To her disappointment, he didn't argue the point. "My apologies," he murmured, and knelt on the pavement. "Allow me to retrieve them for you."

She watched him, still irritated and rather bemused, as he righted her handbag and began to pick up her scattered belongings. She watched his bent head as he gathered her tortoiseshell comb, her gloves, her cotton handkerchief, and her money purse, then began placing them in her handbag with careful precision. So like Phillip, she thought. God forbid one should just toss it all inside and get on with things.

After all her things had been returned to her bag, he closed the brass clasp and reached for his hat, a fine gray felt homburg, which had also gone flying during the collision. He donned his hat and stood up, holding her bag out to her.

She took it from his outstretched hand. "Thank you, Phillip," she murmured. "How—" She broke off, not knowing if she should inquire after his brother, but then she decided it was only right to ask. "How is Lawrence?"

Something flashed in his eyes, but when he spoke, his voice was politely indifferent. "Forgive me, miss," he said with a cool, impersonal smile, "but your use of Christian names indicates a familiarity with me of which I am unaware."

Miss? She blinked, stunned. "Unaware?" she echoed and started to laugh, not from humor, but from disbelief. "But Phillip, you've known me since I was five years—"

"I don't believe so," he cut her off, his voice still polite and pleasant, his gaze hard and implacable. "We do not know each other, miss. We do not know each other at all. I hope that's clear?"

Her eyes narrowed. He knew precisely who she was and he was pretending not to, the arrogant, toplofty snob. How dare he snub her? She wanted to reply, but before she could think of something sufficiently cutting to say, he spoke again. "Good day, miss," he said, then bowed and stepped around her to go on his way.

She turned, watching his back as he walked away. Outrage seethed within her, but when she spoke, her voice was sweet as honey. "It was delightful to see you again, *Phillip*," she called after him. "Give Lawrence my best regards, will you?"

His steps did not falter as he walked away.

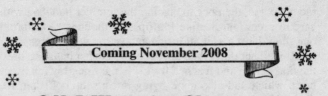
Coming November 2008

All I Want for Christmas Is a Vampire

The latest in the *Love at Stake* series
by *New York Times* bestselling author

KERRELYN SPARKS

Vampire Ian MacPhie is on a mission—he's on the lookout for true love. He claims that all he wants is another vampire . . . . until Toni Duncan comes along. Toni's best friend is locked up in a psycho ward, deemed insane when she confesses that vampires attacked her. The only way to get her out is for Toni to prove that vampires exist. So Toni comes up with a plan: make Ian lose control and beg him to make her one of his kind . . .

✳

Ian felt ten degrees hotter in spite of the cold December air that drifted through the open window and over his white undershirt. The lamp between the two wingback chairs was turned on low, and it cast a golden glow across the room to outline her form with a shimmering aura.

She made a stunning cat burglar, dressed entirely in black spandex that molded to her waist and sweetly curved hips. Her golden hair hung in a ponytail down her back. The ends swished gently across her shoulder blades, as she moved her head from side to side, scanning the bookshelf.

She stepped to the side, silent in her black socks. She must have left her shoes outside the window, thinking she'd move more quietly without them. He noted her slim ankles, then let his gaze wander back up to golden hair. He would have to be careful capturing her. Like any Vamp, he had super strength, and she looked a bit fragile.

He moved silently past the wingback chairs to the window. It made a swooshing sound as he shut it.

With a gasp, she turned toward him. Her eyes widened.

Eyes green as the hills surrounding his home in Scotland.

A surge of desire left him speechless for a moment. She seemed equally speechless. No doubt she was busily contemplating an escape route.

He moved slowly toward her. "Ye willna escape through the window. And ye canna reach the door before me."

She stepped back. "Who are you? Do you live here?"

"I'll be asking the questions, once I have ye restrained." He could hear her heart beating faster. Her face remained expressionless, except for her eyes. They flashed with defiance. They were beautiful.

She plucked a heavy book off a nearby shelf. "Did you come here to test my abilities?"

An odd question. Was he misinterpreting the situation? "Who—?" He dodged to the side when she suddenly hurled the book at his face. Bugger, he'd suffered too much to get his older, more manly face, and she'd nearly smacked it.

The book flew past him and knocked over the lamp. The light flickered and went out. With his superior vision, he could see her dark form running for the door.

He zoomed after her. Just before he could grab her, she spun and landed a kick against his chest. He stumbled back. Damn, she was stronger than he'd thought. And he'd suffered too much to get his broader, more manly chest.

She advanced with a series of punches and kicks, and he blocked them all. With a desperate move, she aimed a kick at his groin. Dammit, he'd suffered too much to get his bigger, more manly balls. He jumped back, but her toes caught the hem of his kilt. Without his sporran to weigh the kilt down, it flew up past his waist.

Her gaze flitted south and stuck. Her mouth fell open. Aye, those twelve years of growth had been kind. He lunged forward and slammed her onto the carpet. She punched at him, so he caught her wrists and pinned her to the floor.

She twisted, attempting to knee him. With a growl, he blocked her with his own knee. Then slowly, he lowered himself on top of her to keep her still. Her body was gloriously hot, flushed with blood and throbbing with a life force that made his body tremble with desire.

"Stop wiggling, lass." His bigger, more manly groin was reacting in an even bigger way. "Have mercy on me."

"Mercy?" She continued to wriggle beneath him. "I'm the one who's captured."

"Cease." He pressed more heavily on her.

Her eyes widened. He had no doubt she was feeling it.

Her gaze flickered down, then back to his face. "Get off. Now."

"I'm halfway there already," he muttered.

"Let me go!" She strained at his grip on her wrists.

"If I release you, ye'll knee me. And I'm rather fond of my balls."

"The feeling isn't mutual."

He smiled slowly. "Ye took a long look. Ye must have liked what ye saw."

"Ha! You made such a *small* impression on me, I can barely remember."

He chuckled. She was as quick mentally as she was physically.

She looked at him curiously. "You smell like beer."

"I've had a few." He noted her dubious expression. "Okay, more than a few, but I was still able to beat you."

"If you drink beer, then that means you're not . . ."

"No' what?"

She looked at him, her eyes wide. He had a sinking feeling that she thought he was mortal. She wanted him to be mortal. And that meant she knew about Vamps.

He studied her lovely face—the high cheekbones, delicate

jawline, and beguiling green eyes. Some Vamps claimed mortals had no power whatsoever. They were wrong.

Their eyes met, and he forgot to breathe. There was something hidden in those green depths. A loneliness. A wound that seemed too old for her tender age. For a moment, he felt like he was seeing a reflection of his own soul.

"Ye're no' a thief, are you?" he whispered.

She shook her head slightly, still trapped in his gaze. Or maybe it was he who was trapped in hers.

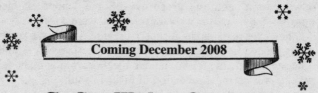

Coming December 2008

To Sin With a Stranger

The first in the new *Seven Deadly Sins* series
by *USA Today* bestselling author

KATHRYN CASKIE

The Sinclairs are one of the oldest, wealthiest, and wildest noble families in all of Scotland. The seven brothers and sisters of the clan enjoy a good time, know no boundaries, and have scandal follow in their wake. They are known amongst the ton as The Seven Deadly Sins. But now their father has declared they must become respectable married members of proper Society . . . This is Sterling, Marquess of Sinclair's, story of how greed and a young beauty, Miss Isobel Carington, almost became his downfall.

✳

"**A**s the Sinclair children grew older, they seemed to embrace the sins Society had labeled them with. Lord Sterling is cursed with greed." Christiana turned her eyes toward the fighter and Isobel followed her gaze. "Lady Susan epitomizes sloth, and Lady Ivy, the copper-haired beauty, envy."

"This is nonsense."

"Is it?" Christiana continued. "Lord Lachlan is a wicked rake. No wonder his weakness is lust. Lord Grant, the one with the lace cuffs, is said to have a taste for luxury and indulgence. His sin is gluttony. The twins are said to be the worst of all." She raised her nose toward the Sinclair with a sheath of hair so dark that it almost appeared a deep blue. "Lord Killian's sin is wrath. Whispers suggest that he is the true fighter in the family, but his anger is too quick and fierce. Why, there is even one rumor that claims that he actually killed a man who merely looked at his twin sister! That's her, there. Lady Priscilla. Just look at her with her haughty chin turned toward the chandelier—here, in a room full of nobility! Her sin is, quite clearly, *pride*."

"Nonsense! I do not believe it," Isobel countered. "I do not believe any of the story. The tale is not but idle gossip."

"I believe it." Christiana set one hand on her hip and waved the other in the air as she spoke. "Why else would they have come to London, if not to leave their sinful reputations behind in Scotland?"

"I am sure I do not know." Isobel saw Christiana's jaw drop, then felt the presence of someone behind her.

"Perhaps I have come to London to ask you to dance with me, lassie." His rich Scottish brogue resonated in her ears, making her vibrate with his every word.

Isobel whirled around and stared up into none other than Lord Sterling's grinning face.

"I apologize, I would address you by name, but alas, I dinna know what it is. Only that you are easily the most beautiful woman in this assembly room." Before she could blink, he reached a hand, knuckles stitched with black threads, and brushed his fingers across her cheek—just as he'd done at the club. "English lasses dinna stir me the way you do. You must be a wee bit Scottish."

Isobel gasped, drew back her hand, and gave his cheek a stinging slap. "Sirrah, you humiliated me, made light of my charity and my attempts to help widows and orphans of war. Why would I ever agree to dance with an ill-mannered rogue like you?"

"Because I asked, and I saw the way you were lookin' at me." He lifted an eyebrow teasingly, bringing to the surface a rage Isobel could not rein in. She slapped his face with such force that his head wrenched to the left. He raised his hand to his cheek. "Not bad. Have you thought about pugilism as a profession?" He grinned at her again.

Isobel stepped around Sterling Sinclair and started for her father. But he was only two steps away. Staring at her. Aghast. She reached out for him, but he stepped back, out of her reach.

She glanced to her left, then her right. Everyone was staring. Everyone.

Isobel covered her face with her trembling hands and shoved her way through the crowd of amused onlookers. She dashed out the door and down the steps to the liveried footman who opened the outer door for her to the street.

She ran outside and rested her hands on her knees as she gasped for breath. Her father would cast her to the street for embarrassing him this night.

No matter what punishment he chose for her, Isobel was certain he would never allow her to show her face in Town again.

And Lord Sterling, the wicked Marquess of Sinclair, was wholly to blame.

At Avon Books, we know your passion for romance—once you finish one of our novels, you find yourself wanting more.

May we tempt you with . . .

- **Excerpts** from our upcoming releases.

- Entertaining **extras**, including authors' personal photo albums and book lists.

- Behind-the-scenes **scoop** on your favorite characters and series.

- **Sweepstakes** for the chance to win free books, romantic getaways, and other fun prizes.

- Writing **tips** from our authors and editors.

- **Blog** with our authors and find out why they love to write romance.

- **Exclusive content** that's not contained within the pages of our novels.

Join us at
www.avonbooks.com

AVON *An Imprint of* HarperCollins*Publishers*
www.avonromance.com